HER RELUCTANT BLUE CAVALIER

A.J. DOWNEY

BOOK SEVEN

COPYRIGHT

Published 2019 by Second Circle Press

Text Copyright © 2019 A.J. Downey

All Rights Reserved

No part of this book may be reproduced in any form or by an electronic or mechanical means, including information storage and retrieval systems, without written permission from the author, except for the use of brief quotations in a book review.

This is a work of fiction. The names, characters, businesses, places, events, and incidents are either the products of the author's imagination or used in a fictitious manner and are not to be construed as real except where noted and authorized. Any resemblance to actual persons, living or dead, or actual events are purely coincidental. Any trademarks, service marks, product names, or names featured are assumed to be the property of their respective owners, and are used only for reference. There is no implied endorsement if any of these terms are used.

The author acknowledges the trademarked status and trademark owners of various products referenced in this work, which have been used without permission. The publication/use of these trademarks is not authorized, associated with or sponsored by the trademark owners.

～

ISBN: 978-1-950222-16-2

Editing by Barbara J. Bailey

Book design by Maggie Kern

Cover art and Indigo Knights logo by Dar Albert at

Wicked Smart Designs

Model - Lovett Taylor

Photographer - Golden Czermak @ Furious Fotog

DEDICATION

To Barbara and John. You know why...

AUTHORS NOTE

It's sad I have to preface this work with this, though in the light of the rampant plagiarism that's shocked our little book world, I feel it's necessary.

This book contains poetry that is not my own. Each work I have included herein is a public domain work, meaning it is not subject to copyright. Each work referenced has been attributed to its original artist and has been meticulously copied in its original form as possible. I have included work from such greats as Robert Frost, Edgar Allen Poe, Shakespeare, and others to honor them and to create something unique and special between my two characters.

Their works stand the test of time and are some of the most romantic words ever written. I hope that you find as deep a meaning and love in them as I do.

PROLOGUE

$\mathcal{S}$kids…

I looked up from where I was running a clean cloth over the bar. The bell above the door usually couldn't be heard above the din of the bar and restaurant on any given night, but it was early yet, and we were closed. Only reason the door was even unlocked was because we were expecting interviews. For a restaurant and bar, we had a decent turn-over rate, that is to say, a low one, but we did have a need to replenish waitstaff on the regular.

We tended to hire on college students, and when they transferred or graduated it was outside our control and we had to hire on new people to keep us running.

The girl that walked through the door was young and blonde. Her long, straight hair was pulled half up and out of her face which had on understated makeup. She was pretty, all wide blue eyes and porcelain skin as she shut the door behind her. An ornate metal clip winking with crystals caught my eye from where her hair was held back.

She turned and smiled at me and asked in a light, but sure, voice, "Are you Marshall McDaniel?"

"I am," I said, tossing my rag up onto my shoulder, putting my hands flat to the bar. I leaned forward just a bit as she walked up, her graceful, long legs almost gliding across the restaurant's floor.

"I'm Colette Bishop. I believe we have a ten o'clock." She held out her hand and I pushed off the bar and shook it. Her hand was soft, but her grip firm and I could already tell I liked her. She was bold, unafraid, and looked like an adventurous girl.

"Nice to meet you, Colette. Most people around here call me Skids."

She raised an eyebrow slightly, almost imperceptibly, but didn't ask. I smiled and gave a nod towards one of the fixed barstools she stood next to.

"Have a seat. Can I get you a drink?"

"Ah, yeah, water with a slice of lemon? If the lemon isn't too much trouble," she said.

I smiled a little bigger and said, "No, no trouble."

I fixed her water-with-lemon and set it on a bar napkin for her, pulling my reading glasses out of the breast pocket of my shirt and putting them on. I picked up her application off of the stack of them by the order screen off to one side and skimmed it.

"So, what's a prima ballerina want to waitress at a dive like this for?" I asked.

"Mm," she swallowed the sip of water she'd just taken and laughed lightly. "One, I'm just a ballerina – entry level, and two, that makes me a starving artist. It doesn't pay for – er – it doesn't pay well at all, and most of us end up holding second jobs. Third, and not the least of which, this place is beautiful and I wouldn't ever call it a dive."

Well, she'd passed that test with flying colors. I smiled and gave a nod, saying, "How is your primary gig going to affect availability for this one?"

She smiled as though she were the cat that'd caught the canary and shot back, "Sounds like I'm hired."

I laughed and said, "Don't go putting the cart before the horse, now…" But yeah. I got a good vibe off of her, I think she was going to be our 'it' girl for the open position. She had moxie and a fire behind those eyes of hers that I liked.

We talked; she answered questions and asked some pretty damn good ones of her own. I was suitably impressed and it took just about everything in me to say I'd give her a call rather than to just hire her on the spot.

"You know, I'll be waiting for that call," she said with a wink, just before going out the door. "Don't disappoint me, now."

I laughed and gave a wave and watched her walk past the windows and up the street. She'd been dressed business-casual in a nice blouse, high-heeled boots, and a pair of nice slacks that hugged her ass. I think I probably lingered on that ass a touch too long as she crossed the alley mouth and went out of sight.

"Can't do that if you hire her, Old Man," I chided myself, and with a chuckle, I put her glass in the dishwasher and swept the bar napkin into the trash.

At the end of the night, as I sat upstairs at my little dining room table, I went back to her application and swept the others aside. I'd call her in the morning. Hers was the only face I could even remember out of the lot of them from today.

I took that as a sign.

1

───────

*C*olette…

    "Ah, ah, ah! Hands off the merchandise, boys!" I called playfully and went onto my toes, holding my tray high and spinning lightly out of reach.

I caught Skids' eye as he worked behind the bar. He didn't miss a thing and I was grateful for it. It was one of the reasons I loved working here. No matter what time, what the occasion, or who was all up in the Cormorant, Skids was a constant and ever-watchful eye and he always backed us servers up.

It was no surprise when I went to the server's station at the end of the bar to load up a tray of drinks that he drifted over to check in with me. He was like that with all the girls.

"Coco." He called to me by the childhood nickname that'd somehow just become my name. "Everything alright over at seventeen?"

"Just peachy!" I called back over the loud cheering as one of the fighters on the television screens went down.

"That guy gets handsy with you again, you shout it out. I'll have him out on his ass in a heartbeat. Not in my bar!"

"That's what I love about you, Boss-man! You always got a sistah's back!" I blew him a kiss and his bright blue eyes lit up, his smile warmed me down to my toes and I whisked the loaded tray off the bar top, raised it high, and threaded my way through the thick crowd.

It was always crowded on fight nights. A healthy mix of city civilians, off-duty cops, firefighters, and yuppies from the nearby business sector who were working the weekend packed the bar and restaurant to capacity. Tonight was no exception. Laine, the hostess, was actually to the point she was having to turn people away. Wouldn't do to go above the mandated capacity and violate fire code with the city's fire code inspector sitting at table five with his wife.

I'd been working here for almost a year and I wouldn't have changed it for the world. We were between shows at the Indigo City Bay Ballet Company and I had picked up a rare weekend shift. Usually, I worked Monday through Thursday in the evenings after practice and I never passed up extra.

As it was, I lived with four other people in a cramped three-bedroom apartment, two streets over and on the other end of Bayside Park. It was, honestly, a two-bedroom apartment. That third bedroom was supposed to be like a little office and wasn't much bigger than a shoebox, but that shoebox was mine to myself, so I was happy. I'd been so done with sharing a room after dance school.

Everyone who lived in the apartment was with the company, but that apartment was still costing each of us over five hundred a month and that wasn't counting bills and the like. City living was expensive as hell and ballet dancers didn't get paid at all what they were worth.

"Hey, you sure you don't maybe wanna come play with me after your shift? Come – aw, come on! You're breakin' my heart!" the guy from seventeen cried when I swept past and wouldn't give him the time of day.

"I'm gonna be breakin' more 'n your heart in a minute you don't leave my waitstaff alone!" Skids boomed out at him.

"Man, why you gotta be like that?" the man cried and Skids shook his head.

"Just leave her alone, rookie!"

I smiled to myself and set drinks down at the table I was serving, two down from the boisterous lot at seventeen, and the guy, my age, maybe a little older, pouted at me but gave it up. I laughed and took empty glasses with me back to the bar.

"Thanks for the assist, Boss," I murmured and went around and back to the kitchen to check on my food for table twenty-three.

"SIT DOWN A MINUTE, girl. You've earned it."

I groaned and dropped onto a barstool and cast a grateful look at my other boss, Reflash, who had spoken. He gave a little laugh and Skids chuckled along with him.

"You know, when you come out here at the end of the night, it's always like watching a dragon come lumbering out of its lair." I told him.

"Oh yeah, how's that?" he asked, pouring himself another pint glass full of water from the bar's soda gun.

"I'll tell yah if you pour me one," I said, looking longingly at the glass in his hand, suddenly parched.

"I got it," Skids said, scooping ice into a glass and dropping a couple lemon slices from the garnish box into the glass. Reflash handed him the soda gun and Skids filled the glass with water and passed it to me.

I took a drink, casting grateful eyes over the rim of the glass in Skid's direction and, lowering it, said to Reflash, "The kitchen is totally your domain, just like out here is Skids'. We don't really see you all night, but we hear you and when you finally come out it's like we get to find out how the night really went."

"Am I that bad?" he asked, and Kristy, another waitress, cracked up, nodding. Skids laughed too.

"You can be," I said. "If the kitchen did poorly, you come out here ravenous for souls. If it was a good night like tonight, no one feels the need to duck and cover. Looks like it was a good night, because no one needs to run from the dragon."

"Fuck me, am I really that bad?" he asked, and Skids laughed outright.

"I'm not trying to hurt your feelings!" I cried, suddenly embarrassed. "I thought you knew…" I felt myself flush, my face heating all the way to the roots of my hair.

"Naw, it's eye-opening. I don't want to be a miserable boss."

"You aren't," Kristy said.

"Easy for you to say, you work out here for this guy. Patron saint of patience," he said jerking a thumb in Skids' direction.

"Well," Skids declared. "Now you know about it and knowing is –"

"Half the battle," Reflash finished with him. Skids shot me a wink behind his partner's back and I tried to cover my smile with the rim of my glass.

"So, it was a good night, I take it?" I said, after I had taken several swallows from my glass.

"Yeah, you know. Minimal screwed-up orders means minimal waste. Wasn't too shabby back there."

"Killed it out here at the bar," Skids said, looking over the print-out from the register.

"Looks like we all live to see another day," Reflash said affably and I gave a feeble, 'Yay', still feeling bad about putting my foot in it.

"Oh, wow, that's my ride. He's early," Kristy said, and I smiled at her.

"Go on, get out of here. I'll do your tables for you."

"Really?" she asked, and I nodded. I would probably regret it, with how tired I was, but Kristy worked just as hard as I did and would do me the same favor some night, I was sure.

"Night, Kristy!" Skids called, without looking up from his nightly paperwork as he went through the drops in the safe.

I finished my glass of water and sighed, standing up, my feet giving me a hard, hot, throbbing ache that went all the way to my knees.

"That's my cue," I said, and started going through my tables making sure the salt, pepper, malt vinegar, ketchup, and whatever else needed the attention was topped off before wiping everything down and putting up the chairs.

We all worked quietly, just dragging through shutdown and prep for the next day over the next hour or so.

"Your friends coming to get you?" Skids asked when they hadn't appeared.

"You mean my roommates?" Most of the time, one or two of them came by the restaurant to walk me home but they were all out of town for the coming winter holidays. We tended to take them before the actual holidays hit, when we had performances just about every weekend for *The Nutcracker.* It was an ICBB tradition.

"Oh, nah, not tonight. Everyone's out of town for 'Christmas' with their families before production starts." I put 'Christmas' in air quotes.

"And you were just planning on walking back to your place alone?" he asked.

I kind of gave a shrug, I mean, I kind of had to when there was no one to walk with me…

"At three-thirty in the morning?" he asked. "In Indigo City?"

"Well, yeah… I mean…" I laughed uncomfortably. It sounded monumentally stupid when he put it that way.

"I'll give you a ride," he said decisively, and I blinked.

"Wait, like on the back of your motorcycle?" I squeaked, excited.

He grinned and he laughed. "I don't own a cage. I could ask Reflash to —"

"No, that's fine!" I cut him off quickly.

He raised his eyebrows, amused and asked, "Ain't you ever ridden before?"

"Nope, always wanted to," I answered. "My mother would have killed me, though."

"Oh yeah, why's that?" he asked.

"Oh, I don't know," I said. "Only daughter, ballet runs in the family, terrified of a career-ending injury, I'm her favorite human on the planet…"

"Okay, okay!" He waved me off. "You've made your point."

"Just don't drop me and we're cool," I declared.

"Let me guess, what your mom doesn't know…"

"Oh, no! I tell her everything. This is sure to drive her up the wall."

He laughed at my matter-of-fact and satisfied tone. My mother and I had a good relationship. A really good one. We were best friends. More like sisters than mother and daughter. She was an *ingénue* with the Pacific Northwest Ballet when she got pregnant with me in the nineties. Sadly, my dad didn't stick around. I never even knew who he was. Having me put a dent in her career as a dancer, but she never, not once, made me feel like I was a letdown. The exact opposite in fact: I was her most treasured thing on the planet.

It was me and her against the world and I don't think either of us would have it any other way. When I'd gotten the opportunity to practice dance at Julliard, we'd squealed and she hadn't had a second thought about sending me.

Dance was our lives, but my mother understood – there was life outside of dance and she was constantly making sure my life and the experiences I had were as well-rounded as possible.

While she would have a motherly fit over her only daughter riding on a motorcycle, she would scold with one breath and before she could draw the next, she would be demanding I tell her all about it. Truthfully, I was excited to have something new to be able to share the next time we talked.

"Hey, kid, you good to go?" he asked and I looked up from where I finished wrapping the cord around the back of the vacuum cleaner. I smiled and gave a nod.

"Just let me bundle up, it's cold out there."

"Now, that it is," he agreed. "Shouldn't be too rough; it's a short ride, right?"

"About eight blocks on foot, I've never ridden or driven it. Might be a little longer with the one-way streets."

He looked impressed that I'd thought of that and gave a nod.

"Gimme a minute to go upstairs and gear up, myself. Be right back down." I smiled and nodded.

"Hang on tight," Reflash said, "and lock this door behind me. Don't open it for anyone but Skids when he gets back down here."

"Okay," I agreed, and he put on his trilby hat when he reached the door, bundled up himself against the cold, although he was likely taking the catering van home. I knew, because he held his leather motorcycle vest draped over one arm reverently.

"Hey, Reflash?" I asked.

"Yeah?"

"Why do you do that?" I said gesturing to the vest with its dull, well-worn patches.

"What? Keep it over my arm?"

"Yeah."

"It's a thing," he said. "You don't wear your colors in a cage. It's not right. Why you ask?"

"Just curious, I guess."

He gave a sharp nod and said, "Well, that's alright with the likes of us, but anybody else in the club or anybody else wearin' a different set of colors, I'd keep questions like that to yourself."

I laughed and said, "I may have been born at night, but I wasn't born *last* night."

He made a derisive noise and said, "You been working here too long, you sound like Oz."

I laughed and he ducked out the front door and into the cold outside. I quickly shut it, trapping the icy air out on the street and threw the lock under his watchful eye. He gave a satisfied nod and headed for the mouth of the alley, disappearing around the corner.

I heaved a big, satisfied sigh and stared out the window at the glittering street. It was so silent and still out there, the frost settling over the pavement in a glittering blanket, giving the illusion of snow which was hopefully just on the horizon.

I loved it when it snowed. The peace, the quiet, the smooth shimmering carpet of white over everything before the city woke up and everything got churned to frozen mud.

The late-night hours with it just drifting to the ground and everyone sound asleep in their nice warm beds was my favorite time to just sit at a window in thick socks and comfortable pajamas with a steaming mug of hot something in my hands to soak it all in.

Movement just outside the door at the edge of my vision startled me. Skids laughed slightly and waved at me, a mass of black leather and denim. I quickly unlocked the door and let him in.

"You alright?" he asked.

"Yeah, just let myself get lost in how pretty it is out there."

"Pretty, eh?" he asked, following me back to the little office behind the bar, beside the banquet room that everyone called 'the fishbowl'. I opened the door marked 'Employees Only' and took down my coat from the line of pegs just inside. He took it from me and held it open, ever the gentleman. I shrugged into the thick white down parka and wound my long gray infinity scarf around my neck.

"Like everything's all sparkly and pure," I said, suddenly embarrassed by the childishness of it.

Skids scratched his bearded cheek, more white than gray anymore, his bright blue eyes silently laughing as he took in my face.

It struck me, and not for the first time, that my boss was extremely handsome. Not that I meant anything by it. I mean, it was just an observation.

I zipped up my coat and put my purse over my shoulder while Skids flipped out the light in the little office and drew the door shut. I followed him down the short little hall as he stopped by the panel outside the kitchen door on this side. He flipped it open and took down the lights a set at a time while I pulled on my gloves. I was already starting to roast but I would be grateful for the extra layers once we hit the street.

I was a dancer and it showed. I barely had any fat on me; I burned far too many calories to really keep it on even though I tried; I really did. Doctors kept complaining at me that I was underweight, and the struggle to convince every new one I had to see for anything that I wasn't anorexic was real.

"Careful," he said. "Frost is thick and the ground is real slick."

"Is it even safe to ride a motorcycle in this? Like at all?"

"Wouldn't recommend a newbie do it, but I'm definitely not new. We'll be fine, but if you'd rather walk, I could probably use the exercise."

I laughed. For a man in his fifties, Skids was perfectly fit. When I'd first met him, months ago, he barely had a bit of a spare tire around his middle, and that was gone now. Things had started in his arms and chest, tightening up and lifting, and for a while, Reflash had been razzing him about trying to impress the ladies.

Skids had laughed him off and denied it, saying it had just been about time he got healthy. I'd wondered to myself if it had been a birthday or something. Maybe a touch of mid-life crisis, but he needn't have worried. He'd been just as attractive with the fluffier dad-bod as he was now, all cut and stuff.

Then again, I was one of those girls that was turned upside-down and inside-out over a pair of gorgeous eyes and a total sucker for a great smile. Skids had both.

Of course, I would never go there! I mean, he was my boss, and he was something like thirty years older than me… It would be weird.

"Okay, what do I do?" I asked, bouncing on the balls of my feet, lifting my heels off the frozen and cracked alleyway pavement. I was already shivering, my teeth trying to chatter as I tried to do anything to generate some warmth.

"First of all, let's get this on yah." He produced a helmet from one of his locked hard-sided case thingies and dropped it carefully on my head, buckling it for me, which was a lot easier for him when he wasn't wearing any gloves.

He put a helmet on his head and dropped onto the front seat, sticking his key in the ignition.

The bike was so loud in the confines of the alley when he started it that I jumped involuntarily and clapped my hands over my ears.

"Okay, come on!" he called over the noise and I got on behind him.

He explained to lean with him and to hold on, and told me whatever I did, to never lean against the curve or I'd throw off the balance of the bike. I snugged against his back as he pulled on a pair of gloves and he asked where I lived.

I told him the address, he thought about it for a second, then called back, "Ah, yeah! I know where that's at. Okay, kiddo, hold on tight!"

I secretly hated it when he called me 'kid' or 'kiddo' but I never said anything. This time was no exception. I held onto him as he put the bike in gear and carefully took us down the alley. He checked both ways, even though it was a one-way street, and turned us out onto it carefully.

My cheeks burned with cold, my nose instantly trying to run, but I was enamored. I'd ridden in countless cars and on public transportation. I'd even ridden in convertibles with the top down, but nothing compared to the exhilaration I felt on the back of that motorcycle.

The ride was way too short, and all too soon, I was stepping up onto the curb in front of my building, struggling with the strap beneath my chin, glowing with excitement.

"That was way too much fun!" I cried and Skids grinned.

"How have I not given you a ride home before now?" he asked. "If I'd have known you would have liked it that much, I would have taken you for a ride when the weather was better."

"God, I don't know, but that was amazing! It's like the difference between watching everything on TV and being there in the moment," I said, and he smiled and pulled off his gloves, reaching up to undo the catch under my chin, his fingertips rough where they brushed against my skin.

"Glad you enjoyed yourself; now you need to go on and get up inside where it's warm. You're half froze to death, girl."

"Thanks so much for the ride," I said cheerily. "I'll see you at work."

"Lookin' forward to it," he said with a wink, and it was nice that he waited until I was safe inside my building's lobby, waited until I turned back and waved, before he restarted the bike and pulled smoothly back out onto the lonely stretch of street.

2

*S*kids…

"Jesus Christ, you dirty old man," I muttered to myself as I watched her go up the steps to the lobby of her building. She used her key fob thing to get in the secured front door and shut it behind her, waving through the glass. I smiled and waved back and fired up the bike.

I hoped the brisk ride back to the *10-13* would act as a cold shower, but no such luck. I was cold alright, but I was still hard as granite, trapped behind the zipper of my jeans. It was uncomfortable as hell, the material of the rough denim pinching with every stride I took and it was pure murder going up the steps to my own apartment.

I'd been fine, everything had been totally innocent and I hadn't thought anything of giving her a ride home, right up until I got back down from my place dressed to ride and spotted her wide-eyed and so-serious look through the glass of the bar's front door.

She was all big blue eyes, those lush lips of hers slightly parted as she stared out over the street without really seeing it. The slight smile that played on those lips just made it click, you know? The realization of just how fucking beautiful she was.

All of a sudden, I didn't see her as the zany and plucky twenty-something kid. She'd gone from zero to all-fucking-woman with that one look and I didn't know how it'd happened.

I'd just… noticed her, that's all.

I keyed myself into my pad and dumped my helmet off on the table by the door, dropping my keys into the basket on its scarred top. My wallet and glasses in their case followed suit.

My colors and jacket were hung on the old-fashioned coat tree next to it, and I worked off my chaps, hanging them up next to my coat. I toed off my scuffed riding boots and set them under the table where they belonged and sighed as my feet found relief in the old scruffy green carpet that was probably a good fifteen years past its need to be replaced.

I took my tired ass in to shower, pulling down a fresh towel from the hall closet where the washer and dryer lived. I stripped out of my clothes right there in the hall and dumped everything directly into the washer, ditching the odd pocket change into an old Tide pods container that was nearly full.

I tried to make a mental note that I needed to take it to one of those Coin Star machines, but anything I threw at my mental wall was refusing to stick – all except Coco and that beautiful dreamer's look she'd had on her face.

"Shit, Skids. Get your fuckin' mind out of the gutter!"

But it was no use, I stood under the shower spray for I don't know how long, just willing my cock to go down. I even went as far as to try and will the erection out of existence by picturing shit that'd always been my go-to before. I had a lot of fucked up shit locked away in the old brain-trust for just such an occasion, but my damn hard-on was being tenacious.

"Man." I shook my head and bowed it beneath the shower spray, letting the water try to pound some sense into me but no dice.

Frustrated, and even a bit borderline angry with myself, I fisted my cock and gave it a tug. I figured that what no one knew wouldn't hurt 'em and as long as I kept shit to myself and didn't act on anything, I was good to go.

Still, all the rationalizing in the world didn't stop me from feeling vaguely dirty as I wanked it with Colette 'Coco' Bishop on my mind.

I tried to keep it clean. Tried just sticking to that look, that one singular moment in time, but no dice. My imagination had other ideas, because before I knew it, the pressure built at the base of my spine, my balls tightened up, and I spilled over the back of my hand picturing her stretched out beneath me, those long dancer's legs wrapped around my hips, my dick buried in her hairless pussy balls-deep.

"You fucking sicko…" I muttered.

Ain't nothing sick about it… she's a woman, of age. Younger, yes, but totally legal, and this is just your imagination.

Just my imagination.

I let go, let the images flood my mind, let the euphoria take over, picturing that smile of hers as she lowered her lips to mine, and I can honestly say I've never wanted anything more in my life. I braced my hands against the tile of the tub surround, let the water beat on the back of my neck, ease the tension between my shoulders and let myself have this because if I didn't, I'd be tempted to drink, and I couldn't ever go back to that life.

I'd already lost everything I'd had once. Lost the love of a good woman, watched her turn bitter and broken… I wouldn't be that guy ever again for anyone, let alone a twenty-something young girl who had the whole world in front of her and the pick of any guy she could ever want.

I sighed and shut off the tap, sliding the glass shower door aside and reaching through the steam for a towel off the rack. I set about drying myself off roughly and hoped like hell that when he came along, whatever guy that was lucky enough to have Colette in his life, that he'd realize just what he'd got and be good to her.

Because if he wasn't and I found out about it? There'd be a good, old fashioned, wood shampoo in his future. I'd beat his fucking brains out with a baseball bat. I liked the girl that much.

Just, no one can know about it, I told myself resolutely.

3

*C*olette…

"Oh, my God! Oh, my God! Coco!" Bridgette squealed from the living room. It was Monday, and we were due to get to practice soon. I looked up from where I was throwing things together in my dance bag for practice and frowned at my half-closed bedroom door.

"What?" I called.

"Not 'what'!" Orion called. "Get your ass out here!"

I rolled my eyes and went out to find out what the fuss was about.

All of my flat mates and fellow dancers were all standing around looking stupid excited, all eyes trained on me. I blinked and looked from Bridgette to her boyfriend Jess and from Orion to his girlfriend Genevieve.

"What?" I demanded.

"Lacy went skiing and tore her ACL," Bridgette said, excitedly.

"Oh, my God, that's awful!" I cried. "Why would you be excited about that?" I demanded, horrified.

"Oh, please," Genevieve rolled her eyes. "Lacy's a bitch and you –"

"You're her number one understudy." Orion grinned at me and it hit me.

"Oh." I dropped down to sit on the edge of the ottoman. "My God." I let it sink in what it meant. I dropped my head and stared at my limp hands in my lap.

"You're the company's new principal dancer, baby! Congratulations!" Bridgette dodged around the lot of them and nearly bowled me over hugging me.

I laughed, a bit in shock. I mean, you could knock me over with a feather. It wasn't that hard, but –

"Holy shit, I'm Clara."

"You're Clara," Jess said, grinning.

I snapped out of it and stood like I'd been electrocuted, and shrieked. We all jumped up and down in our living room excitedly until the neighbor banged on their ceiling, at which point several of us collapsed on the couch in a fit of giggles.

"We have to celebrate, the whole company, after practice," Orion said judiciously.

"Oh, I don't know," I said.

"Oh, come on!" Genevieve cried.

"It'll be fine. We'll go to the Cormorant. You get an employee discount, don't you?"

I laughed and said, "I don't know about that. It sure doesn't extend to you guys!"

"Oh, we'll be fine. You just be ready," Bridgette declared.

I rolled my eyes.

"Whatever, if we're late to practice, the Madame will kill us." We all had a laugh. Our director was strict but not awful. Not like she could be, not at all, but she was very poised and very French and even though I don't know where the nickname had come from – it'd stuck.

We shared a Lyft to Bay Water Hall and sure enough, I was pronounced Clara. The Madame seemed well-pleased with the outcome and I was surprised by that. I mean, I had worked really hard to get this far, and I knew I was better than Lacy, but Lacy's father had money and you know how that goes…

I'd never relied on my mother's name to get me anywhere, even though she'd been one of the best in her prime, and most of the company didn't even know I was her daughter. They just knew me as Coco, thanks to my roommates, who did know, and who had leaked my childhood nickname the first time my mom had come to stay with us.

I practiced hard, and the Madame was, surprisingly, not even close to tougher on me like I had expected. At the end of the run-through of the first act, she corrected one or two minor things and I asked her if she was sure.

She'd winked and told me, "Darling, no one here could be half so hard on you as you are on yourself."

I'd smiled and had been grateful. It was high praise coming from her, and I almost felt like I was drifting along in some sort of dream-state. I was sure the euphoria and excitement would be worn off by the next day's practice, though.

My roommates made the announcement about celebrating that night at the Cormorant, and I blushed and tried to make myself look busy rooting through my dance bag. I was happy for the attention when I was on stage; not so much when I was off of it. Still, we didn't allow ourselves much in the way of opportunities to cut loose and party, so who was I to deprive them?

We went home, got showered and all dressed up for a night out. Of course, 'dressed up' for me was a pair of skinny jeans, a nice, clingy, light-gray angora sweater that, though it hugged every inch of my body, still had a modest cowl neck to it, and a pair of my favorite knee-high boots. Over the sweater, I put on a cropped leather jacket that paired nicely with the boots, and I was quite pleased with my reflection in the mirror.

I swiped some neutral lip gloss with some shimmer to it across my lips and called it good just as Bridgette shouted at me to hurry my ass up from the living room. I snorted softly and threw my tube of gloss into my little clutch purse with my ID, bank card, keys, and my phone. Those objects alone filled it to capacity, and slinging the chain across my chest, I called "Alright, alright! I'm coming!"

We walked to the Cormorant, laughing and talking. Though a couple of my roommates bagged on Lacy, I didn't join in. I felt sorry for her. It was true, she could be nasty to people and mean without cause and there was probably none among us who had escaped her sour attitude, but I felt sorry for her. It felt like, at least to me, she didn't know any other way to be and that was likely a product of her own misery. I wished her well and a speedy recovery, but knew that she would likely never again be what she once was, on stage.

That made my heart break for her a little. Dance was my life, a never-ending source of joy for me. I couldn't imagine what it would be like to have an injury cut me off at the proverbial knees, not when I was just getting started.

I smiled to myself, and nodded at something Jess asked as we walked up the frozen street, breath pluming the night-dark air, even though it wasn't that late. Not yet.

Despite the celebrating we still had dance practice the next day, so I was going to make it a point to ask Skids to keep the drinks coming with very little to no alcohol in mine.

There was no way I was going to try and get through practice for the lead part in *The Nutcracker* hung over. I was crazy about dancing, but I wasn't crazy.

We went through the door, laughing. The restaurant was busy, the bar not-so-much. Skids looked up from behind the bar and I realized belatedly, it was Monday. He shouldn't have been there.

"What are you doing here?" I asked.

"Took the words right out of my mouth, kid. Was just about to ask you the same thing."

"Our girl got the lead!" Genevieve crowed and Jess echoed her with, "We're celebrating."

I blushed and said, "Ah, yeah, drinks all around!"

"Well, I'll be! That's great to hear. What'll you have?" he asked.

I let my friends place their orders first, and was just about to place mine when a black AmEx appeared over my shoulder.

"Put it all on my tab," a familiar smooth voice said. I turned and smiled up at Brooks, one of the other performers. He smiled down at me, his dimples out in full force and I nodded.

"Thank you," I murmured. He was Lacy's boyfriend, and I had no idea what he was doing here and not with her. Still, I knew he had more money than God, and if he wanted to do something nice, far be it from me to argue.

"This must be a little awkward," I stammered, and his smile grew slightly and he shook his head.

"Lacy dumped me," he said matter-of-factly. "Just before going off on that ski trip with Gregory. I can't help but think 'instant karma.'"

"Oh, God, I'm so sorry!" I put a hand on his arm and he smiled and gave me a wink.

"Always liked dancing with you better anyway; we kind of just flow."

I blushed and he laughed and said to Skids, who was listening, "I'll have a gin & tonic, and, of course, whatever the lady will have."

"Hey, Brooks!" Brooks turned his head to whoever had called his name from over at the pool tables and I thrust my chin in their direction.

"I'll catch up and bring it over," I said.

"Thanks." His green eyes flashed under the fall of his dark hair over his forehead and he went over.

"And what will the lady have?" Skids asked.

"Honestly, whatever you can throw together that looks like it's girly and boozy without any actual booze in it." I stretched my bottom lip and ducked back slightly, guilty at not joining my friends in their hang-over and he laughed a little.

"You don't have to feel bad for not drinkin'," he said. "Good on yah for not caving to the peer pressure."

"Celebrate, yes, but I still have practice tomorrow and I really don't want to do it hungover."

"Ain't gotta explain it to me," he said, and though we talked, his hands never stopped moving as he poured and mixed with precise efficiency borne of long practice.

"Thanks for the assist, Boss," I said as he put something that looked like a Tequila Sunrise in front of me. I picked it up and took a sip with raised eyebrows and smiled appreciatively.

"You're the best," I said and took my mocktail and Brooks' drink over to the pool tables, where an impromptu mini-tournament was beginning.

It was a good evening full of laughter and just cutting loose.

"Another drink?" Brooks asked from behind me as I sat on one of the tall stools usually taken up by one of the Indigo Knights, but we'd arrived first and had usurped them. Instead, several of them had taken up residence along the actual bar. A couple of them turned this way, talking to Skids behind them. I smiled at Skids and he gave a nod.

"Sure," I said and Brooks wandered over to the bar.

I went to use the restroom and found Lys and Claire, two of the Indigo Knights' girlfriends in front of the mirror at the sink. I think they were with the twins, Angel and Golden.

"Uh-oh, breaking the seal?" Claire asked with a wink.

"Hardly." I checked to make sure the stalls were empty and none of my roomies or the other dancers were around. "I had Skids hook me up alcohol-free. I'm not trying to dance hungover tomorrow."

"Oh, God! I don't blame you," Claire said. "Been there, done that; pretty sure I left the tee-shirt covered in puke somewhere in Prague."

I laughed, "That's right! You dance too, don't you?"

"Not really, dance was part of it, but I'm a silk dancer, which is so not the same thing."

"Oh, right, that's more acrobatics than dance-dance," I answered and went into one of the stalls.

"Impressed you even know what it is," she called out.

"What kind of dance do you do?" Lys asked, and I knew she had to be asking me.

"I'm a ballet dancer with the ICBB," I answered, relief filling me up. I had waited way too long to go.

"ICBB?" she asked.

"Sorry, Indigo City Bay Ballet."

"Oh, wow! Really?"

"Yeah," I buttoned my pants and zipped them, smoothing my sweater down over everything before turning and flushing. I waited for the noise to abate as I stepped out of the stall and found Lys and Claire standing off to the side, giving me room at the sink.

"One of the principal dancers just tore her ACL on vacation. I was the lead understudy so my friends insisted that we come out and celebrate since I'm to take her place. I'm having some serious mixed emotions about it," I confessed and it felt kind of good that they didn't blow me off and wave it away.

"Dude, I would too. That's awful but so awesome at the same time," Claire said, making a face, and I could tell she really got me.

I shut off the tap and shook my hands into the bowl, Lys dispensed some paper towels for me and ripped them off, handing them over.

"Thanks," I murmured.

"Well, good luck," Lys said, smiling innocently, and Claire and I traded a look.

"She means 'break a leg,'" Claire said ushering Lys towards the door. "Come on, I've got to educate you some more on stage talk," she said laughing. "You don't want to jinx the poor girl."

I laughed and turned back to the mirror, refreshed the gloss on my lips, and smiling, stepped back out of the restroom to walk past the tables I didn't have to serve tonight and rejoin my friends. The little talk with Lys and Claire had done me some immense good, surprisingly. It was amazing what a small confession to someone who truly listened could do to unburden your soul.

"There she is! Come on, you're up," Brooks held out the pool cue to me and I smiled, taking a sip of my refreshed drink from our tall table. I frowned slightly at the slightly-salty taste to it, wondering if some of the rimming salt had gotten on or in the glass. I took the cue and, deter-mined, leaned over the table.

"Look out, now! She's concentrating," Orion called and I busted up laughing.

"Shut up!" I cried. "You're going to ruin my shot."

4

———————

*S*kids…

It picked up for a minute and I almost missed it when Lys said to Golden, "Baby, something's not right, we ran into Coco like an hour ago in the bathroom and she said Skids wasn't mixing any alcohol into her drinks. How did she get that drunk that fast?"

I looked up, freezing in what I was doing, and sure enough, Coco was staggered up against the young guy who'd handed over his daddy's black AmEx to pay the tab.

"Claire, go get Reflash up front for me. Angel, Golden, with me."

I went around the bar and marched up to them. The guy was already half-dragging Coco out the front door.

"Hey, yo, don't you want to wait for your card and close out your tab?" I called, sarcasm edging my voice.

"Oh, no, I think I'd better get her home. I can come back for it later." He looked nervous and I got in their way. Coco's hand reached out and touched my chest and she looked up at me, her eyes glassy, face flushed.

"I don't feel well," she slurred. "What's happening to me?"

"Angel," I barked, and he was there. Golden already had the guy by the arm and was on his cell with dispatch as Coco fell against me. I put my arms around her and helped her out onto the sidewalk, leaning back against the building, I leaned her back against me to protect her from the rough brick and to hold her up. Angel was in front of her, asking questions gently, checking her eyes with a penlight as she groaned and tried to cover her face.

"Call a bus," he called out to his twin. "We get her to Trinity Gen, we can get blood and urine samples – we got this guy dead to rights. No way will it metabolize fast enough out of her system before we get it.

"No, no hospitals, can't afford it…" Coco mumbled.

"Don't worry about that now, sweetheart. I'll get it if I have to. You're okay, I've got you."

"What's happening to me?" she repeated.

"Baby, we think you've been drugged," Angel tried to explain, and she whimpered and pressed back tighter against me.

"Easy," I murmured in her ear. "I've gotcha, ain't nothing gonna happen now."

Her friends came piling out once the party lights showed up, and Reflash came out and said, "Arrest that guy," pointing at the rich kid. "I got him on our surveillance dosing up our girl's drink while she was in the bathroom."

"What? No!" he cried.

"Skids, don't leave me!" she cried, terrified and confused, when Angel and the arriving EMTs tried to get her in the back of the ambulance.

"Not going anywhere, Coco," I murmured to her. "Can I ride with her?" I asked one of the medics.

"Um, typically we don't let non-family ride with –"

"Put me down as her father," I grated. "I don't care."

I picked her up and climbed up into the back of the bus, and set her down on the gurney before either of them could say anything.

Angel was trying not to laugh and said, "You heard her 'daddy', get goin'!" He lost it after that, and the ambulance's bay doors shut just as her friends started this way. I scowled at them and sat aside to let the paramedic do his work.

Coco wanted to try and fight through her confusion and altered state, and was giving the medic a hell of a time until I took her hand and gently put my face in front of hers. She clung to the familiar face and I got her to settle down. Seems she trusted me. Probably a lot more than she should have, but right now, I would take it.

She kept a death grip on my hand as we wheeled her in to Trinity Gen and set up in one of the nearby curtained-off bays. The nurse got her out of her clothes, but she still wouldn't hear of me leaving even through that, pitching a screaming fit when they tried to make me leave. I had to settle for keeping my back turned while they got her out of her clothes and into a gown behind my back.

They took blood, got her started on an IV, and she went out on us, the drug forcing her under when the adrenaline had worn off. I stepped out when they put a catheter in her to get their piss sample to test and ran into the cops outside the curtain. Both of them were cops I knew.

"Her father, huh?" one of them asked looking down at his notebook.

"Her boss is more like it," I said with a heavy sigh. "Any port in a storm, right?"

"This happen at the *10-13*?" Kovacs asked. I nodded and rubbed the back of my neck.

"Right in fuckin' front of me, man. I didn't even notice."

"Walk me through it; how'd you guess?"

"I didn't. One of my patrons, the girlfriend of a patrol officer noticed. Coco – sorry, Colette asked me to keep her dry at the start of the night, so I kept making her up virgins. She ran into a couple of my regulars in the ladies' room and even told them as much, like an hour before. So when she started acting drunk, my regular, Alyssa Glenn, said something. That's when I knew something was wrong."

"And the guy she was with, the one you think dosed her, ever seen him before?"

I shook my head. "No. He's somebody she knows from the dance company she's with. He's never been in. She wasn't part of his clique before now, I guess."

"What changed that?" Kovac's partner asked. She was a feisty Latina. Cortez, I think her name was.

I told them everything I knew. That Coco had just gotten the lead part or whatever, because the previous girl got hurt.

"He's her boyfriend," she slurred from behind the curtain and the nurse whisked it back for us to come in. "Or he was. That's what he said anyway – that she dumped him right before the ski trip."

"Think this is some kind of a revenge thing?" Kovacs asked.

"I don't know," I said, looking over Coco, who had closed her eyes and was swallowing hard in that way that said she was fighting not to puke. I went to the wall and snatched down one of the plastic-ringed emesis bags and opened it up quick. I held it for her when she lost it and I winced. "That's your job to find out, ain't it?" I asked and instantly felt bad.

"Sorry, not trying to be an asshole, I'm just pissed. She's a good kid," I said, stroking her blonde hair back from her face.

"Yeah, I get that, thanks," Cortez said and some of her hard-ass that'd she'd been ramping up dissolved at the apology.

The doctor came in and said, "Ah, good, everyone's here. Ms. Bishop, do you mind if I talk about your status in front of these officers and your father?"

"Father? Who, Skids?" she asked and blinked. "No, go ahead," she mumbled and it seemed she was coming out of it.

The doctor sighed and said, "With as altered as she is, I shouldn't be taking her permission to heart…" he said, and looked like he wrestled with it some.

"She's doing much better," Cortez said.

"Yup, looks like it's mostly worn off now," I agreed, deadpan, staring the doctor in the eyes. He heaved a sigh and nodded.

"She tested positive for Rohypnol," he said. "She's going to likely remain altered for the next few hours, but I don't think she's in any physical danger at this point. Just let her puke, keep her hydrated, and let her sleep it off… it's all you can do."

There was a long silence as we all looked over to her prone form in the hospital bed. She seemed smaller than usual, more fragile.

The doctor drew a breath and said, "I'll have a nurse come and help her get redressed, but at this point her case is no longer considered an emergency and there's no need to admit her, so we really need the bed down here." He turned to me specifically, "I take it you're going to take her home and look after her?"

I braced my hands on my hips, dismayed, but damned if I would show it. I nodded and said, "While she's getting dressed, I'll get us a ride."

"We can help you out with that," Kovacs said.

"Yeah," Cortez agreed. "You're on the way back to the station house," she said.

"Thanks," I said softly. They didn't owe my disgraced ass anything.

"No problem, and thanks for your time, Doc," Kovacs said.

"Her story has a happy ending. You stopped what was sure to be a sexual assault. I wish it ended like this more often," the doctor said, eyeing me again and I shook my head, my eyes on Coco where the curtain was being whisked along the track, cutting her off from view.

"Wasn't me," I said.

"But you responded," Cortez said.

"You can take the man out of the job…" Kovacs said.

"But you can't take the job out of the man," I agreed.

"Thin blue line's still wrapped around your heart. You should be proud of that," Cortez said, and I couldn't help but smile at that, though it was filled with a bitter irony.

I'd left the job voluntarily. Retired before they could fire me, but I still was, and always would be, disgraced, no matter who disagreed.

We waited for Coco, and by the time the nurse pulled back the curtain, another was there with her discharge paperwork. I blinked in surprise at how efficient they were being. Usually it was a whole lot of restless hurry-up-and-wait to get out of these places.

"Busy night," the second nurse said unhappily as I signed off on things. I nodded and understood her. A busy night for the cops on the street, for the medics, for the hose boys… for ER nurses like her? It meant a whole lot of bad was going down in the city that night.

I went over to Coco and helped her up. She leaned heavily into my side and I didn't think she'd want her roomies swamping her. I took her bag of personal effects from the nurse and helped her stagger out the ER's doors, Cortez on her other side to catch if she tried to go down. Kovacs had disappeared to get the car and we only had to wait a couple minutes in the freezing air for him to pull up.

"Thanks again for the ride," I said as Cortez handed Coco down to me in the back seat.

"You bet, where are we taking you?" Kovacs answered.

"Back to the *10-13,* if you don't mind. I live upstairs and have a guest room she can sleep it off in."

"Wish my boss was as nice as you," Cortez said. She had the passenger side sun visor down despite the dark, and I caught sight of her speculating deep dark eyes in the mirror on it.

"She doesn't got any family here. She's from San Francisco originally and her mom's still there."

"Long way from home," Kovacs said.

"No," I disagreed, "this is her home; she's just a long ways from family. I guess it's always been just her and her mom."

She whimpered and shifted against my chest and I looked down at the back of her blonde head, wincing as she lost it and threw up.

"Shit," I swore, and was grateful we were in the back of a squad car with the hard plastic seats. An uncomfortable ride, sure, but a lot easier to clean.

"Shit is right," Kovacs said sardonically.

"No good deed goes unpunished," Cortez said as we pulled up to the curb in front of my building.

"It's no worries, we'll make one of the rookies hose it out," Kovacs said, and I chuckled.

"Feel sorry for the kid," I said and tried to take the worst of the mess with me and Coco onto the sidewalk. We were both pretty well slaughtered.

"Need help?" Cortez asked but Reflash came out the front of the *10-13* and said, "Naw, we got it."

"Good deal. See you guys around," she said.

"Come in for a free drink on me," I told her.

"Yeah, you got it."

"Going up?" Reflash asked.

"Ah, yup."

"You get her, I got the keys," he said, and was already unlocking the street-level door to the stairs leading up to the apartments above. I picked Coco up easily and followed him up.

"Ain't takin' her home?" he asked.

"The doc said she'd need some attention until this shit wore off."

"She pop positive?"

"Oh, yeah."

"Little fucker's going down for sure, then. Good. You want I should stick around?"

I stepped past him into my place and Coco groaned. I shook my head.

"One of us has to stay 'the boss,'" I told him.

He said to me, "No one's gonna think twice you takin' care of her. I don't trust her 'friends' to do it."

I could practically see the quotes around 'friends' when he said it and I shook my head.

"Ain't their fault, but I don't trust them to know what's right. I mean, they're just kids themselves."

"Uh-huh." My best friend gave me a knowing look and I closed my eyes and felt my shoulders drop slightly. As slight as Coco was, she was all muscle and that muscle was getting heavy.

"Later, huh?" I asked, and he nodded.

"Take care of our girl," he said. "We'll talk later."

"Thanks."

"Glad she's okay," he said, eyeing her in my grasp, and he tossed my keys into the basket on the table by the door before he ducked out. I was glad for it. Her puke had cooled and it was getting chilly against my skin.

I took her into the bathroom and stood her up. She clung to me, shaking like a leaf and I helped ease her onto the closed lid of the john.

"Can you keep yourself up for just a few seconds?" I asked.

She nodded, makeup running down her cheeks in muddy tracks.

"Okay, hang tight, we're gonna get you all cleaned up."

I turned on the tap and pulled up on the tab to block the drain, to run her a bath. When I stood up, her hands went to my belt and worked at the leather holding it closed.

"Woah, hey, not about me, it's about you, slow down there," I murmured and tugged on her jacket sleeve. She let me have it, and I took it off her gently.

"You think you can finish getting undressed and get in the tub on your own?" I asked.

"I think so," she whispered thickly.

"Okay, I'm going to get some towels in the dryer and warmed up for you. You just dump everything in a pile here and I'll get it in the wash. You holler if you need some help, okay?"

"I just want to be clean," she murmured and I smoothed her hair back. She startled and looked up at me, and her blue eyes were still glassy from the drug and from her emotional fragility.

"I'm right here, you're safe. Wasn't gonna let anything happen to you, kid."

"I hate it when you call me that," she said, and then looked surprised that she'd said it.

"I didn't know that," I said softly. "I'll knock it off."

I took her jacket out into the hall with me and shut the bathroom door to where there was a sliver left open. She had her privacy, but I'd hear it if she called.

Her jacket had some vomit on it, but her sweater had taken the brunt of it. I laid the faux leather out on the dining room table and wet a washcloth at the sink, wiping it clean but keeping an ear out for Coco.

When I was satisfied it wouldn't stink too bad, I got the towels in the dryer and going, in the closet across the hall from the bathroom door.

"You good?" I called, and heard the water slosh as she got into the tub.

"Okay, you can come in," she said faintly and I peeked. She was beautiful, crouched in the bottom of my tub, her knees drawn to her chest, the knobs of her spine and her ribs a little too prominent against her pale skin. Everything was pretty much hidden, and I didn't want to scare her so I tried not to look and moved slow, shutting off the tap and closing the curtain.

I loaded up a spare toothbrush with paste and handed it to her behind the curtain. She took it and I listened for a heartbeat or two as she brushed her teeth.

"You just take as long as you want in there," I said. "I'm going to get cleaned up myself. You just holler if you need anything, now. I mean it."

"Okay," she whispered and it was a sound on the edge of total heartbreak.

"I'm right here, babe. I'm not going anywhere."

"Did you just call me 'babe?'" she asked.

I stopped what I was doing, picking up her discarded clothes off the floor and said, "I think I just did, I'm sorry."

"Don't be," she said. "I like that much better."

Shit.

"You just take it easy," I told her, and tried not to let on how her words affected me. Instead I ducked back out into the hall and went through her clothes. Nothing in her pockets, I ditched her jeans, her panties – which were satin and lace and some strange mix of wholesome and racy with them being white, and the matching bra.

Good Christ, get your mind off her underwear!

I listened to the water gently trickle and shush against the sides of the tub through the cracked bathroom door behind me and checked the care instructions on her sweater.

Dry Clean Only

Because, of course it was. But with her socks and the rest of her shit in the washer, a shirt was the least of her problems. I could send her home in one of mine; that was no problem. Her sweater, though – I found a used plastic grocery sack and dumped it in there, tying off the top. I stripped out of my things and put them in the washer with hers, ditching the change in my pockets, setting my wallet and phone aside.

I had a flood of inquiring texts that could be answered later. Reflash knew all was cool, and as my Deputy Chief, he could handle things club-side for a while.

I took a fresh washcloth off the shelf up top after I started the washer and went bare-assed into my kitchen to bird-bath myself with the hand soap at the sink. It wasn't perfect, but my place only had the one bathroom, so it was all I had.

I'd shut the doors on the closet to muffle the washer, and put the towel I'd pulled down for myself on the dining room table, which pretty much sat in the kitchen, a part of it.

Part of the charm of this place was that it was laid out so funky. You walked in the front door to the dining room table and kitchen right in front of you. To the left was the doorway to the living room, to the right the hall leading to the bathroom, the guest room door just past the wash closet. At the end of the hall was the door to the main bedroom, my bedroom, and I contemplated what it would be like to have Coco in my bed even if I wasn't in it with her.

I could stay in the guest room.

I thought about it, while I pulled a clean white tee over my head and a pair of blue and gray plaid patterned flannel pajama bottoms up my legs.

It was good timing; Coco was calling out, "The water is getting cold!"

"I'm coming," I told her and opened up the hall closet's sliding doors and pulled open the dryer. I fished out a big, fluffy, fresh, hot bath sheet for her and asked at the door, "You good to get up on your own?"

"I can try."

I heard the water slosh and trickle and she gave a slight yelp. I pushed open the door and caught her in the towel before she could fall, wrapping the warm absorbent material around her as she held onto me.

"Take it easy and step over," I told her. She got out of the tub and stood, shaky, on the mat.

"Dizzy," she complained and I helped sit her on the john again.

"I gotcha, you hang tough and let me get you a shirt."

"Okay."

"You okay?" I checked, only halfway letting go.

"I'm okay," she affirmed and I let her go. She hugged the towel against her chest and was, mercifully, mostly covered. Her face freshly-scrubbed and free of the disaster her makeup had turned into she looked entirely too wholesome, too sweet and innocent.

"Be right back," I said, and went for my bedroom closet.

I pulled down my favorite flannel shirt; I wanted her to be warm. It was a button-down, a blue-and-gray plaid, similar to, but not the same as, the pajama pants I had on. I grabbed a soft, thick pair of natural-fiber wool socks out of my drawer for her feet.

She was already shivering when I got back to the bathroom, but she'd dried herself off.

"Here." I knelt in front of her and put the shirt around her shoulders. She slid her arm through one sleeve then the other, keeping the towel mercifully in place. I started buttoning the shirt while she looked down at me, blinking owlishly like she'd never seen me before but I was suddenly fascinating.

"You're so good to me," she murmured and her hand came up and cradled my cheek.

I looked up sharply; her blue eyes were locked on mine and I think I forgot to breathe. Her cheeks were still flushed, her lips slightly parted and her expression was so… open, hopeful.

I pulled her hand gently down from my face and swallowed hard around the lump that'd taken up residence in my throat. It was the same kind of lump you got when you looked at something so beautiful it'd like to break your heart because it filled it so full.

I gently cupped the heel of one foot with my hand and she sucked in a sharp breath. I froze when I looked at them, her feet. They were so battered, so bruised and painful-looking from her dedication to her craft.

"Sorry, did I hurt you?" I asked.

"No," she murmured, but her cheeks flamed and she looked embarrassed.

On impulse, I bent and placed a feather-light touch of my lips to the top of the foot I held and said against it, "Tell me if anything I do hurts."

I sat up and opened up the sock wide, and carefully eased it over her foot and ankle. She sat like stone, her breath held, and I asked her, "Alright?"

"Okay," she said, breathless.

"Give me the other foot," I ordered gently, and she moved as if my words pulled her by strings, giving me the other one. I slipped the heavy sock on it and let it go; she lowered it carefully to the floor. I stood up and held down my hands, and she stood, sucking in a sharp breath and closing her eyes, swaying on her battered feet as the world must have spun for her.

As far as I was concerned, it did.

Dammit.

"I've got you," I murmured, and thinking the better of having her in my bed, I told her, "Just have to make it across the hall, babe. Guest bed is waiting for you."

"Okay," she said. "Thank you."

"You're welcome," I murmured, and she let the towel slip out from beneath my shirt covering her slim body. She went to try and bend to get it and I said sharply, "Leave it," before I gentled my tone. "I'll get it later, right now let's get you to bed so you can sleep the shit that asshole slipped you off."

"Okay," she said, and it sounded like it took her great effort and concentration to even say that much.

I let her go out ahead of me, my hands on her hips, steering her gently and carefully where I needed her to go. She paused in the open doorway of the guest room and I reached inside the bedside lamp's shade and pushed the switch to turn it on. She winced and shied back against me and I held her for a heartbeat or two while her eyes adjusted.

"Come here and lay down," I ordered and pulled back the blankets on the bed. She got in and I tucked her in.

"Stay with me," she begged and captured my hand with hers. I wanted to, believe me, but I chose to intentionally misinterpret what she was asking.

"Shh, you're all good, babe. I'm not going anywhere. I'll be right down the hall in my room, I'll even leave the doors open. All you need to do is holler."

"Okay," she said, dejected, and when I was sure she was snug, I clicked out the light and backed out of the room. I picked up her towel in the bathroom, switched the laundry from the washer to the dryer and got it going, and finally, shut the laundry closet doors and went back to the end of the hall with the hall light switch so I could turn it out. I paused, making sure everything was where it needed to be. Her personal belongings at the dining room table, my own in the basket on the table by the door. I plucked my phone out of the basket to take in to my room to charge it and paused one more time outside the guest room door.

I didn't hear anything, and satisfied she was okay, I took myself in to my own bed.

5

Colette…

I lay in the close dark and it was like my head was stuffed with cotton, my head swimming, thoughts jumbled and confused. I was alone, and scared, and I didn't want to be alone. I closed my eyes and tried to sleep, but it was like every nerve cried out for attention, something to hold onto, to anchor me to the here-and-now. I'd felt that in Skid's arms. Anchored. Like he would keep me from floating away. I was desperate for that secure feeling again and so I pushed back the blankets and sat up, gripping the edge of the mattress and squeezing my eyes shut as the wave of vertigo swept over me.

When it passed, and I was sure I could get my feet under me and not fall over, I stood. I paused again at the edge of the doorway and waited for another wave of dizziness to pass.

I tried to tell myself I was being crazy as I inched my way up the hall, but I knew I wasn't. Childish, maybe, but not crazy. I paused in the doorway and let my eyes adjust to the dim light coming through the slatted blinds. The windows of his apartment faced the alley, but the

45

roof of the building next door was low enough to let the bluish-white rays of moonlight pass.

I lifted the blankets and slid into the bed behind him, and he jerked awake. I didn't care, I cuddled myself against his back and felt that wash, that tingling wave of sensation like no other, a pleasurable blush of heat across the skin that preceded a throbbing ache of need at the apex of my thighs.

I both was, and wasn't the least bit, surprised I wanted him. I'd had the odd fantasy about my boss a time or two before; I just had never dreamed of actually following through on anything. I mean, I still didn't intend to, did I?

"Coco, what are you doing?" he asked, softly.

"I don't want to be alone," I said, and felt on the verge of tears, expecting him to push me out, to send me away. He turned sharply and I cringed.

"This probably isn't a good idea, babe," he whispered.

"I don't care. I'm scared."

"Shit," he swore softly and with feeling, but his arms went around me and I cuddled against his chest, laying my head on his shoulder, folding myself against him in the dark.

"I won't tell anybody," I whispered. "It can be our secret."

He snorted slightly and said, "Don't talk like that. You're gonna make me feel like a pedo."

"Don't you talk like that, I'm not a child," I said, sensitive about it. I wasn't tall, I didn't have a great chest, and I was tired of the comments and people treating me like a child when I'd probably grown up faster than a lot of them.

The dance world was demanding, and my own mother hadn't treated me like a child for a very long time. Since before I was even eighteen. I think she'd stopped sometime when I was sixteen or seventeen, around the time I'd confessed I'd lost my virginity to another dancer, Mia Thomas.

I'd been afraid how she would take it, but she'd laughed lightly and had told me about her experimental phase with women when she'd been my age. Then in the next breath, she had told me she didn't care if it wasn't just a phase. She loved me, unconditionally, and I believed that of my mother wholeheartedly. It would break her heart to find out what had happened to me tonight.

"I'm sorry," he murmured somewhere above my head. "You're right."

"I know I'm right," I said and he chuckled. I smiled with him and closed my eyes. "I feel the safest I've ever known right now," I confessed.

He grunted, rubbing a hand up and down my back and said gruffly, "Good, that's good."

"Thank you for not pushing me away," I said.

"I should," he said, "but I can't."

"Good, that's good..." I parroted back to him dreamily, I was drifting, so very close to sleep. He kissed my forehead, jostling me slightly to do it and it was like the press of his lips against my skin flipped my switch and I just powered-down and was out.

I WOKE ALMOST TOO-WARM, wrapped in the muscular steel bands of Skids' arms. I closed my eyes and breathed him in, a mixture of his cologne, which was quite nice, and anti-bacterial hand soap. I didn't get the hand soap. It wasn't something he usually smelled like. Usually it was a mixture of his slightly spicy yet modern cologne and the smell of clean laundry. I had no idea what he used for laundry soap, but it was wonderful.

I sat up slowly and looked down at him. It was still pretty much dark out, but the sky was lightening out there, so it was closer to sunrise. You would think the spell of the drug would have been broken, and it was, I mean, I felt like me again. I wasn't dizzy anymore and the world didn't tip or try to slide out from under me when I sat up… but I still felt different.

Horny, for one, and it wasn't hard to figure out why.

I was totally attracted to my boss and had just spent the night cuddled up to him. Some of which I had spent with his erection poking me, but not where I decided I wanted it. I bit my lips together and tried to make a decision.

I felt like I was teetering on a tightrope. Fall to one side and it would be awkward for a few days, but we could pretend this never happened and go back to the way things were… hopefully, maybe …eventually. Fall to the other side and I risked courting a rejection that I was surprised to find would be soul-crushing the more I thought about it… but if I weren't rejected, what then?

I decided that fortune favored the brave and there was only one way to find out. The image, the feeling of his lips gently and reverently pressed to the top of my instep deciding me, I swung a leg over his hips and settled across his lap, my hands trailing over his chest to rest on his sternum and wait.

He woke with a start, looking up at me through a squint before it seemed to dawn on him through the fog of sleep that he wasn't dreaming and I was really straddling his obvious boner. I was acutely aware that the only thing separating us was the thin layer of his flannel pajama bottoms and my body responded accordingly, my pussy giving a throbbing, wanton pulse. A deep wanting ache settling in my core, a fire sparked in my middle that quickly rose, licking through my body. My nipples tingled and perked, growing taut as he eyed me carefully from where he lay beneath me, his hands on my hips.

"Coco, what are you doing?" he asked, uncertain.

I didn't answer with words. I didn't know what to say. I think, in some ways, I was afraid to speak and so I let my body do the talking. I ground against him and he sucked in a sharp breath. When I was sure that the slow roll of my hips had brought about the reaction I was looking for, I slowly lowered myself over the length of his body, bringing my lips close and closer still.

"Babe, I don't know about this –"" I silenced him with a light kiss, my lips skating over his in a barely-there sort of butterfly touch.

I closed my eyes, savoring the sensation of his lips against mine, his warm breath ghosting over my skin as he let out a shuddering sigh.

"I'm sure," I whispered, and his hands belied his stiff posture below me, sliding down my hips to dip below the hem of his shirt, his palms slightly rough but warm against the outside of my thighs.

"The drug has the effect of lowering inhibitions. It's not you, okay?"

"Stop," I ordered, and he stilled and fell silent. "This is me, not some drug. So just stop, okay? Just touch me."

He sucked in a steadying breath, his bright blue eyes capturing mine as he smoothed his hands slowly in a caress that made my own eyes slip shut, over my thighs, under his shirt, to capture my hips in his hands. I moaned slightly and ground against him again and was relieved when his hands, though they tightened against my hips, didn't stop me but rather helped me to grind against him.

"Shit, I'm going to hell for this," he said, his voice strained.

I opened my eyes and said, "Good, you can save me a seat on the bus," before I lowered my lips to his and kissed him for real.

His tongue clashed with mine, his hands skating up my body beneath the flannel shirt, pressing his forearms against my skin, as if, suddenly, there wasn't enough skin-to-skin contact in the world.

I half-whimpered, half-moaned into his mouth as I pulled his simple white tee up so I could touch his stomach, run my hands over his hard, chiseled body beneath all that warm soft skin.

"Jesus, Colette," he growled against my mouth and I sat up, shoving at his pajama pants, down, over the ridges of his hipbones.

His cock sprang free, lightly tapping against my inner thigh, the sensation of all of that velvet-wrapped iron, scorching to the touch, brushing that sensitive skin that close to my pussy sent me wild in my passion. I pressed my sex against him like a horny teen and rubbed myself up and down along his length.

He groaned like it was the best thing he'd ever felt and sat up abruptly, dragging his shirt off over his head, his arms going around my body, caging me, holding me still.

"Shit, fuck! I ain't got any condoms."

"I'm on the implant. Stop it already and fuck me," I said breathlessly and he didn't hesitate, thrusting his hips, the tip of his cock stabbing at my wet heat looking for purchase, which he found on the second or third try – I couldn't keep track.

I cried out as he entered me, long and almost too thick.

He slowed down and asked, "Did I hurt you?"

"No," I gasped, "more!"

He relinquished his control to me and fell back, the act driving him up inside of me just a little bit more, but then I had the reins; it was me who decided how fast, how hard, how much to take at once. He watched me as I went for the buttons on the shirt, undoing them as quickly as possible as I sank onto him, taking him in, taking him deeper, until I had the offending cloth keeping his hands off my skin out of the way and had taken him into my body to the root.

"Oh, Jesus, Colette. Don't stop now," he begged.

"Stop? I'm just getting started," I murmured and I rolled my hips in the best way I knew how to both take him deep and to please myself completely.

I threw back my head and let out a harsh breath as I gave myself over to the pleasure coursing out from my middle.

I bowed my head to look at him and Skids looked up at me through heavy-lidded eyes, lust and some sort of stronger emotion I couldn't readily identify painting his features. Everything was close to the surface, communicated on a deep sub-level I'd never experienced with any other man I'd been with, and I loved that.

It felt good. It felt right, and so I fucked him with everything I was worth, hips rolling and finding that cadence that made me feel like I was spiraling higher and higher on some invisible pleasure thermal while simultaneously plunging Skids into a deep erotic pleasure of his own.

"Mm, oh!" I cried and threw my head back again. I was close, so very maddeningly close.

"That's it, babe, you're close, yeah, good, that's good," he murmured, and I'd never been encouraged, edged on by a lover's voice before.

He licked the pad of his thumb and reached between us, settling it against the slick wetness at my clit. I cried out and arched, riding him faster, bouncing, pumping his thick cock in and out of me as he teased the hell out of my clit with gentle touches, driving me wild, making easy scorching circles against it with the pad of his thumb.

I gasped, the fragments of me flitting around his room suddenly drawn into the center of my being, my pussy contracting around his thick shaft as he called out, encouraging, screaming my name as all that I was exploded into so many pieces, so many fragments there was no way I would get them all back.

I collapsed over him, his strong arms going around me, holding me down, anchoring me tightly to his body as my own convulsed around and on top of his.

"Easy, baby, yeah, that's a good girl, come on back now," he urged quietly, as I lay panting and gasping, our bodies between us slick with wetness from my center, the rest of us lightly dewed with sweat.

"Oh, my God, that was the best sex of my life," I swore to him.

He chuckled and kissed the side of my neck, his hand buried in my hair at the back of my neck.

"Shit, yeah," he agreed, and heaved out a satisfied sigh. I leaned up and looked him in the eyes and, smiling, lowered my lips to his to seal things with a kiss. He kissed me back, and it was beautiful, fragile, and new.

"We gotta talk about this," he said finally, reluctantly.

"After," I said.

"After what?" he asked.

"After you make love to me this time," I murmured and he blinked, taken aback.

He thought about it, eyes calculating, and finally he flipped me onto my back, pulling me around my thighs so my head wasn't so close to the headboard.

"You got it," he murmured and lowered his mouth to my tit, sucking on the nipple there, his hands smoothing over my skin like I was a work of art.

I closed my eyes and fell away, and let him do whatever he wanted with me.

6

*S*kids…

She was a beautiful mess by the time I got done with her. Her body lithe, strong, and mesmerizing. I lost myself in it, making love to her with long, slow strokes, going at my pace no matter how much she writhed, no matter how much she begged 'harder' or 'faster'. She'd had her way with me, and I would have my way with her… except the more I drank her in, the drunker I got, and man, did I think I had a problem with alcohol? This girl was a more dangerous addiction yet.

"Coco…"

"Don't say it," she begged, covering my mouth with both of her hands. I blinked and she scowled. "Do not say this was a mistake," she insisted. "You'll break my heart."

I stared at her, mystified, until she finally lowered her hands.

"What could you possibly want with an old bastard like me?" I asked and she sighed.

"And there you go breaking it a whole different way," she whispered.

I shook my head. "I don't understand."

"I'm not sure I can put it into words just yet," she said. "But for one, you make me feel safe, protected in a way I don't think I've ever felt."

"You are safe with me, and I will protect you; you're so beautiful and I don't mean out here," I said, brushing my fingertips against her cheek. She turned her face into my hand and kissed the heel of my palm and it sent shivers through me.

"So, what happens now?" she asked softly. "Do I have to pretend this never happened?"

"No," I shook my head, "I wouldn't do that to you."

"Why?" she asked. "Seems like the easiest course of action."

"It probably would be," I agreed, "but not at the cost you'd have to pay." I swallowed hard. "To pretend this didn't happen would mean pretending you don't mean anything to me, and I think I've already blown the lid off that one, beautiful."

We lay on our sides, facing each other, her fingertips lightly playing against my chest. The sensation of her fingertips against my skin was out of this world, sending a tingling sensation racing across my chest, gooseflesh marching in its wake.

"You… you've wanted me for a while, too?" she asked.

"Yeah," I confessed. "I know it wasn't right, thinking about you like that when I'm supposed to be your boss, and an adult –" Her fingertips found my lips and silenced me again.

"I may be young, and have the body of a thirteen-year-old boy –"

It was my turn to silence her with a derisive snort. She lowered her hand and I caught it with my own.

"Not sure who told you that," I said, "but it ain't true. I love your body."

She bit her bottom lip and nodded, her eyes welling like I'd given her a most precious gift. That hurt me in ways I couldn't even begin to describe.

"You're something beautiful inside and out, Colette. I don't think I've ever fantasized so much about what I've wanted to do to your body. I just never thought I would get the chance."

"You can have as many chances as you want," she whispered, and leaned in to kiss me.

I kissed her back, still completely stymied over why, out of all the men around her, she would want this, with me, at my age. I would be lying if I said it didn't bother me.

"How are you feeling, really?" I asked when this round of kissing concluded. I resolutely thrust everything else away, choosing to focus on one problem at a time.

"Tired, and like I was run over by a Mack truck. I'm still sort of fuzzy on the details, and I really don't remember anything – It's like one minute I was in the bar, and the next minute I was naked in your bathtub and I don't remember anything but glimpses and flashes of light and sound in between."

"Okay, let me tell you what happened…"

I spent the next God-knows-how-long filling her in on all the dirty details. She paled and went very still and I tried and failed to resist the urge to hold her tight.

"I… I should probably get my phone," she said finally. I nodded.

"I'll get it for you, it's in the dining room. Just stay here for me."

I got up and pulled my pants back on, padding barefoot down the hall and grabbing up her personal effects bag from the hospital with her purse and what looked like a cami or something in it.

She frowned and asked suddenly, "Did I throw up? I think I remember throwing up."

"A couple of times, yeah."

"Oh, God and you kissed me!" she cried and put her hands over her mouth, horrified.

I lost it, I couldn't help it. I laughed until I damn near cried and said, "Guess you don't remember brushing your teeth."

"I did?"

"Yup, in the bathtub last night. I had a spare toothbrush. I always keep one around, you never know."

"Oh, thank God," she said. She lit up the screen on her phone and blanched.

"Wow, okay, so my roommates are seriously freaking out and don't know where I am, the company wants to see me at my earliest convenience, and," she looked at the time, "I'm not late yet but if I don't move my ass and get home and changed, I'm going to be.

"I'll give you a ride. I washed your clothes last night, let me get them for you."

"Are you sure?" she asked, anxiously.

"One crisis at a time, babe. We'll get you squared away with your roomies and the ballet then we can tackle whatever's next."

"Feels like I can do anything when you're there to keep me grounded," she confessed and my hardcore reluctance softened some. I didn't know what the hell we were going to do about us –if there should even be an 'us'– but we had plenty of time to figure it out after the rest of things got squared away.

I wasn't worried about her housemates, but I'd be lying if I said that I wasn't worried about the ballet. Especially after the thing last year with Claire and the Night Circus. These kinds of places could be a real bag of dicks where victim-blaming and shaming were concerned, and I didn't want to see Coco's dreams snatched away from her as soon as she'd grasped onto them, for something she didn't do and was completely outside her control.

We'd have to see, but I was going with her. I couldn't let her face that kind of thing alone.

I got dressed and she did, too. I didn't want her to be cold without her sweater, and so I let her keep my favorite shirt for now. I also pulled down one of my old jackets out of the closet. It was definitely what you would call a boyfriend jacket, the way it fit her, something like two or three sizes too big as it was, but it would afford her a lot more protection than the skimpy fashionista pleather thing on my dining room table.

I took her down to the bike and we rode over to her place. She was surprised when I actually got off the bike with her. I raised my eyebrows and she sort of glowed a little and took my hand, leading me up the steps to her lobby.

She took the stairs despite feeling like garbage, and we came out in a corridor on the fourth floor. She barely got her key in the lock when the door flew open and one of her harried roommates flew out of it and wrapped Coco in a tight hug.

"Oh, my God! Coco, where have you been?" she demanded.

"Inside," I said and glanced up and down the hall.

"You, get ready to face whatever music at your ballet company," I told Colette before turning to her roommates. "You, you, you, and you, sit your asses down. It's time for a chat."

All four of them looked taken aback, but they all drifted in the direc-tion of the couch and chairs in the living room. They dropped onto the couch and Colette grabbed and squeezed my hand twice before disap-pearing.

"What the hell were y'all thinking last night?" I demanded sternly. All of them stared up at me like deer in the headlights, completely mute.

I lit their asses up, lectured them up one side and down the other about peer pressure, not listening to their friend, and their total lack of situational awareness and how they almost got her raped by not checking in with her.

I was used to giving rookies a rip, and even the occasional kid on the street, but this was new, and somehow more personal, so I had to keep a tight rein on my anger. The guys looked miserable and sick with guilt, the girls cried softly and all of them looked mighty sorry.

I finished off with, "Y'all need to treat each other better and look out for each other. Every one of you was drunk, and if shit had hit the fan for you, Colette would have been the only one with her shit together to take care of you. Not a damn one of you were there to take care of her last night, and it was supposed to be her night. I don't care what you do or how you do it, but you need to fix that shit."

"Skids." Her soft voice dragged our attention to the hallway. "I need to get to the company."

"Right, let's go."

I held out a hand and she tucked herself against my side telling her roommates, "I'm sorry, you guys…"

"Don't you dare!" one of the girls said and rushed forward wrapping her in a hug. "We're sorry," she said, muffled by Colette's borrowed jacket. She'd changed clothes and had a gym bag slung across her chest, but she'd kept my coat, which meant she didn't have a good enough one of her own for the ride.

"I've got to get to the company," Colette told her. "They want to see me. I don't know why."

"Okay, we'll be there as soon as we can," one of the boys said.

"Okay," she murmured. "I still have to call my mom," she added unhappily.

"One thing at a time, babe." I put a hand to her back and guided her to the front door. I didn't give her roommates a backward glance. I think I'd shook them up enough.

The ballet company's hall or whatever you call it was intimidating. It was on the other end of, and almost part of Bayside Park, one of the older and more impressive buildings of Old Town, the original part of Indigo City. I found easy parking in a motorcycle slot at the curb and killed the engine. Colette got off the bike and I got off with her. She blinked up at me in surprise. I gave a one-shouldered shrug and told her, "Not letting you go in there alone when there's a potential for bad news. I mean it, you're not alone out here anymore."

She nodded and went up the wide, flat, easy-riser stone steps surrounding the building on its grand pedestal. I went up just behind her and followed her through the front doors and down an administrative side-hall to a set of office doors. She knocked and a light, heavily accented female voice called out, "Come in!"

My dread eased off when the slender older woman, her auburn hair pulled into a severe bun, dressed in a black leotard and one of them pink floaty skirts all but leapt up from behind her desk.

"My poor girl! The hospital called late last night and said you had been there, what happened?"

She looked up at me in the doorway as she fluffed some of Colette's hair and asked, "And who are you?"

"I'm Skids. Coco stayed at my place last night after she was discharged from the hospital."

"I'm fine now, Madame, honestly."

"What happened?" the Madame or whatever demanded.

"I was at Skids' bar last night. I work there most of the week and we –

my roommates and I – other dancers in the company, decided to go out to drink to Lacy's health and sort of celebrate me moving up." Coco blushed furiously, getting a little tongue-tied and the Madame frowned and shrugged.

"It is only natural to celebrate upon becoming a principal dancer in any company," she said and Colette looked grateful.

"Um, long story short, I wasn't really drinking, I didn't want to compromise my body for practice today."

The Madame smiled at that.

"So, why the hospital?"

"Because one of your boys slipped something into her drink and she got real sick," I said.

"Pardon? One of my –""

"Brooks put a date rape drug in my drink," Colette said, and she was looking at the floor, dejected, scared, and I hated that for her.

"No!" The Madame looked aghast and I waited for the hammer to drop like it so often did.

"He's probably still cooling his heels in lockup. I've got video footage from my surveillance cameras at the bar that caught him dead to rights if you need to see it."

"I do!" The Madame declared and I pulled out my phone. Reflash had sent me three clips: the dose, Colette's reaction, and the rescue. I played them all in succession for the dance lady and she turned positively stormy.

"Yet you are still here, to dance?" she asked Colette, and before my girl could answer, the Madame waved her hand in the air and said, "Preposterous! You must go home and rest. Tomorrow, you come back."

"So I'm not fired?" Colette asked meekly and her instructor lady looked horrified.

"Absolutely not! However, Brooks is no longer welcome in this company – we shall replace him immediately."

"His number one understudy is Bennett, isn't it?" she asked.

"Oui."

Colette nodded. "I dance well with him; we should be okay. I don't want the production to suffer."

I fought not to roll my eyes, but couldn't help the urge. The Madame seemed to have a decent head on her shoulders. Thank fuck for that. Usually these artsy types had the reality of shit completely ass-backwards.

"Take her home," she said and looked me up and down. "The hospital said her father was with her?"

"Oh, my God, you didn't!" Colette sputtered, laughing.

"Damn right I did," I grated, and she smiled big.

"And they bought that?" she asked.

"It is the blue eyes, I think," the Madame said, smiling appreciatively. "Thank you for taking care of my star dancer."

"Any time," I said, and meant it.

"Please, take her home while I deal with this."

"You got it."

And that was that.

I took Colette back to her place just as her roommates were coming out and she filled them in. I had to leave her at the door, it was getting late, and I had to open up shop back at the restaurant. We were open and did a decent lunch business during the week.

7

––––––––––

$\mathcal{C}$**olette...**

    "Oh, my God! I am totally coming out there, and don't you say no!"

I laughed some and said, "I'm not going to say no! I miss you."

"I can't believe someone would do that to my baby – well, I can believe it," she sighed. "I'm grateful to your boss. What did you say his name was?"

"Skids, he goes by Skids, and there's more."

"Oh?" My mother's voice took on that dry, interested tone that she got the second she scented blood in the water. She adored gossip, and I never held back.

"I sort of fucked him this morning and I know, I know, he's my boss but I really like him and he's just so wonderful and so safe, and oh, my God! He's a total heartthrob; Mom, I can't even."

She laughed through the line and said, "And what else aren't you telling me?"

62

"He's something like in his fifties?" I said, wincing, not sure how that bit of news was going to go over.

My mother made a dismissive noise. "Pfft! I'm the one that told you that you were always going to end up with an older man, if you ended up with a man at all. This is no surprise to me."

"Ah! You did not!"

"I did too! Or maybe I just always thought so and never actually told you, but whatever – I always knew you'd end up with someone older. So, he's your boss, huh? What does that mean? He's the manager? He's the –?"

"Owner," I said. "Well, half-owner. He runs the bar, but doesn't drink. His partner is the head cook in the kitchen. He's a retired cop, his partner is a retired firefighter, and they run a motorcycle club."

"What?"

"And I may have ridden with him a couple of times."

"Colette Bishop! Need I remind you how dangerous those things are?" she demanded.

"So, let me get this straight: you don't mind that I boned my boss this morning, you don't mind that he's something like thirty years older than me, but you're totally freaking out over the fact I rode on his motorcycle with him?"

Silence on the other end of the line and then a petulant, "Yes!"

"Oh, my God, Mom, seriously?"

"Coco, you are my only child! I don't know what I would do without you. I swear sometimes you'd like to send me to an early grave."

"Okay, okay, all of this contradictory bullshit aside, I saved the best news for last."

"Oh?"

I knew that would distract her.

"The reason we were in the bar in the first place last night? Lacy Colbert tore her ACL; I've been moved up to principal for *The Nutcracker* production."

My mother lost her shit and I couldn't help but laugh. I can't tell you how much better I felt unburdening my soul to her. She didn't always know what to say, but she was honest with me like no other human being on the planet… until Skids.

A soft knock fell at my bedroom door and I looked up as Bridgette poked her head inside.

"Hey," she said hesitantly.

"Hey," I said back.

"We, um, made dinner. We were hoping to talk to you. I mean, we've got some things to say and we thought it'd be nice to have a house dinner. We haven't really done that in a while."

"Sure," I said quickly, to cut off her babbling. I got up off my bed and stretched before padding across the carpet in my socks – well, in Skids' socks. I had put on some comfortable heather gray leggings when I'd gotten home, returning the thick wool socks to my feet and Skids' over-sized shirt to my body. It hung on me like a dress and the ensemble was probably the coziest thing I'd ever worn.

I was reluctant to give it up. I hoped I didn't have to.

I went out to the dining room with Bridgette and everyone looked up from around the table. The guilty looks on their faces told me they'd really thought about what Skids had said to them that morning and they all felt horrible. The knot of anxiety in my chest eased and I slid into my seat at the round table.

"Peace offering," Jess said.

"We know you have every right to be mad at us," Genevieve said, and I shook my head.

"I'm not," I said. "Not mad, disappointed, hurt a little, but not really mad."

"Ouch, that's almost worse," Orion said.

"We deserve it, though," Bridgette said bitterly.

"We're really sorry." Genevieve looked like she was going to cry again.

"I'm sorry Brooks was a douche, but I had a really good time leading up to all of that," I said.

"Your boss was right," Jess declared. "We were being selfish, and we should have looked out for you."

"We didn't know you weren't drinking," Bridgette said.

I shifted uncomfortably and said, "That was my fault."

"Only because we made you so uncomfortable you didn't trust us enough to say something. We made it tough on you for no reason. I've been thinking about it all day…" Orion shook his head. "We make fun, sure, but if it gets to the point you feel like you gotta lie to us to get us to back off?"

"God, that makes us shitty friends," Bridgette said, and then she did cry.

Their guilt was a little overwhelming and I felt bad that they felt bad.

"Well," I said, "I guess it's all out there now." I sighed.

"Just tell us where we should go from here. We'd do just about anything to make this up to you," Genevieve said and she sniffed, tears falling out of her bright hazel eyes, too.

"Dinner looks good," I hazarded. I had never really been good with my feelings. At least, not being out in the open with them. Especially in front of and with so many people. The dance world was sort of a miniature cross-section of the worst of schoolyard bullying sometimes. You learned fast to keep certain things to yourself and to not rock the boat or let blood into the water. The sharks, like Lacy, like Brooks, would circle almost immediately.

I couldn't fault my cast and roommates, it was like the culture could be slippery, oily, getting under your skin and twisting you to it without you even really noticing – until something like last night. Now they were starkly reminded in one of the most in-your-face ways possible that they'd let the worst parts of dance culture get in.

"Look," I said softly. "I know you guys are all really good people. I also know you love me and you wouldn't knowingly do anything to hurt me or even knowingly let someone else do it. We all just took our eye off the ball for a second."

"Yeah, and it smacked us in the face," Orion said unhappily.

"So we don't let it happen again," I said.

"So you forgive us?" Genevieve asked hopefully.

"There's nothing to really forgive. Like I said, I'm not mad at you."

We talked over our chicken, grilled vegetables, and couscous.

Finally, it was Orion who said, "We need to take turns. One of us needs to stay sober every time we go out as a group. If we're all here, at the apartment? Fine. We can all get smashed, who fucking cares when we're like ten feet from our own beds, but when we're out?" He shook his head. "One of us has to look out for the others."

The rest of my roommates made noises of agreement and Bridgette asked, "So who goes first for the next time we go out? How do we decide the order?"

"Alphabetical by last name?" I suggested.

Genevieve rolled her eyes, "Okay, Ms. Bishop – you're not going to be the first designated roomie after last night. That's hardly fair."

"Fine," Jess said. "We'll go Z to A, then. She'll be last in line that way."

We all kind of paused and thought about it for half a second.

I nodded. "Sounds good," I said and took another bite of my food. It warmed me that they cooked for me, that they were taking everything seriously and that everyone was trying to just plain do better. After all, all of us were far away from home, from where we'd come from, and none of us exactly had any family that was local.

We were supposed to be each other's family in absentia, and we hadn't necessarily been doing a very good job of that. I couldn't say I blamed any one of us for it, though. When you're a dance kid, it's very competitive, very focused and that focus is, and always will be, solely on yourself and how well you do. Sometimes, it was easy to lose sight of the fact that there was a bigger picture. Like losing sight of the forest for the trees.

A production on the scale of *The Nutcracker* wasn't just one dancer. It took all of us. Still, everyone strove to be the best dancer they could be. To be noticed, to get that part above them, to be the next rising star.

It made what happened last night entirely too easy. It'd been a wake-up call to the household. For sure.

A soft knock fell at our front door and we all just sort of froze. We weren't used to visitors all that often.

"I got it," Jess said and rose. We all followed him with our gaze as he went to the front door and opened it, but whoever it was, was hidden by the door itself.

"Hey, uh, is Coco here?"

I smiled at Skids warm, rich voice and said, "I'm here."

I got up from the table and Jess stood aside. He stepped into our apartment and asked, "Can I talk to you for a sec?"

"Sure, um, my room okay?"

He rolled his lips together and nodded, and I smiled.

"Right this way."

8

———————

kids...

"I know that look."

I looked up from the clipboard in my hands as Reflash walked back down the alley toward our side door and I sighed inwardly.

"Yeah, what look is that?" I asked.

"The look that says you're beating the shit out of yourself for somethin'. What happened?"

I jerked my head in the direction of the interior of our bar as the produce distributor rolled his empty dolly out and onto the lift on the back of his truck. Reflash slid past me and I shut the side door with a final nod of thanks to our delivery guy.

"So, what happened?" he asked.

"What makes you think something happened?" I asked coolly, wrestling with how the news I'd fucked one of our employees, a girl less than half my age that morning, was going to go over.

69

He gave me a baleful look like I shouldn't talk stupid and I sighed and swore with feeling. He bucked up and looked alarmed and I nodded.

"Yeah," I said.

"Still have no idea what we're talking about, but if I had to guess, it probably involves the cute blonde that works for us, bein' that she –" He stopped cold and his eyebrows shot up.

"Did you score with Coco last night?" he asked.

I shook my head and he looked relieved.

I said, "This morning."

It was not the reaction I was expecting. I expected heat. I expected fire and brimstone. What I got was hysterical laughter.

"How is this even remotely funny, Flash?" I demanded, put out.

"Oh, come on! How is this not funny?" he demanded.

"She's our employee, or did you forget that?"

"What? No I didn't forget it. I also didn't forget that she's young but she's a woman, not a little girl. So quit standing there lookin' like you just sucked on a lemon. You should be happy."

"Happy?" I demanded. "I should be happy?" I shouted at his back as he wove his way through the standing produce crates and made his way back into the kitchen.

"Yeah, you should be happy! Not many twenty-two-year-olds wanna get it on with guys like us!" he called back.

"That's another problem entirely," I said sourly.

"Oh, yeah? How's that?" he asked, ducking out the kitchen door tying on his apron.

"She's twenty-two," I said. "I'm fifty-four. We got a thirty-two-year age gap going on here. You don't think that's even slightly fuckin' wrong of me?"

He looked like he actually thought about it for a second, then, picking up one of the flats of butter lettuce said, "Mm, nope."

I threw up my hands.

"And the fact that she's one of our employees?" I demanded.

"Well, that depends. Who started it?" he asked.

I sputtered, "Does it really matter?"

"Well, yeah. If it was you, bad boy, you shouldn't fuck the employees, but if it was her – you're free and clear. So which was it?" he asked.

"Her," I ground out.

"You lucky son of a bitch," he said, chuckling dryly.

"You don't see a problem with this?" I demanded.

"Yeah, I think you're being a pussy about it. Why the fuck can't you just enjoy it, man?"

"You're serious?" I demanded.

"As a fuckin' heart attack. What's the worst that could happen?" He looked at me sharply, eyebrows raised, and waited for my answer.

"She could get her heart broken," I said finally and he smiled and bounced his eyebrows once and said, "She's twenty-two. Heartbreak is a rite of passage at her age and I know you. You'd let her down easy."

"Don't joke, not about this."

"Who said I was joking?" he asked and took the flat weighing down his arms around the bar and into the kitchen's side-door at the end of the bar. I sighed and rubbed my eyes.

I guess the only question left was did I break her heart now or did I *really* break it later?

"Fuck me," I grumbled and hefted one of the next flats in the stack.

I went through the motions, helping Reflash get everything back into the kitchen and put away as some of his kitchen staff started to show up for the day's prep.

It was a busy lunch rush, dinner equally so, but a relatively slow bar night.

"Hey, Brandon."

"Yeah, what's up?" My bar lead in my absence looked up from where he was reloading our speed well.

"You got this?" I asked. "I got something I gotta head out and take care of."

"Yeah, man. I'm good," he said with a rakish grin.

I rolled my eyes and shook my head. "No banging the patrons," I said conspiratorially as I passed him by and he laughed.

"I flirt for tips, no matter what form they take," he said, eyeing a brunette at the end of the bar.

"Yeah, just as long as they pay their tab," I said and he grinned.

"Always."

Brandon was a stand-up guy. I didn't have to worry about him handing out freebies to get his dick wet. He had charm for days and was perfectly capable of scoring on his wit alone. I sighed inwardly and asked myself for something like the millionth time that day, *Just what the fuck does she see in you?*

I was about to find out. I rode over to her place, her apartment number burned into my brain from her employee file. It was too easy piggy-backing into her secure building. I just walked right in as soon as someone came out, and with a friendly smile and a nod, they even held the door open for me. I didn't like that one bit, but there wasn't much I could say about it.

I rode the elevator up to her floor, sparing my fucking knees the stairs, and went down the hall to her apartment door.

I heaved a sigh and felt like a douche that I had to stand there a second and literally pluck up the fucking courage to knock.

You're fifty-four, asshole. Not a teenage boy.

Her roommate, Jess, opened it up and looked surprised.

"Hey, uh, is Coco here?"

"I'm here." Her lyrical voice drifted around the door from somewhere off to the left.

Her housemate stood aside and held the door wider to let me in. I stepped around it and there she was, beautiful in the simplicity of her comfort, wearing my socks and heather gray leggings, my shirt on her lithe body.

I swallowed hard at the sight of her, in her home, wearing my clothes, and asked, "Can I talk to you for a sec?"

I'd come here determined to end things, but looking at her, dressed like that, I felt my resolve already begin to weaken.

"Sure, um, my room okay?"

I rolled my lips together, wishing I could talk to her anywhere but where there was a fucking bed in the room, but had to admit, it was likely the only place in the apartment that could and would afford us any privacy. I nodded, and she smiled and I had that tight sensation in my chest again. The one where my heart swelled so damn big I felt like it cracked.

"Right this way," she said and I followed her around the couch and toward a hall, turning almost sideways to go through a narrow bedroom door.

Bedroom, my ass, this was a closet, but it would have to do. She went in first and I stepped in after. She waved at me to close the bedroom door behind me and I did.

I was jammed between an open closet on one side and a desk on the other. The closet didn't even seem that it had any doors to begin with, just an open rod in an alcove with some shelves to one side. On my right was the desk, and even with the mesh office chair pushed in, there was barely a foot of walking space left to get by to what I guess was supposed to be the main part of the room.

The bed was a twin and shoved up against the wall in the little nook left by the closet. The foot was right up against the lip of wall left by the closet to close it off, while the head of the bed was right up against the wall just below the window – at least she had a window. If there hadn't been one, and I lived in here? I'd go claustrophobic bat-shit crazy inside the first day.

She had a tall bookcase across from the bed, a trashcan between the desk and the bookcase and still, somehow, managed to have a soft microfiber gray wingback chair in the corner draped with a throw, positioned so she could look out the window.

She used light colors, and her choice of decorating was decidedly different. She had wrecked ballet slippers hanging from picture nails along the wall over the bed. Probably a pair of them for every year that she danced. The first pair small and all of them the same pale pink, the ribbons frayed, the toes all but worn through and gray to black.

Opposite the bed, above the chair, was a photo portrait of a woman who looked like her, only older. Maybe in her thirties, the photo lit softly, the woman wrapped in a shawl, her shoulders bare, a rose in her hand as she posed delicately, lips slightly parted, eyes cast down, demure.

"My mother. I always loved that picture of her from when I was a little girl. It was taken for a playbill for one of her productions with the San Francisco Ballet. I believe it was *Sleeping Beauty*."

"You look just like her except for the red in her hair," I said.

"I wasn't even born yet when that photo was taken. She was, I think, nineteen."

"I would have guessed thirty," I said, blinking in surprise.

"Makeup," she said grinning. "You should see some of my shots, they can be completely unflattering. That one, though? I don't know… she looks like her age on the inside at the time. You know?"

I pursed my lips into a fine line and took a deep breath, holding it for a few seconds before letting it out. "Listen, Colette, that's what I'm here to talk to you about…"

The transformation her face went through smashed my damn heart into a million fucking pieces. It went from open and happy to wary and almost defeated. Like someone had walked up and literally just wiped the smile off her face.

"Please, don't," she murmured, and swallowed hard.

"Look," I said, as she sank down onto the edge of the bed. I moved quickly to take the seat in her cozy reading chair and put my mitts on her knees, giving the tops of her thighs a reassuring squeeze. "I just don't think you've thought this through. What it means to get involved with a man as old as me… I only have so much time left while you've got your whole life ahead of you."

She didn't speak, just let me. That was really the crux of it. That, and what if she met someone younger? The novelty with me would wear off pretty damn quick. At least that's what I kept telling myself… the way she was looking at me right now, though? I think, in my heart of hearts, I knew I was doing her a disservice.

"So what are you telling me?" she croaked out between vocal cords tight with emotion.

"I'm telling you, that while it was nice, and I do mean 'beyond wonderful', this morning, that it can't happen again. Not just because

I'm older than dirt, but there's just so many reasons why it was a bad idea and –""

"Stop it!" she snapped, and sniffed, swatting angrily at the tears that finally crested her bottom lashes.

"I'm not a child, Skids, and I know what I want."

I let out a frustrated sigh. "And I'm telling you, you can't have it," I said harshly.

Better to break her heart now than to let this linger, let it fester, I told myself but I'd be lying if I said it was easy. Doing the right thing never was…

Bullshit. You can tell yourself this is the right thing, but look at her, man.

I was. She was so beautiful it hurt, and the pain in her eyes, the tears on her lashes, only made her more so. She was so lovely, too lovely for the likes of me.

"Am I fired?" she asked, coldly, and I could tell her heart could barely take me sitting here anymore.

"No," I said, my heart betraying my hand as I reached out and smoothed it over her silky hair one last time. "I wouldn't do that to you, but if you need anything it'd probably be best if you went to Reflash for a while. Give whatever this is time to settle between us. You know, the sting to fade."

She laughed bitterly, but quietly, and murmured, "Don't think that's going to happen anytime soon."

"I know it probably feels like that now, but I'm sure it'll be okay."

"You really have a low opinion of yourself, don't you?" she asked and her voice held an underlying heat like she was pissed about that, but I think it was only half at me.

"Well, there's a reason for that," I said. "I'm not a good man, sweetheart. This morning proves it."

She looked crestfallen, and I couldn't stand it. I stood up and she stood with me and it was made doubly hard having to do this when she was standing there cozied up in my fucking clothes.

"I'll, uh, see you at work, I guess," I said, and she gave a stiff nod.

"I guess so," she said quietly.

I didn't say anything else. I didn't know what else to say… So I let myself out, nodded politely to her roommates at the table with their curious stares, and with one backwards glance at her closed, silent bedroom door, I let myself out of the apartment.

God, I felt like a total dick.

9

———————

*C*olette…

Dumped in less than twenty-four hours. That must have been some kind of a record. I know it was for me. I pulled one of my pillows off my neatly-made bed and hugged it tight to my chest, squeezing it, hoping it would stem the tide. I felt cracked wide open, right down the middle, and it felt like everything, from last night through this morning all the way up until right then, just came pouring out of me in a torrential downpour I just was not ready for.

A light rap at my door; Bridgette's voice, "Coco?"

"I'm fine!" I called back but my voice betrayed me. Too high, too tight, it cracked right down the middle like I did.

"Oh, honey," she said, an empathetic whimper and my bedroom door opened and she rushed in, closing it quickly before anyone else saw me. She came over and sat on the bed beside me and pulled me into a hug.

Girl power. I broke, and sobbed my broken heart out onto my friend's shoulder.

"What did he say to you?" she demanded, but the question was clearly rhetorical for now. I was so busy crying, I couldn't answer her anyway.

Of all the things to have happened in the last twenty-four hours, his putting a stop to us before there could even be an 'us' hurt the absolute most.

"I MEAN, I guess I don't understand," Genevieve said. "I mean, he's hot, don't get me wrong, but he's so… old."

I rolled my eyes at her and blew my nose, for like the thousandth time, into a Kleenex. It was a war zone of tissues across my lap and littered around me on my bed. Genevieve sat in my reading chair, her legs crossed under her while Bridgette sat with her back against the wall. Bridgette and I traded a look and I could tell she got it even if Genevieve didn't.

"It's not always about age," Bridgette said, trying to help me. "That's just a number. It's about how you feel when you're with someone."

"Right," I said, nodding tiredly, emotionally exhausted. "And around Skids I feel… God, so many things."

"Like what?" Genevieve asked, still trying to understand.

"Safe and looked after, for one. Even though he doesn't have to do it, it's like he wants to, and that's so nice…"

I also, for all of his talk about being too young, felt like he took me seriously, like deep down inside on some sub-level. He listened to me, valued my opinion, made me feel pretty without making me feel like all I was, was pretty. We talked books, we liked the same cinema, and we meshed really well when it came time to hustle at the bar, moving in almost this sort of dance with and around each other when the need called for it.

"Give it some time," Bridgette said gently and sagely. "He'll either snap out of it, or he won't, but he'd be stupid not to. You're one in a million, girl."

I sniffed, "Thanks."

"He really cares about you, too," Genevieve said softly and took a sip of her tea she'd brought in here with her, her hands wrapped around her snarky unicorn mug.

"I know," I said with another sniff. "Nobody just does all the things he did without caring," I said, and she nodded.

"Exactly, and nobody tears into four total strangers over somebody if they don't care."

Or touches them like he touched you. Or kisses them with such an epic amount of passion like he kissed you.

God, I ached at the thought of never being touched like that again, because as childish as it sounded, I was sure Skids was the right man for me… Because I didn't think any other man would even compare after what we'd shared this morning. I was no stranger to sex, and Skids was definitely the best sex I'd ever had. I mean, I guess, let's hear it for experience, right?

"Besides," Bridgette said, "it sounds to me he's broken it off with you *for* you. I think he thinks he's being noble or something." She rolled her eyes.

"Boys are dumb," Genevieve said with a sigh.

"Throw rocks at them," I finished. Which is something we just said any time Jess or Orion decided to get stupid about things.

Bridgette snorted and we all kind of fell out in a peal of laughter. It helped. I felt lighter. I also felt like I could do this, weather this storm, and hold out hope that Skids may come around after all.

I missed him already.

THE FIRST DAY back to work was awkward, to say the least. It was like Skids and I had lost our easy rhythm. I would turn around and nearly crash into him and vice versa. It was like we knew each one of us was there but we'd closed off somehow, it was like we couldn't feel each other; our awareness was suddenly stunted.

I kept stammering out apologies every time I found myself underfoot and at least once I had to have a quick cry in the ladies room before I fixed my makeup and got right back out to it. It was a good waste of one of my ten-minute breaks but it let off enough pressure that I could finish my shift.

We barely spoke. It was too hard now, and that hurt the most. I was so used to our laughing, easy banter, and its sudden absence left a vacuum. It was one that, while I was eager to fill it, couldn't be filled by anyone but Skids. I knew that, so I didn't even try.

After the last customer had gone and we were about to begin clean-up and do the bit of prep for the next day we usually took care of at closing, he appeared at my back, his presence looming large, reflected in the glass of the front door as I locked it. I jumped, startled, and pressed a hand to my chest. It was just so unexpected.

"Sorry," he said gently, and held out a glass of ice water, two slices of lemon in it.

"Thanks," I murmured, taking the glass.

"Welcome," he shifted his stance and asked softly, "Doing okay?"

I couldn't look at him, I didn't want my face to betray me even though I knew it would anyway.

I sighed out, a heavy defeated thing and said, "No."

"I'm really sorry," he whispered, and it sounded pained.

"Yeah, well, me too." I was a little angry at him then and took a big swallow of the cold water, ducking past him to the waitress station to do what needed doing. He let me go, but it didn't go unnoticed that he stood, rooted to the spot for several heartbeats, simply staring help-lessly in my direction.

You can fix this. I urged him silently. *All you have to do is take it back...* but of course, closed mouths didn't get fed and I resolutely kept my own mouth shut.

I knew it wouldn't fix anything but I didn't know what to say, what to do, to change his mind about me, about trying for an 'us,' even though I badly wanted it. I desperately wanted a rainy day spent cuddled on the couch watching bad movies, to go out to dinner someplace that wasn't the *10-13* and maybe catch a play or a show. I wanted to go for a Sunday ride where it was about the journey, not the destination. I wanted to spend all day in bed with as little clothing as possible, napping and making love.

I wanted so much for us, like I'd never wanted with anyone else, and it was difficult to understand the why of it. I didn't know why, I didn't know why him, but I didn't feel the need, unlike Skids, to pick it apart and worry it to death.

I sighed, and let my hands mechanically go through the prep work laid out in front of me as I let my mind wander back to the conversation with Bridgette and Genevieve the night he'd come to the apartment.

"You know he's like, totally going to die first, right?" Genevieve had said. Bridgette had leaned over and hit her with a pillow, but I knew Genevieve didn't mean anything by it.

I knew that. I knew that our time was limited and that he would grow old and I would still be young enough to care for him and strangely, that actually appealed to me. Having the ability to love someone so completely, so beyond what was considered the norm. I knew it was different, but I also knew I could do it. That it wouldn't all be a bowl of roses all the time, that it would be hard, but I was used to doing hard things – I thought I was pretty good at embracing the suck, but for some reason I wasn't willing to embrace this suck.

I wanted a bigger suck.

Starting with his dick would be nice, I thought to myself and sputtered a laugh.

"What's so funny?" Reflash asked, coming out of the kitchen.

"If I told you, I'd have to kill you. Secret espionage spy stuff," I said, deadpan.

"Oh, you're funny, been watching too many Bond flicks lately?"

"Actually," I said lightly, tucking silverware into napkins, rolling, and securing them with the elegant fold method Reflash had taught me my first week here. "It was a John Wick double feature at our apartment last night.

He pulled out a chair at the table I worked at and dropped into it, "Oh, yeah?"

I nodded and he eyed me for a second. I swallowed hard and waited for it…

"You doin' alright, kid?"

There it was.

Of course Skids told him, they're best friends, and of course he would ask… he's Skids' business partner. He needs to know things are cool and that you won't try to fuck with the business.

"Everything's fine," I lied easily, except I was a crap liar.

"Yeah," he said. "Right."

"Yeah," I nodded and forced a smile, "right."

He chewed indecisively on his bottom lip and eyed me, the wheels turning in his head as he said, "For what it's worth, I think he's an idiot, but I can see where he's coming from and it's his life."

I swallowed hard and nodded.

"Um, it's true with the, ah, age disparity there's a lot to think about and I'm not stupid," I said. "I mean, I know I haven't thought through everything but I've thought through a lot of the bigger points. At least I think I have. I'm, um…" I blushed furiously and finished with, "…Yeah."

Reflash huffed a big sigh and nodded. "Skids is stubborn," he confided. "If there's a patron saint of torturing yourself, Skids probably prays to that guy nightly."

I smiled and laughed a little, but of course Skids came out of the back office and asked, "What's so funny?"

Reflash cleared his throat loudly and stood up, walking past his partner, he clapped him on the shoulder, looked him right in the eye and said, "You're a fuckin' idiot."

"What'd I do now?" Skids asked, throwing up his hands, but Reflash didn't turn, just waved over his shoulder and went back into his kitchen while I studiously paid extra careful attention to my prep work and refused to look in Skids' direction.

"Aw, Jesus Christ," he snarled under his breath and Reflash shouted from the kitchen, "I heard that!"

I rushed through the rest of my prep, suddenly just wanting to get the hell out of there and go home. I went back to the office and pulled on my puffy down coat and scarf for the walk home and paused at the sight of the corner of the gold ticket envelope sticking out of my purse.

The Madame had given it to me. For Skids. For opening night. A 'Thank you' for taking care of her new principal dancer. I bit my lips together and drew in a deep breath, in through my nose and out through my mouth. I slung my purse across my chest and slipped the envelope free, holding it in my suddenly shaking hands.

Opening night was next week, and I doubted Skids would want to take time away from the *10-13*. Still, she'd made me promise I would deliver it, and I followed through on my promises so…

I nearly crashed into him as I went to leave the office. I looked up into his so-handsome face, swallowing my nervousness, my fear, and held out the envelope and blurted the truth, "The Madame wanted me to give you this. I've got to go."

I thrust the envelope at him and he took it, and I was off, striding up the short hall, past the banquet room, past the kitchen door on the other side, ducking around the end of the bar and making quick strides for the front door.

"Night, Coco!" Reflash called from the kitchen as I swept by.

"Night!" I called back and unlocked the door and swept outside. I didn't even wait for Bridgett and Jess to get there. I met them two blocks away in the direction of home.

10

S kids…

I pulled at my collar. I was used to wearing collared shirts, but I wasn't used to buttoning them all the way or putting a tie with them anymore. Still, I figured, opening night for the fucking ballet called for a suit. I'd been invited as her guest, and I wouldn't disrespect that. I was a fifty-four-year-old man not some punk millennial.

Watch it, buddy. She's a millennial.

I waited in line and breathed out, the lobby opulent and gold, the ceilings soaring. I'd gone to Lys' flower shop and had stared at all the different blooms for over an hour trying to decide. I'd finally gone with some pale pink and white carnations with baby's breath.

I guess I was in some kind of VIP section; when I showed the ticket-taker my ticket, they'd pointed to another, much smaller, line, and I was ushered in to some side room where a glass of champagne was thrust into my hand.

I stared at my long lost love, alcohol, and looked up, shaking my head.

"No thanks, I'm an alcoholic." The waiter blinked, eyes wide at my admission and I didn't care. I wore it out in the open on purpose. I could never forget, never go back there, and the night Coco had given me the ticket to this thing was the first night in over a year I'd needed to take my ass to a meeting.

My sponsor, who I hadn't contacted in longer, hadn't picked up his phone. Of course, I couldn't guarantee he'd even recognized the number.

"Can I get you anything else, sir? Coffee? Sparkling water?"

"No, thanks," he nodded and I thought back to that meeting. I'd spoken. Confessed I was fighting the urge to drink to cope; it'd always been my number-one coping mechanism. Rough tour? Have a beer. Except one beer had turned into six, which had eventually turned into a shot, which had quickly turned into a glass, until I was putting that shit in my coffee in the morning just to get through the next tour.

Eventually, I fucked up so bad I was given the option to take an early retirement and get into treatment or just lose my shield, period. By the time anyone insisted I needed the help, it was too late. Too late for my marriage, too late for the Washington family, and too late to take back any of the mistakes I had made, which were many and all-consuming.

Reflash and the club were the only ones to stick by me. If it weren't for Reflash and the Knights, I would probably be in an alley somewhere. Not standing in the fucking VIP area of the fucking Indigo City Bay Ballet.

I still wasn't one-hundred-percent sure what I was even fucking doing here.

We were escorted one by one to our seats and I found myself three rows back and center stage. There was a nice woman, tall and slender, wrapped in a rich, white fur stole, her dress glittering in the stage light with some sort of metallic thread, already seated to my left when I sat down.

"Sorry," I muttered when my elbow nudged her arm while I was trying to put the flowers between my knees to keep them upright. These seats were made for a generation much slimmer than ours and while she fit in her seat, I was a bit wide. At least in the shoulders.

"Oh, please, don't worry about me," she said smiling. Gentle crow's feet fanned out from her hazel eyes. She patted the back of my hand with hers, which was covered in a long white satin opera glove, an expensive tennis bracelet glittering with diamonds over it.

She looked vaguely familiar, but I would be damned if I could place her. I didn't have time to dwell on it. It seemed the performance was waiting on the last of this section to be seated and I was, embarrassingly, that guy – or at least one of them. As soon as the couple behind me were seated, the house lights dimmed further, the music from the orchestra pit blared to life larger than life, and the curtains swept up and out to the sides revealing the stage set as a perfect Christmas living room albeit from a long fucking time ago. I'm talking like the Victorian era or some shit.

I settled in and focused on the stage, the sweet, slightly spicy scent of the carnations in my lap filling my nose as the dance began.

She was the only thing I saw the entire night. I couldn't tell you what the other dancers did. I didn't care. The second she tiptoed onto the stage, she was the only thing I could see and she was magnificent. Every wave of her hand painted the scene with vibrancy and grace. She really outdid herself, so beautiful, so lithe and light on her feet, she defied gravity, defied convention.

She earned herself a standing ovation and I don't think there was a dry eye in the house. She was everything I knew she could be and more.

When I exited the row, an usher was waiting and asked me to follow him. I did, through a door past the stage and down into the backstage of the hall. He stopped beside a door, and gestured with a hand, giving a slight bow.

"Thanks," I muttered, uncomfortable, but I wasn't used to this high-end production made out of every little thing. I raked my bottom lip between my teeth and knocked.

"Yes?" a light voice called out from the other side of the door and I sucked in a breath and opened the door.

She sat at a dressing table scattered with makeup, her back to me; her wide blue eyes capturing mine in the mirror.

She sucked in a sharp breath and stood up, turning saying, "You came." Her voice was light, breathy with her shock and surprise.

"Uh, I was invited, remember?"

She blushed and I stepped past the door and closed it behind me. I turned back to her and she was rooted to the spot, almost like she was afraid to approach me, like I wasn't really real, which was pretty much exactly how I was feeling after watching her up there like that.

I don't understand what she saw in me.

"Um, these are for you," I murmured and held out the flowers. She took a tentative step in my direction, the sequins and rhinestones of her costume winking in the overhead lights, and she was pure magic in motion.

I wanted so badly to pull her to me, to tell her I was a fucking idiot, but I honestly didn't know if there was any fixing this.

"They're beautiful," she murmured, taking the flowers from me, smelling them, her eyes closing as she breathed them in. She set them aside on a table near the wall and I just stood there, mesmerized by her every movement as she turned back to me.

Like before, she was the brave one, the bold one, and made the first move. Coming to me, wrapping her arms around me, and hugging her body to mine, her eyes closing as my arms went around her. I realized she was breathing me in, just as she'd breathed in the scent of the flowers a moment before, only her body relaxed, easing into the bigger cover of mine and I swear to God, the feeling was mutual, like coming home.

"I'm so sorry," I muttered and she didn't say anything, just held me as I held her.

"Sorry enough to try?" she asked.

Against my better judgment I said, "Yeah," and was surprised to find that I meant it.

"Yeah?" she echoed, her tone and inflection rising at the end, the question a tremulous one, with her fear of my rejection a second time.

"Yeah," I said and tipped her face up to mine with gentle fingertips. She deserved my honesty. "But we've got to talk about some things."

"Tonight?" she asked. "After this?"

"Good a time as any, I suppose," I murmured and this moment felt so fragile, so surreal. She leveled her deep blue gaze at me, and I stood there feeling half my fuckin' age. Standing there like her reluctant blue cavalier when the look in her eyes telegraphed clearly that she needed me, that she wanted this with me more than anything in the world.

"I don't understand why you want me out of anyone in the world you could have," I said.

She bit her bottom lip slightly and sighed before she said profoundly, "I don't know where you came by such insecurities, but I'm telling you I know what I want and what I want is you. All of you."

"I'm not a young man, Coco..."

"I can do math, Skids. I know that," she said and I flinched slightly on the inside. *Shit.* I kept telling myself she wasn't a kid but the back of my brain still hadn't fucking got with the program.

"Kiss me," she whispered and I hesitated for only a moment before my lips found hers, her arms snaking around my neck, her fingers buried in the back of my hair, massaging my scalp. A sweeping wash of sensation swept down my back, heated my blood, as her sweet taste filled my senses, more intoxicating than any damn drink. I pulled her body tight against mine and she groaned into my mouth.

Okay, so we're doing this thing, this... where the fuck do we even start?

She had an answer for everything, even the unspoken questions.

"I want a do-over," she murmured against my lips.

"Yeah?" I asked, my voice husky with desire.

"Yeah. Take me back to your place, let's do things right. I want to be there for everything this time."

A light knock fell at the door and we both jumped. I let her go, stepping further into the room to give her and whoever was at the door some room. She opened the door enough to duck her head and upper body out into the hall with whoever it was and I had to smile, appreciating her backside as she traded words with whoever was out there.

"Yeah," she murmured.

"Alright, I'll just go back to the hotel then, shall I?" a light but cultured, older female voice.

"Okay. I love you, Mom."

"I love you, too, baby. You did so well. I am so proud of you."

I stood there, a little shell shocked and grateful I wasn't meeting her mom now, that she'd run some interference. Colette ducked out the door and hugged whoever was on the other side before coming back into the room with me.

"Okay, bye," she whispered and shut the door tightly.

"We can do this later," I said, "I mean, your mom is in town and –'"

"Has been in town for over a week now, and will be here tomorrow, and likely the day after that," she said gently.

"Okay," I said and held up my hands in surrender. Tonight was her night. She could be in charge.

She smiled then, and it was the first genuine smile I'd seen on her face in the weeks since I'd left her apartment. She smiled at work, but things just hadn't been the same. It had been a fake-ass plastic customer service smile, the cheerfulness she usually exuded effortlessly having become painfully forced since I'd broken her heart, thinking I'd been doing her a mercy.

Fuck me.

"Let me get some of this makeup off and change clothes," she said quietly and I nodded slightly.

"Fuck the makeup, just get dressed. You said you wanted a do-over, right?"

"Yeah," she said, cocking her head lightly.

"You puked all over us in the back of the car on the way to my place from the hospital. If you don't mind skipping that part this time, I'd appreciate it, but first thing that happened when we got back to my place was I put you in a bath."

Her forehead wrinkled slightly and she said, "Where did you clean up?"

"Kitchen sink."

The furrow in her brow smoothed and she said, "That explains why you smelled like hand soap."

I laughed lightly and nodded and asked, "What are you waiting for?"

She startled slightly and sprang into action, gathering herself and stepping around a screen in the corner to change.

I let her have her privacy for now. If I were going to embrace this, I would have her nude in my shower, writhing against the tile as soon as

I got her home. Despite my patience and virtue having all but run out, I could at least be patient until I got us back to my place.

"Are you hungry?" I asked.

"I could eat," she said.

"Takeout from downstairs work for you?"

"The *10-13?* Sounds fine."

"You know what you want?"

"My usual."

Okay, chef's salad it was. I texted Reflash, who usually had his phone stuck to the stainless-steel shelving by its magnetic phone case above his prep station. He shot back a text saying it would be ready when we got there and that it was about fuckin' time I stopped being an idiot.

I shook my head and shoved my phone back in my pants pocket as Coco stepped out from behind the screen in street clothes, twisting her hair into a loose knot at the base of her skull, a plastic clip to pin it clutched between her teeth.

She took the clip from her mouth and worked it into her hair asking, "Did you bring a coat?"

"Yeah, uh, it's at the coat check."

"I'll have a valet get it." She held out her hand for the ticket and went to the door once I handed it over. She cracked the door, murmured a few words and passed the stub of paper along before shutting it firmly again.

"It'll be just a minute," she murmured.

"You're really serious," I asked softly. "Out of all the guys you could have your own age you still want me?"

She smiled and said, "Out of all the guys my own age, none of them are you… so, yeah. You need to quit selling yourself so short." She came to me and wrapped her arms around my waist, looking up at me with those eyes made soft and filled with desire.

"Still got some things to talk about," I said softly.

"Like what?" she asked demurely.

"Need to know you get what you're signing up for, babe."

"Mm, you mean like snarky comments about being out with my dad?"

"Or granddad," I said. She crossed her eyes and I laughed a little.

"People calling me a gold-digger behind my back?" she asked.

"Haven't heard it yet, but I'm sure it's coming," I said softly and it already pained me thinking anyone could think of her that way. I knew just how damn hard she worked, busting her ass day in and day out just to maintain her dream.

"Or how bitches are going to be trippin' calling you a sugar daddy," she said, and then with a shrug, "Of course, they won't be trippin' once I've pushed them down a flight of stairs for it."

I laughed again and pressed my forehead to hers, holding her close. She giggled with me and things just clicked for me. She knew. She knew at least a fraction of the shit that would come our way for this, and she wanted it anyway. It boggled my fuckin' mind.

"I only got so many good years left," I murmured and her fingertips traced my bottom lip, her eyes fixating on my mouth.

"And I want to wring every last drop of love and life out of them before they're gone," she said. "Then when they are, I want to be there for you until the bitter end, because that's what you do for the people you love."

Holy shit. She was fuckin' serious.

"You really mean that; you've really thought about all of this, haven't you?"

"Not all of it," she said with a smile. "I'm sure I've missed some things, but I'll deal with those, too… if and when they come up."

Goddamn, I was so hard right now.

"What happens when the sex isn't great anymore?" I asked.

A knock fell at the door and she shrugged, slipping out of my grasp, and said, right before opening the door, "That's what masturbation is for."

I lost it, I couldn't help it.

She took my coat from the valet outside with a 'thanks' and shut the door again. She smiled and held it out to me and I took it, shaking my head.

I took her back to my place, and I have to tell you, it was oddly freeing holding her hand as we left Indigo Hall. It made my chest swell to hold her close in the back of the car for the ride back to Muller Street.

I took her upstairs and let her into my place and the nerves started up. I closed the door behind us and she drifted further in, towards the dining room table, slipping her purse strap from her shoulder and hanging it on the back of the chair.

It made me wonder if she'd really been as with it as I thought she'd been the next morning, when we'd left and I'd taken her home.

"I didn't really look the last time I was here, you know? I mean, I was here and I saw everything, but it's like watching a movie while distracted and then watching it a second time. You see all new things, you know?" Her voice was soft, a little sardonic, and even a little bit sad.

"Don't feel bad," I said. "You had plenty to be distracted about." I went to her and put my arms around her, cuddling her back to my front. It felt so good, but still slightly strange.

"How about that shower?" I murmured in her ear.

"I would like that, more than you could know," she murmured back.

With the thousand or so pounds of stage makeup on her face and as hard as she'd worked it up there, I didn't have any doubt.

I hooked my fingers in the front of her jacket and she let me take it from her. I hung it on the coat tree and ritualistically divested myself of my own coat, wallet, and keys into their proper places.

She watched me, a slight smile playing on her lips that rivaled the Mona Lisa's and my heart melted. Again, my chest swelled, a mix of contentment and pride as I held out a hand to her to lead her to the bathroom. She came to me and took it and trailed me up the hall. I told her to go ahead and get started, I wanted to put some towels in the dryer for us and she smiled, biting her bottom lip in anticipation.

She started the shower, I got the towels going and went into my bedroom to hang up my suit.

Her clothes were neatly folded on the edge of the sink when I walked into the bathroom and she was already shrouded by the shower curtain, her lithe silhouette tantalizing as I stepped up, cock bobbing as it stood at attention between my legs.

I got into the shower behind her and she immediately cuddled back against me, her skin warm, her body fitting against mine so perfectly it was like we were two matching pieces of the same jigsaw puzzle. Our edges perfectly aligned, she craned her head back against my shoulder and offered up her lips.

I groaned and kissed her sensually, my hands smoothing over her slick body, just feeling her supple skin beneath my palms, my fingers gently kneading her taut muscles. She moaned into my mouth and relaxed against me, trusting me to hold her up and I did, easily.

"Mm, baby…" I murmured against her lips.

"Yes, Daddy?" she whispered, a mischievous edge to her lilting voice.

I jerked back as if scalded, a horrified look overtaking my face as her laughter echoed off the tile surround.

"Right, I can see I made my point. Pick something else – anything else but that."

She turned in the circle of my arms, blue eyes still laughing and threw her own arms around my neck.

"Ah-huh, I see your point and I'll raise you…" I thought about it for a second, "Pookie?"

Her face fell into a flat, unamused expression that was ruined by the sparkle in her eyes, the barely-suppressed smile on her lips.

"Mm, Sugar?"

"I'm not a stripper, Skids!" she said, smacking me lightly on the chest, and it was my turn to laugh.

"Sweetheart?"

"Warmer," she cooed, voice husky with desire.

"I'll figure something out." I know my tone matched hers as we quit playing and fell easily back into kissing once again.

I tipped her head back into the shower spray and told her gently to hold onto me. Soaping my fingers with face-wash, I bid her to close her eyes and worked in a feather-light touch around her eyes, across her nose and cheekbones to rid her beautiful face of the caked-on makeup.

It took three washes to get it all off, and she patiently stood, her body pressed to mine and let me work, sighing out in contentment as I indulged myself in caring for her. It felt good to have a woman in my arms again. Felt good to run my fingers through her hair, to gently soap the strands and rinse them for her, to wash every inch of her skin with my bare hands.

The anticipation of having her body slide against mine, of being inside of her was becoming almost too much to bear.

It felt even better when she was invested in giving me the same treatment, her light touch eliciting delicious shivers as she soaped my skin, her lips touching against my shoulder as the soap rinsed away.

We spent I-don't-know-how-long caring for each other, engaging in little sensual delights until both of us were absolutely breathless with anticipation.

I got us calmed down to where I could shut off the tap and snatch the towel off the bar to wrap around my hips. I tucked the edge and kissed her quickly as she stood glistening and shivering in the tub.

"Two seconds, a couple warm towels coming right up," I murmured and went to fetch them out of the dryer. I handed her one and she wrapped her dripping hair, and, that done, I wrapped her up tight in the second, rubbing her down through the warmth of the material.

"How am I doing so far with this whole do-over thing?" I asked her.

She smiled up at me, adoration in her eyes and practically purred, "Perfect."

I took my time drying her well as she returned the favor with her towel, both of us laughing and giggling over the struggle that ensued over the bath sheet, which though big, wasn't nearly big enough for the both of us to be using on each other at the same time.

"What happens next?" she asked softly.

"Next, I put you to bed in the guest room, but you didn't stay there," I said, bypassing the door and leading her to my bed.

"Mm, then?"

"Then we slept in mine, but I think we'll skip that part, too," I answered.

"I like the sound of that," she said and her voice was coy.

"You won't need that," I murmured and took the towel from around her body.

"You won't either," she said, loosening the corner tucked into the hastily-fashioned waistband of my own.

"You started it last time," I murmured.

"I remember," she said grinning, stepping into me and raising her face to look at me.

"It's my turn," I growled and captured her mouth with mine.

She melded her body against mine, the heat shimmering between us and I couldn't wait to lose myself in her completely. Her sweet scent was overwhelming, her taste as intoxicating as any whiskey, smooth and mellow, dissolving on the tongue like sugar.

I could get used to this.

Still, the best part? The look on her face as she gazed at me down the length of her body, between her small, but pert breasts, the look of liquid sensuality in her eyes. The erotic heat in her gaze as she lived this waking dream with me.

Flawless, she was absolutely flawless.

11

*C*olette…

The way he went down on me was – God, I had no words. The lightning in his eyes, the satisfied grunt as he hauled me down against his mouth, the way he positively devoured me, tongue darting in and out of my opening, lapping at my lips, teasing over my clit until I nearly climbed the walls with ecstasy. He was perfect, he was everything; he was almost too much for me.

I couldn't hold still, I squirmed and writhed, and when I came he was relentless. I arched and finally sat up completely and tried to get away from him as he continued his assault on all of my senses, teasing me with his tongue even as I became completely over-sensitive and he just wouldn't stop even as I begged him to through my laughter. He wrung every last drop of pleasure out of me until I was a weak, sweat-dewed, panting mess sprawled across his sheets.

He pushed himself up, a self-satisfied, smug look on his face, his bright blue eyes sparkling with pride and mirth and I bit my bottom lip and shook my head, laughing.

"Was that as good for you as it was for me?" I asked.

"Better," he grunted, pressing his lips against my skin, low on my stomach, working his way up a gentle peck at a time while I giggled and laughed, elated to be here with him like this.

He reached my mouth and I grasped his bearded cheeks lightly between my hands as I opened my legs further to take him in. He didn't disappoint. He slipped into my wet and waiting pussy with barely any effort. Of course, after an orgasm as intense as what he'd wrought with his mouth, it wasn't a surprise I would be so ready for him. My body was eager, my back arching, my arms and legs wrapping around him and pulling him down on top of me, the weight of his bigger body felt so good. Solid, warm, and safe. Powerful, as he drew back and surged forward, the hard length of him sliding in and out of me easily, despite how hard I tried to hold onto him, the way I gripped him with my pelvic muscles.

"God damn, woman," he groaned into my ear. "Fucking grip that cock, just like that, yeah."

I tried to grip him even harder and he slowed, having to work at thrusting, but it all felt so good, so right, I didn't want it to end. He set a rough but sweet cadence, his strokes sure and true and it sparked that same feeling deep in my soul as when the music started to play and I let my body tip and fall into the easy, practiced movements of whatever dance was required.

This dance, however, was infinitely more intimate, more meaningful than any I had performed on stage.

He fucked me into a pleasure-filled, blissed-out coma, until all I could do was lay there, sated. He stretched out beside me and cuddled my listless body to his chest, my head on his shoulder, my leg draped over the both of his. One of his big hands rested at my back, the other at my knee where it rested atop his thigh, holding me close.

"You're too good to an old man like me," he murmured.

"Shut up," I said. "You're not old." He laughed and I rolled my eyes and amended, "Okay, you're not that old. You keep acting like you've got one foot in the grave and you don't, so just…" I faltered, afraid of how he might take what I had to say but in the end, I plucked up my courage and went for blunt honesty. "Just shut up and be happy with me, please?"

His breath caught, and I was almost afraid to look. Instead I listened to the steady beat of his heart in the close, hushed dark of his bedroom, listened as he let that captured breath out slowly and relaxed when he kneaded the back of my neck with gentle fingertips.

"I am," he said finally. "Enjoying being with you. You do make me happy, babe." I snorted and he chuckled. "I said, 'babe', not 'baby', now don't let yourself get distracted. We're having a moment here."

I laughed and he laughed with me, when we settled down, he said, "I think I'm fallin' in love with you, woman. I'd be lying if I said that didn't scare me for a lot of reasons…"

I pushed myself up so I could search his face. He was giving me cop-face, though. That not-unpleasant expression that gave absolutely nothing of what he was thinking or feeling away. I couldn't get a read on him even if I wanted to when he did that.

"Explain," I said softly, "because I seriously can't see what you're thinking or feeling right now."

He hummed and urged me back down to how I'd been laying before with a gentle hand. I cuddled close and waited him out.

"People are going to talk," he said, and his voice was rough with emotion.

"So what? Let them. I don't care." And I didn't.

"It's not just the talk that bothers me, it's how they'll treat you."

"And you're not worried about how they'll treat you?" I asked.

"Not particularly."

I rolled my eyes again and gave an exasperated sigh, "Well, I don't care how they'll treat me either, but I worry about you."

He chuckled, "Guess we're more worried about each other."

"I guess so. There's not really a word or phrase for that but 'we'll have to agree to disagree' comes closest in sentiment."

He raised his head off the pillow and pressed a kiss to my forehead a bit awkwardly. It warmed me through, even more so that I could feel the curve of his sensual lips quirked into a smile when he did it.

My eyes drifted shut and I sighed in contentment as we cuddled beneath his blankets into the stupidly comfortable cloud of his bed. I was happy. With a man I was insanely attracted to. A man who, for all his emotional insecurities, was secure and had his shit together. Who, by all accounts, wouldn't play me. Who'd already gone out of his way to protect me, who made me feel beautiful; not with words, but with how he looked at me, how he treated me with respect, and how he actually listened to what I had to say.

Maybe that was due to his age, maybe that was due to his experiences; whatever it was, I was incredibly happy and incredibly grateful to be with someone who was past all the stupid games people my age, of my generation, seemed to like to pull on each other.

I drew a breath and told him, "I am so grateful for you, you don't even know."

"Oh?" he asked, intrigued. "How's that?"

And so I told him. I told him everything I'd just been thinking and he lay silent beneath me, that silence so very loud with the way the wheels in his head turned, the gears grinding away as he thought it through.

"That's fair," he said finally, his voice edged with an emotion I couldn't readily define. He gave good cop-voice in addition to his cop-face. He swallowed hard and asked, "You sure you aren't putting too much faith in me?"

I snorted dismissively, but I answered him.

"The fact you would even ask me that tells me no, I'm not."

"Babe, there's still a lot you don't know about me…"

"Name one."

"I'm an alcoholic," he said, and I frowned.

"You don't drink," I said. "I mean, I've never even seen you taste anything. You usually have Cody make new drink recipes."

"You're right, I don't drink – not now. Doesn't mean I'm not an alcoholic, though."

"How long have you been sober? If you don't mind me asking, that is…"

"Course not, and I've been sober a little over five years."

"Relapses?" I asked hesitantly, feeling like I was overstepping but my curiosity would not be assuaged.

"Close, a couple of times, but no…"

I swallowed hard and forced out, "Any of those close calls because of me?"

He kissed my hair and tightened his hold on me but answered me honestly.

"Ah, yeah…"

"I'm sorry," I whispered and my heart dropped into the pit of my stomach.

"Not your fault, babe. I think, mostly…" He choked up a bit and I held my breath.

I wanted him to say it, needed to hear it so badly, to know he trusted me and believed in me as much as I did him. He didn't disappoint, even though I would probably never tell him if he'd faltered.

"I think mostly it had to do with me wrestling with things – demons from my past. Wrestling with the 'what ifs', you know?"

I nodded, eyes growing hot with my own emotion.

"I understand," I murmured.

"I think, the truth of it is, I'm afraid I'm not perfect. That I'm going to let you down – disappoint you…" he trailed off. "That you'll get tired of taking care of an old man…"

"That I'll find someone else? That I'll leave?" I asked, voicing what I was sure he couldn't.

"Yeah."

He was afraid I would break his heart? Oh. Oh, no… I couldn't fault him for thinking that way. I mean, I was young and my generation wasn't exactly known for its dependability. I knew I was wildly outside the norm when it came to other people my age but his confession still stung deep down.

I pushed that feeling down and away and in a determined tone of voice, asked, "Just tell me what I have to do to prove to you I mean it, that I'm here to stay, and I'll do it."

He chuckled lightly and snuggled me even more and said, "Only time'll tell, won't it?"

I pushed myself up and climbed on top of him, the air of the room cool after our warm cocoon of blankets and body heat. He smoothed his hands up my thighs and eyed me in the dim blue light through the windows. Unfortunately, the windows were now at my back and I doubted very much he could see my face. I could see his, though, carefully thoughtful as he gazed up at me.

I rolled my hips when his cock grew warmer against my body and began to grow hard, sliding my pussy lips over him, causing a delicious friction.

He hummed out appreciatively, his hands wandering over my skin and my eyes fluttered shut, soaking in the sensation.

"I won't leave you," I whispered into the dark, lowering my mouth over his. "But you can't see that, so I'll show you." I kissed him and he kissed me back, his chest rising and falling with deep breaths borne from strong emotion.

I loved that about him. That even though he said he was afraid to feel so much, he did it anyways. How could I not give him everything that I was in return?

12

*S*kids…

I woke in the middle of the quietest hours of the night and realized Colette wasn't with me. I pushed myself up into a sitting position, my body protesting after the unfamiliar workout I'd given it. I stayed fit nowadays and discovered I hurt less and had more energy, but a gym workout didn't exactly work the fine muscles involved in giving and getting great sex. At least, not all of them, anyway.

I sat on the edge of the bed and listened hard. When I didn't hear anything from the rest of the apartment, I grew concerned. *Had she thought about what I said? Did she leave? If she did leave, are you really surprised? Did she get home okay?* Too many questions and I needed some answers, so I pulled a plain white thermal over my head and found a pair of my blue, black, and gray plaid flannel pajama pants. It was fuckin' chilly in here, the building old, the windows a shitty single pane of glass that didn't do squat to keep the heat in.

I went down the hall, scuffing along the old worn green carpet in my slippers. I didn't find her in the kitchen and dining area, but I did find her things right where we'd left them on the coat tree and at the table.

"Colette?" I called softly.

"In here," came her quiet reply, her voice clear and lilting despite her subdued tone.

I slipped around the corner into the living room and froze at the beautiful sight in front of me.

She'd pulled one of my recliners over to the window and had raised the blinds. She wore one of my light blue dress shirts, or it could have been a white one. It was hard to tell with the night-blue light coming through the window. Her face was serene as she stared outside, shadows flitting across it, making me edge further into the room.

She watched the snow. Falling in these great fat flakes from the heavens, my mother'd always told me the angels were having a pillow fight.

I smiled and went to her and said, "Up you go."

She smiled up at me and uncurled her legs from beneath the black-and-blue plaid throw from the back of my couch, a big ceramic white coffee mug steaming between her hands. I dropped into the recliner and she laughed lightly and curled back up like a kitten in my lap. I reached down and tucked the throw around her, careful not to spill the contents of her mug.

She smiled and kissed me lightly before settling back against me and handing me her cup. I took a drink, warm and comfortable with the weight of her body back against mine.

Fragrant herbal tea flooded my mouth and I swallowed, the warmth radiating out from my chest. I handed it back and she wrapped her slim fingers back around the cup.

I slid a hand down her leg beneath the throw and she sighed with contentment as I rested it over her instep, warming her poor battered foot, making sure the other was tucked in the throw.

"What're you doing all the way out here?" I asked after some quiet, just the both of us watching the snow fall from the sky.

"I woke up and it was snowing," she murmured, as if that would explain everything.

I chuckled and gave her a questioning, "And?"

She bowed her head and smiled and it was a sight that'd like to stop your heart with how beautiful she was.

"I don't know, it's stupid…" she whispered.

I tipped her chin and her blue eyes flew to mine, wide and innocent, edged in fear of some kind of a rebuke.

"Not stupid at all, babe. Tell me."

"It's like the world is always so busy," she whispered, turning her gaze back out the window. "It's my favorite thing when it snows like this. When it's deepest night and the whole city sleeps, to be the only one awake… to experience time-stop." She sighed and it held such an edge of romanticism I fought not to chuckle. "It's the closest thing to magic I've ever felt or seen."

I held her tight, close in my lap, and cuddled her, immersing myself in what she spoke of, living the moment with her and I have to say – it was the closest thing to true peace I'd felt in a long time… maybe ever.

We sat together in silence, neither of us needing to say anything, sipping her tea and quietly passing the mug back and forth as the snow fell from the sky in great, fat flakes, blanketing the city in white, the edges softened, blunted, and I swear the sight was a match for what Colette did to my very soul, blanketing it in a soothing touch, blunting the sharp edges of pain I'd felt for so long.

God, I loved her for it. It was like when I was with her, I could breathe again. Like I'd been suffocating and I hadn't even known it.

The feelings she evoked in me were so pure. As pure as the freshly fallen snow outside my window.

∽

I WANTED to tell the guys. I didn't want to keep things on the down-low, but I didn't want them finding this shit out through gossip and whispers, so I found myself in a bit of a quandary.

"Not sure what I should do," I said, and Colette sat down across from me at my little table.

"Reflash knows," she said.

"Of course, he does."

"It's not like you want to keep it a secret." She shifted, visibly nervous and I knew she was sensitive about it, which was why I was asking her.

"I don't," I agreed.

"You just think it would be better coming from you," she said.

"I do."

She laughed, a bit on edge, and I understood her nervousness. I felt it too. Truthfully, I was relieved I wasn't alone in that. Of course, when you partnered up with a woman, you were never truly alone. I'd learned the hard way, by being a real fucking idiot, that everything you did was a 'we' proposition. There really wasn't an 'I' anymore. I wouldn't put Coco through the same shit I'd put my ex through.

If whatever powers that be were handing me some kind of a do-over here, I wasn't about to fuck it up. Even though I'd done a bang-up job of that so far, up to this point. I searched her face while she searched mine and she reached across the expanse of table between us, putting her hand over mine.

"When do you see them all again?" she asked.

"This week, for our poker game. Not all of them, but enough of them. Church first, then up here," I said.

She rolled her eyes, "So, like, a few days?"

"Yeah."

"I think I can handle a couple of days of keeping it on the down-low." She smiled, but just as quickly as it flickered to life, it faded.

"What?" I asked.

"Um, what about my job?" she asked.

"What about it?" I raised an eyebrow.

"Should I find another?"

"No fucking way," I said. I heaved a big sigh, not entirely sure how to tackle that one, but sure I didn't like the idea of her working someplace else. Too many disreputable places, too many opportunities for shit to go sideways anywhere else. I didn't like it. Especially with how close a call she'd had, right under my own nose.

"But how should we handle it?" I asked.

"I'll talk with Reflash, we'll see what we can come up with."

She nodded and sighed herself. "I have to get to the Bay Water," she said.

I nodded, "You want I should walk with you?"

"Don't you have to open?" she arched a brow.

"Yeah."

"Then I'll see you soon," she murmured, but didn't sound terribly happy about it. She wrapped her scarf around her neck from the coat rack. I got up and stood near her, helping her into her coat.

I murmured at her back, "I'll miss you every minute." The smile she gave me when she turned around was the light of my life.

"I'll miss you, too," she cooed, her arms going around my neck as she stood on tiptoe so her lips could reach mine. I ducked my head and kissed her carefully, reluctantly letting her go only when I had to.

"I'm really starting to love you," I grated, my voice rough with emotion, my hands still on her hips. I guess the emotion swamping me was mostly the fear at expressing myself. It just wasn't done, you know?

She smiled and winked and leaned into me, offering her lips for another kiss. I took it and she leaned back, lowering herself back down to the floor again as she said, "About time you came around to my way of thinking."

I laughed and she grinned, biting her bottom lip impishly and I was fucking done for.

"Sure you don't want me to walk you?" I asked, and she touched the side of my face.

"I'm sure. I'll see you soon enough." She was half way out the door before she leaned back and said, "I love you, too."

Before I could even open my mouth to say anything, she'd shut my apartment door firmly behind her and I could hear her light step through the gap beneath it as she practically skipped down the hallway outside it, heading for the stairs.

I drew a deep breath, one hand on my hip, the other at the back of my neck as I tried to think just what the hell I was gonna tell the guys.

"So why you look so down?" Reflash asked as we hung around waiting to open up, and had our daily little chat that was usually half business meeting.

"She wanted to know if she should find another job."

Reflash leaned back in his seat and looked thoughtful.

"Looks like my instinct about her was right," he said and I arched an eyebrow.

"Care to share with the rest of the class?" I asked.

"Girl works her ass off around here," he said. "If anybody is gonna worry about anything it's gonna be that she's some kind of gold-digger. I knew otherwise, had a hunch that if you ever did pull your head out of your ass, that the business would be safe – yah know?"

I nodded; I had thought about that myself. "I told her I'd talk to you about it, but that when it came to her finding another job that I didn't want her to, and I don't. I also said I'd talk to you first and see what you thought before we committed to any course of action. If you said she needed to drop it, I think she would. She brought it up in the first place, not me."

"Good help is hard to find," my best friend said, leaning his elbows on the table, capturing one fist in the other and pressing them to his lips in deep contemplation. I let the wheels in his head turn. Whatever he decided I would be good with. I had to be. I couldn't at all be objective in this one, now could I?

"You know, we've never had a problem where the kid's concerned. Why borrow trouble? Something comes up, I'll handle it, but until something does, let's roll on business as usual."

I winced and said, "Sounds good, just do me a solid, man."

Reflash's eyebrows went up.

"Don't call her 'kid' anymore. You're gonna make me feel like a pedo."

His laugh boomed out across the empty dining room and before long, I was chuckling right along with him. Still worried, but not as bad. Of course, we'd have to see what today brought. It would be mine and Coco's first shift back – only this time as a couple.

Fuck, that felt weird!

13

*C*olette...

I was slightly dreading going to work, how different things would feel, but I needn't have worried. Things went as smooth as butter. All except for the part where my mom crashed the party a bit.

I hadn't even seen her come in, just one minute I was at table seventeen taking drink orders and when I looked up, bam! There she was, sitting on a corner bar stool, laughing it up at something my boyfriend had said.

I am so going to get you back for this, I thought, my lips curving into a genuine smile. She'd wanted to know when she was going to get to meet him, said she wanted to feel him out and make sure her baby was in good hands. I'd rolled my eyes and had given her a non-committal 'Soon'. Not good enough for that diva, apparently.

Also, with how easily Skids was moving around behind the bar, his polite expression of customer service on his face, he had no clue who she was. Still, there was a spark of recognition in there somewhere. He kept glancing back at her like he was trying to place her. I sighed and dropped the menus back at the hostess's stand and went to the bar to put in my table's order.

"Mom, what are you doing here?" I asked, and I fought not to laugh as Skids visibly blanched.

"Mom?" he asked, gobsmacked.

"Surprise!" My mother said mock-meekly and gave a throaty laugh. She flicked my braid back over my shoulder and said, "I was thirsty, and I wanted to have a look at your new beau."

"Riiiight," I said, and I was honestly irritated with her. Things were so new, and I didn't want anything to be overwhelming, or to jinx it somehow… of course, to be fair, I hadn't said any of those things to my mother.

"Ah," Skids said, like something had clicked. "The theater. We sat next to each other."

"I knew you would get it eventually," she said playfully.

I rolled my eyes so hard and said, "Don't mind her, she's a professional flirt."

"Only got eyes for you, babe," he said softly and I blushed and put in my table's drinks. Skids got busy mixing them up for me.

"Behave yourself," I snapped at my mother, but there wasn't any bite to my words as I went off to perform my primary function, which was to do my job.

She stayed and had something to eat, chatting with Skids when he had the time, his posture easing when he realized he had earned my lifegiver's approval. Of course he had. He was him, and I hadn't had any doubt about it.

It remained busy and I caught my mother – or rather, she caught me, before she left for the night, giving me a quick hug and murmuring "I like him. You did good, baby girl," in my ear.

I smiled and rolled my eyes slightly and said, "Of course you do, and I know I did! Be careful. You going to my place or back to the hotel?"

"Hotel. I'll see you tomorrow if that's alright?"

I rolled my eyes again. "Of course, it is!"

By the time I got another chance to stop and breathe, the restaurant was nearly empty except for one of my tables and two of Kristy's. We went about getting as much of our closing work done as we could while still having guests in the place and I finally ended up at the bar, Skids setting down a glass of ice water with lemon for me.

"Well, that's another one in the books," he said with a gusty sigh.

I nodded, chugging water. When I came up for air, it was with a satisfied sigh as I said, "Indeed it is," and the first bit of awkward silence ensued.

I suddenly wasn't sure what to say or what to do without it appearing I was shouting from the bar top how happy I was and that Skids and I were a thing.

"Relax," Skids murmured, and put his hand over mine where it rested on top of the bar.

I did, feeling the tension ease out of my shoulders and a smile paint my lips.

"My place after this?" he asked, softly.

"Wish I could," I whispered. "Early practice and I would rather not be sore, if you know what I mean." I raised my eyebrows and he laughed a little, blushing, his expression chagrined.

"Yeah, can't exactly say I'm sorry about that."

"Oh, me either!" I declared. "I just need to stay on top of my game. It is my main livelihood."

"No, I get it," he said. "Maybe later this week?"

I felt my expression soften and my face warm slightly as Kristy walked near. "Absolutely, wouldn't miss it," I murmured.

He took his hand off of mine and I went to check my table. Back at the waitress station Kristy paused and leaned back from the order screen as she closed out her ticket and I waited my turn.

She eyed me and asked hesitantly, "So, um, you and Skids?"

I bit my lips together, my mind scrambling on how best to answer. I just gave her a deer in the headlights look, suddenly tongue-tied, and she smiled and shook her head finally. "You know what, it's totally none of my business. It was rude of me to even ask."

"I really don't know what to say or how to answer that," I said softly.

"It's okay," she put a hand on my shoulder and gave me a most sincere look. "Just, um, be careful, okay?"

"Careful?" I echoed.

"Yeah, well, I mean…" She blushed furiously and dropped her hand from my shoulder and said, "Um, never mind," and hustled through putting her guest's ticket into one of the little black payment folders, rushing over to their table and handing it over, chatting with them cheerfully.

I glanced in the direction of the bar where Skids stood, arms crossed, a slight smile on his lips that didn't quite reach his eyes. Worry radiated from the sparkling blue depths as he raised an eyebrow, asking silently if all was good. I gave him a hesitant nod and went in to the system to retrieve my own ticket.

A few minutes later the place was cleared out, and Skids came out from around the bar and up behind me, resting his hands on my shoulders and pressing his thumbs in that spot that was impossible to reach but seemed to always hold all the tension. I sighed and closed my eyes, momentarily forgetting Kristy was still there.

"Oh, my God, you guys are totally an item," she blurted out and Skids' hands trembled where they rested on my shoulders with his nod.

"That may be, but it ain't nobody's business but theirs," Reflash said from the kitchen doorway and I saw Kristy jump slightly out of the edge of my vision. She blushed fiercely, ducked her head and went to bus her last table.

I took a step to do the same and Skids sighed behind me, reluctantly dropping his hands, which I mourned internally; that'd felt so good and I wanted more.

Reflash was over talking to Kristy, but whatever he was saying was gentle, not harsh, as they both looked our direction. I smiled a little sadly at Skids and said sardonically, "And here it was I thought we were doing so well."

He laughed and tossed a bar towel over his shoulder saying, "One of the things I love about you?" I arched a brow in silent interest. "You read like an open book."

"Well," I murmured, "if your living room is any indication, that's another thing we share."

"Oh, yeah?" he asked.

"Oh, yeah." I answered.

The entire wall opposite the windows in the living room, the same one that shared the apartment's front door, was lined floor-to-ceiling with bookshelves filled with books, lovingly dusted, the rich wood of the shelves gleaming with varnish. It was a small portion of the apartment almost easily missed behind the small lip of wall separating the kitchen and dining area from the living room, but it had quickly become my favorite part of the apartment aside from watching the snowfall outside the old-fashioned windows. I wanted to take more time to explore that wall of books when I had more light to do it.

"How did I not know that?" he asked, drifting along in my wake as I went to bus my last table.

"Because I don't have many books in my room? Not enough room for them. I have to keep everything on my phone or my Nook."

"Nook? What's that?"

"It's Barnes & Noble's version of the Kindle," I answered. "I like supporting the underdog when I can."

I smiled when he smiled and he nodded, arms folded across his broad chest as he said, "Somehow I knew that about you already."

We parted ways to finish up and by the time I was ready to head back to the office to get my coat, my roommates were there to walk me home and Skids was already trailing up the hallway with my coat and purse in hand.

I smiled and turned as he held my coat open for me, sliding my arms into the puffy, warm, down jacket. He laid my scarf at the back of my neck and I zipped up and finished winding it around my neck. When I turned he held my purse out to me.

"Thanks," I murmured, and suddenly felt a bit awkward and put on the spot, with Kristy still looking on.

"Welcome," he murmured, walking me to the door.

"Should we, um–"

He grinned and leaned down, kissing me goodbye, which had been precisely what I'd been about to ask. Kristy kept at her final cleanup, studiously not looking in our direction. I wondered what Reflash had said to her, but my head couldn't stay on it because Skids captured my soul in the palm of his hand with that kiss and I felt myself melt into his arms, a peace and happiness settling into the center of my chest the likes I'd never experienced before. Not even on stage, not even dancing, which was saying something.

"Wow," I whispered, breathless, when he let me go flatfooted back to earth.

"Sure you can't stay?" he whispered, voice husky with desire.

"I'm sure," I said, regretting being such a responsible adult for once. *Irony of ironies…* I thought with a silent chuckle.

"Okay, babe. Be careful. Call me when you get home, please?"

"You got it," I whispered, and he opened the door and turned me loose into the cold, dark night.

My friends were silent for several blocks; finally Orion was the one to break it.

"You guys seem really happy," he said and I smiled to myself.

"We are."

"You're sure?" Genevieve asked, concerned, and I felt my smile grow.

"Look, you guys, I'm sure and I promise, we both know it won't be easy and what lies ahead and we're both willing to take it on. I promise, I'm not going into this blind and I'm really happy." I hated the note of desperate pleading that entered my tone, but I couldn't help it. "So please, can you guys just be happy for us too, and let us enjoy this?"

Orion put an arm around Genevieve and hooked his other arm around me, hugging us both into his sides.

"Yeah, Coco. We can do that," he said simply and my heart grew three sizes in my chest for my friends and my new man, and the life I had chosen to live. I honestly couldn't remember being happier.

I couldn't wait to call Skids or talk to my mom.

14

*S*kids…

So much for playing it cool or on the DL, but you know what? It was cool. I was alright with it and Reflash had done his duty as my best friend and brother and had headed off any trouble with the employees and gossip at the pass.

I waited for Coco to call me, and she had. We'd kept it short, and I'd gone to bed early. Her mom was a trip, and I could see where Coco got it. But, her mom seemed to approve, and I was grateful for it. I didn't want to drag her down or make her life more complicated. I wanted her to be happy, and unlike my last relationship, I realized now that I couldn't put her happiness on a pedestal. I could make some sacrifices, and she would have to, too, but we both needed to be happy together.

I was cautiously optimistic, but still nervous about how the guys would react. So, as I sat at the head of the table, waiting for the rest of who could make it to arrive for our weekly meetup, I felt every bit of my nerves being worn raw. I kept trying to tell myself to hold my horses, to slow down, to stop putting the worst reactions on them before they'd even heard the news or had the chance to have their own feelings about it, but I was a cop before anything else and it was pretty much ingrained into every fiber of our beings to expect the worst-case scenario.

I tell you what, though. I was definitely aware that civilian life was starting to take a toll on my edge. I didn't like it, but I also didn't exactly know what to do about it at the same time.

My thoughts on the subject were interrupted by Youngblood coming through the door, the sharp squeaking scrape of the metal door frame against the metal lintel making me wince. I needed to fix that shit, I really did.

"Skids, man, hey! What's up?" I got up and greeted my man with a clasped hand and a big bear hug. If any of my boys were gonna be a voice of reason in this, it'd be Youngblood. Young? Yes, but also wise beyond his years. If there was anybody I had to worry about getting upset, I'd put my money on Golden.

Of course, think of the devil and he shall appear. Oh, wait, no that was Angel walking through the door. Golden was just coming in through the main door out in the bar. Reflash came into the fishbowl after Youngblood, and gave me a nod.

His words about underestimating our squad came back to haunt me a bit as we waited for some more of the guys to arrive.

So far, there was Youngblood, the twins, Blaze, Oz, Driller but no Narcos, and Yale. Looked like that was going to be it. We were missing Backdraft, Poe, and as I said, Narcos. It was a good majority, as good as it got, usually. Still, while I was pleased with it, I was also even more nervous which made me realize with a jolt just how much I wanted this with Coco, how addicted I'd become to her vibrancy, her warmth, and her headstrong, can-do attitude.

When I was with her, I didn't feel like a washed-up, has-been cop. I felt like a man on top of the world.

I glanced out the glassed-in box of my restaurant's banquet room and found her bright blonde ponytail bobbing over at table six as she animatedly talked to the patrons there, laughing at something one of the young bucks at the table said. It didn't make me jealous, not when I could see her profile and the secret smile that played across her lips, the one that was basically a different form of rolling her eyes, which would have been rude and beneath her – at least until it was just me and her when the place closed down.

I was sure I would hear about whatever it was later, if it was funny enough or stuck with her enough to tell me. She'd walked up with some doozies before when it came to stories. People were generally outrageous when it came to what they thought was acceptable flirting.

"Yo, Skids! I think we're all here, you wanna get this party started?" Oz demanded from down the table.

"Yeah, sure, hold your damn horses," Reflash called back to him, but my best friend raised his eyebrows at me and I had to sigh inwardly.

Time to face the music.

I started the meeting with the usual BS and was coming this close to chickening out, which I had told Reflash I might and asked him not to let me.

So, of course, my best friend gave me the kick in the ass I needed to keep me honest by saying… "…And in other news, Skids got himself a new girlfriend."

Silence rang sharp around the table for a good couple of heartbeats and then grins and smiles broke out.

"Seriously?" Golden demanded. "You're not pulling our leg?"

"You've been single as long as I've known you, dude. What made you decide to give up the bachelor's life?" Blaze demanded.

I caught Coco's eye out on the floor and gave her a chin-lift. She headed up this way and I took a deep breath and said, "Well, I guess you could say she wouldn't have it any way."

She stepped into the room and Oz called up the table, "So who is she?"

"You know her already," I answered, and pulled my girl into my lap.

Coco laughed and said, "You're telling them, I take it?"

"Damn right," I said, as the looks around the table went from happy to surprise. Some of them immediately shut down to disguise what they were thinking, some of them immediately went back to happy, some of them remained cautiously neutral as they thought things out for themselves.

"Uh, surprise!" Coco said meekly, and raised her hands and waggled her fingers in a pale imitation of jazz hands. She put her arms around my shoulders and smiled at everyone down the table, but I could feel her anxiety, her body tense and thrumming with a low-key energy that practically crackled with her anxiety.

I knew exactly how she felt, and nervous laughter swept through a couple of the guys.

"You're joking, right?" Oz demanded.

"Dude!" Driller scowled at him and I felt Coco stiffen.

I gave her a reassuring squeeze and looked up into her true blue eyes. I smiled at her, I couldn't help it, and let the deep fondness I held for her flood my gaze. She smiled in return, and we just clicked. We knew it would be hard, and we were here, together, ready to face it head on. The boys would either get on board or they wouldn't… but she wasn't going anywhere. It was as simple as that.

"Go on back out there," I murmured.

"K," she whispered, and defiant little shit she was, she bent her head and kissed me sweetly before she got up to go.

"Don't be too hard on him," she called over her shoulder and went back out onto the floor.

I turned my attention back to the boys and said, "Okay, let her rip."

"What? Naw!" Youngblood was smiling, genuinely, and said, "Ain't nobody got nothing to say, right, guys?"

"Not so fast, man," Oz sat up and leaned forward. "You havin' some kind of a mid-life crisis, bro? Jesus Christ! You can still smell the Similac!"

Okay, even I had to laugh at that one. We all sat around the table, fallin' out laughing, but even though Oz was smiling I could see the worry.

"Go on, say your piece," Reflash said, wiping tears out of the corner of his eyes.

"She's what? Nineteen?"

"Twenty-two," I corrected.

"And you're what?"

"Fifty-four."

"Jesus Christ," he repeated. "That's a thirty-two-year age difference. She don't want a boyfriend, she wants a daddy."

I gritted my teeth, but before I could say anything unfortunate, Reflash stepped in once again.

"You're dangerously close to disrespect, there, Oz," he said quietly.

"Ain't mean no disrespect, but what's she fishin' for?"

I leaned forward and put my elbows on the table and scrubbed my face with my hands.

"I think the word you're looking for is 'digging', am I right?" I asked.

Oz had gone too far; I knew his heart was in the right place and that his ex was a piece of work, but he'd definitely crossed a line I hadn't even realized I'd drawn in the sand.

He stared down the table at me, defiant, but he knew he'd overstepped. He didn't have shit else to say.

"Look, I get where you're comin' from is a good place, in your heart. That you're just lookin' out for me, but I'd like to think I've earned a measure of trust out of the lot of you."

Surprisingly, it was Golden to the rescue; I'd misjudged him and thought sure he'd have been the Oz in this situation, but here came the star with the rainbow tail… the more you know.

"You have, Chief. Oz just doesn't know when to keep his mouth shut. You know corrections – they're all professional assholes. You can take the guys out of the jail, but –"

"You can't take the jail out of the guy," everyone responded and it was Oz's turn to look embarrassed, a bit.

"All I'm asking for is you give her a chance. Get to really know her past just being a waitress here, or my 'too young girlfriend.'" I put the last in air quotes. "She's something, and I tried fighting it, believe me, but all it did was make me miserable when Jesus fuck, that girl has managed to make me so damn happy. It's still so fragile and new, and I was as surprised as you all that I want this. I really do."

That seemed to sober them up and make them think past their initial shock.

"It's all any of us want," Golden said into the resounding silence. There were grunts of agreement around the table and more silent introspection.

"All I'm asking is that you give us a chance," I said. "I know it ain't conventional, but then again, since when have any of us really given a shit about that, huh?"

"You're damn right, buddy." Reflash held up his beer and I picked up my Sprite, we clicked glasses and Oz picked up his and held it high.

"To the chief," he said. "Crazy son of a bitch, you know we all wanna be like you when we grow up."

"Speak for yourself," Golden piped up. "Some of us are happy with the women we're with, but salute all the same!"

"Thanks, guys. Not gonna lie, I was worried how you all would take it."

"Not well in Oz's case, but the rest of us'll get over it. Just give us a chance to really get to know her."

"And don't die of a heart attack when you're fuckin'," Oz said just as Coco came back in with fresh drinks for me and Reflash, lookin' to get everyone else's orders.

She laughed and said, "Not likely, I'm the one that has to beg off on the rare occasion. I need my legs to work to dance."

"Oh yeah? You a stripper on the side?" Oz demanded.

She went up on her toes, did a perfect pirouette and a couple of other ballet moves I had no names for and said, "Ballet. I'll let your pervy mind fill in the blanks."

She did me proud, giving no fucks and no quarter. I was proud of her bulletproof sense of confidence and found it sexy as hell. She really didn't care what any of these guys thought of her, at least not on the surface.

Her eyes, though, when they met mine, were filled with questioning worry as she smiled and said, "Now what can I get the rest of you?"

THERE WAS MORE TALK, some questions, a lot more jokes, and though some of the guys were still tense about it, I think we all had an understanding about my new relationship. I didn't expect all of them to like Coco, but I did demand they respect her, just as I expected them to respect any woman. We were men in good standing, the good guys, the knights sworn to defend this city – chivalry wasn't dead, we lived and breathed it. It was a rule. One of our most closely held tenets.

My only regret was that the table in here wasn't round. They may look to me for answers, they may see me as their leader and their chief, but I saw us all as equal. Still, I took the honor they bestowed on me by looking to me as all of those things and I was careful to make sure I was worthy of it. I strove to be, and I would live it every day, by taking care of the woman out there who put the same kind of faith in me.

"Alright, alright," I said, breaking up the chatter by rapping my knuckles against the tabletop. "Who's up for a round of poker upstairs?"

We couldn't play down here, not legally with all the laws surrounding gambling, bars, and what-have-you. So we usually went upstairs to my place after the weekly meeting if there were enough guys interested. This time around it was Driller, Oz, Blaze and Reflash. It'd be a bit tight around my four-person table, but I had a card table we could bust out if we needed to. With five, we generally didn't; anymore and we would have to.

"You sure, man?" Oz asked Golden.

"I'm sure. I gotta get back to the family."

"Claire is waiting for me," Angel said.

"Cool, cool," he said and I tried not to feel… I don't know.

'Betrayed' wasn't the right word at all, but Oz's reaction to my decision to try with Coco hadn't gone down well. It'd hurt, vaguely, and I felt a bit at odds. I didn't like feeling like there was some kind of a rift between me and any of the guys, so I tried to figure if this was something that needed talked about or if it was one that, if let alone, would heal on its own.

We sat and shot the shit for a while more before we headed upstairs to play some old-school five-card stud. Before we left, I stopped and said good night to Coco, who knew the plan.

She looked up at me and murmured, "That went well," and though her expression didn't betray it, I could see she was a touch hurt too. Though with her, I couldn't tell if she was hurt or if she was hurting for me.

We'd have to talk about it later.

I hated leaving it, though. I hated leaving anything undone or unsaid. I didn't do unfinished. I tended to unravel, which is part of how I'd gotten into trouble in the first place when it came to the drinking and shit. Some cases just went unsolved. Some going unsolved tended to kill you inside, little by little, day by day.

Coco was more important than any case I'd ever worked, though. Making this work had suddenly become all-consuming, not just for her, but for me, too.

"It'll be fine," I promised her. "Just give it some time."

"Want me to just text you when I get home?" she asked.

"No, but tonight, yeah."

She smiled up at me and said, "You got it," and though we agreed to keep it on the DL around the restaurant, and had handled it up until tonight for the most part, I broke the rules a second time by leaning down and kissing her – a quick, chaste press of lips.

"Love you, babe."

"Love you, too," she said softly, and I went out and met the guys staying for the game on the street.

"Not going to lie, that's gonna take some getting used to," Oz said.

"Why?" I grated, sticking my key in the lock for the street side door. "Because you ain't never seen me with someone, or because of her age?"

"Both. Look, I ain't got nothin' against her, Skids. I'm just sayin' –"

"You don't know what a girl like her wants with a guy like me except money?"

"You put it like that I sound like a dick."

Driller spoke up, half-laughing, "Dude, you are a dick."

"Yeah, I get that, but I ain't trying to be that kind of a dick."

We were working our way up the stairs by that point and Blaze called out from the back of the line of us, "A little late for that."

"Man, you guys wanna quit bustin' my balls for like two seconds?" Oz snapped.

"You make it so easy," Reflash said, as I keyed my way into my apartment's front door.

I had the cards and chips out on the table already. We didn't play for actual money very often. Just chips. Every once in a while we played for loose change and dollar bills, but that was it. It was more about the game and camaraderie than money.

"I'm honestly not tryin' to be a dick," Oz said as we took our seats. "I just look at a girl like that with a guy like you and –"

"You totally realize how fucked up that is, right?" Blaze demanded.

"What?" Oz asked, holding out his hands like he really didn't get it.

"Motherfucker, you're black," Driller said.

"What the fuck does that got to do with anything?" Oz demanded, scowling.

"I think what our white compatriots are trying to say is that it's fucked-up that you would judge Coco based on her appearance or age given that we brown folks gotta put up with it, like constantly," Reflash said, shuffling the deck of cards while I doled out the chips. I kept my mouth shut and just listened. I didn't have anything to add to the conversation just yet.

"It's not even the same thing," Oz protested.

"Oh yeah, how's that?" I asked coolly.

"Age and color ain't even the same thing."

"And the gender bias?" Driller asked.

"Oh, here we go," Oz complained and I had to smile. They were a bit like comparing apples and oranges but I could see where the guys were coming from all the same.

I sort of tuned them out for a bit while I thought about it myself and tuned back in when Oz asked me a direct question.

"I mean, what do y'all even have in common anyway?"

"Things are still new," I said. "We're still exploring and finding that out."

"Sex must be damn good," Driller said, with a bit of a laugh.

"That it is," I agreed, "but it's not everything."

"She come onto you or the other way around?" Oz asked, and I didn't like it, it felt like a leading question to lob yet more accusations or to go *'Ah-ha! Just as I thought, gold-digger'* I didn't want to answer it, but did anyways steeling myself against the outcome.

"She did, but the attraction is and probably always has been mutual."

"Ah. Uh-huh," he said knowingly, stacking his chips.

"Why do you do that?" Driller demanded.

"Do what?" Oz asked.

"Get these ideas about people in your head and stick to them like they're gospel. You don't even know the girl but you already got it in your head she's all these things without finding out of she is or not, first."

"Man, I work in the jail. You know how often we see the same people come through for the same shit, day in and day out all singin' the same ol' song about how it's not really them, and how they're gonna change, and blah, blah, this and blah, blah, that?"

"Sounds to me like maybe you're lettin' the life get to you too much," Reflash said, dealing cards and getting the game started.

"Naw, I'm just tired of watching all these motherfuckers tryin' to ice skate uphill," he said. "If it walks like a duck, you know?"

"So because you deal with the worst of the worst all day every day that means everybody out here on the outside is rotten to the core, too?" I asked and he paused.

"No, I ain't sayin' that."

"Really?" Reflash asked. "'Cause you're sure acting like it."

"Dude, no, that's not what I mean at all," Oz protested.

"We ain't trying to bust your balls," Driller said gently, "just trying to point out that there's other lines of thinking."

"Let me ask you this," I interjected. All eyes turned on me. "You look at me with a woman like that, what do you think?" I asked.

"That you're a stud," Blaze provided.

"Really?" I asked. "Why not that I'm a pedo?"

The guys laughed and Oz said, "Man, we know you."

"Yeah, that's right, you do, but a lot of these other motherfuckers out here don't. You don't think we're gonna come up against it?" I shook my head and said, "That's not even my point. My point is, why do I get to be the stud and she's automatically some kind of gold-digging whore?"

"Well, she works for you, for one thing," Oz pointed out.

"Doesn't have to anymore," Reflash stated. "She's a principal dancer at that fancy-ass hall now. That came with a hefty pay raise. So just because she chooses to still work for us and earn even more, that makes her a whore?"

Oz was lookin' a little green around the gills at this point.

"All I'm askin' is that you give her a chance," I said. "That ain't so much is it?"

"Naw, man." Oz met my eyes. "I can tell I really came in below the belt. I didn't mean to. Seriously, I'm sorry."

"'S okay," I said.

"We all know your heart's in the right place, man. That you're just lookin' out," Reflash put forward.

"Just asking that you keep an open mind about things," Driller said.

"Guess it's kind of hard to," Oz muttered and Driller sighed.

"We all know you got a shitty ex, man. Just know that the path to happiness doesn't lie through pegging everyone you meet for her sins, yah know?" Reflash said.

"Starting to sound like Angel," Oz grunted.

"He's a solid dude and seems pretty happy with Claire," Blaze pointed out.

"Yeah," Oz nodded.

"I think we've given our man enough food for thought for one evening. Who's betting?" I asked.

We were a little over an hour into playing when a knock fell at my door. I frowned and wondered if one of the guys who hadn't made it to the meeting was late showing for the poker game. I was surprised to find Coco on my doorstep.

"Hey, everything okay?"

"I didn't know where else to go, um, Orion called just as Jess and Bridgette got here to walk me home. I guess Brooks is at my apartment. They're trying to get rid of him but I don't feel like I should go home, you know?" She huddled in on herself a little meekly as she said it.

"Yeah, no. Get in here." I stepped aside and she slipped past me.

"Hi," she greeted the curious stares of the guys.

"Guy who drugged her is at her place trying to start some shit or something," I said.

"I don't want to interrupt anything, I could always get a car to my mom's hotel now that I think about it."

"Naw, no, you're fine!" Reflash said.

"Play poker?" Blaze asked.

She smiled and shook her head.

"To be honest, I just want to chill."

"Sure, babe. Go on in the living room, make yourself at home."

"Thanks," she murmured. "You're sure it's okay? That I won't be putting a damper on things?"

"Naw," Oz called out. "It's cool." I met his somber brown gaze and gave a barely imperceptible nod.

The guys stared at their cards and stacked their chips while I took her scarf, purse, and coat and hung them up for her.

"Get you anything?" I asked softly.

"Naw, I'm good, go play. I'll just watch some TV or something."

"Whatever you want." I kissed the top of her head and she smiled, giving my hand a quick squeeze before she drifted into the living room. She folded her slim frame into my favorite recliner, all but disappearing into it, and I watched for half a second as her slim hand appeared and picked up the remote and switched on the TV, lowering the volume.

I went into the kitchen and started some tea for her, even though she had said she didn't want anything. Her hand had been frigid when she'd given mine a squeeze, so cold, I had to believe that she'd been standing outside downstairs for a minute, trying to decide if she should come up here. I'd talk to her about that later. I didn't want her to ever hesitate to come to me. I hated the thought that she would, for any reason.

I sat back down for a hand while the water came to a boil and was getting my ass handed to me. Driller and Blaze were both going back and forth on killing it tonight. Made me real glad it was just poker chips and not any actual money at stake. Also made me glad that booze, not gambling, was my vice of choice. While it wasn't easy to quit, at least when I had, I still had my shirt and the ability to open up downstairs.

By the time the tea water gave a whistle from the stovetop and I'd doctored it up, Coco's eyelids were getting heavy. I brought her the tea and she smiled up at me tiredly with a murmur of thanks, cradling it between her hands and breathing it in.

"No problem," I murmured.

She sipped carefully and gave a purr of appreciation and I went back to the game with a hot cup of tea of my own.

Me and the boys had played for probably another hour or so when finally, Driller leaned back with a gusty sigh, a neat pile of chips in front of him, and said, "I gotta say, fellas, it's getting tiresome kicking y'all's asses like this. It's like taking candy from a baby. I think I'm gonna quit before my luck turns."

"I'm with Junior over there," Oz said throwing down his cards. Even his decent-sized pile of chips was much diminished.

"Night, kid, try not to kill our chief tonight, huh?" he called out to Coco. Silence drifted from the living room and Oz raised his eyebrows and leaned forward, pushing out of his seated position with his hands on his knees. "Okay," he said.

"Yeah, she is out," Blaze said from beside the recliner, where he'd wandered to check on her.

"Let her sleep," I said. "I'm sure she'll be sad she missed you."

I said goodbye to my squadmates as they went out the door one at a time and crept over to the living room. She was sound asleep in my chair, one leg curled under her, her face smooth and angelic in the wavering blue light from the television.

I had to smile and reached over her, plucking the remote from the side table, her tepid cup of tea sitting beside it. I switched off the set and left the remote in its place before straightening up. I wanted to be all romantic and just carry her off to bed, but the way she was sitting was awkward for a good grab and I didn't want to scare or startle her.

I settled for stroking a thumb lightly along her cheek and whispering, "Coco, come on babe, let's get you to bed."

15

*C*olette…

    I woke with a slight jolt and unfurled my foot out from underneath me. I was groggy, bleary-eyed, and just wanted to go back to sleep. Skids chuckled lightly and before I knew what was happening, I was airborne. I put my arms around my neck and held myself up, taking some of my weight off his arms.

"You alright?" he asked softly.

"Mm, sleepy," I murmured back.

He chuckled, and it was deep and rich like dark chocolate. I let him carry me across the threshold into his bedroom and was almost sad when he put me down on the edge of the bed, his warmth retreating as he leaned back and knelt on the floor at my feet.

"What are you doing?" I asked softly.

"Getting you ready for bed," he replied simply.

And he did just that, stripping me out of my clothes with a gentle yet firm sensuality, fingertips grazing my skin in all the right places to

137

make me catch my breath, causing my blood to pulse through my veins with a wicked desire.

If only I weren't so tired.

"Kiss me," I begged, my voice tremulous, always low-key afraid he would say no. He didn't, though. Just knelt up, putting his hands on my knees and placing his lips against mine in a butterfly kiss, deepening things slowly until we kissed one another ravenously.

He was, of course, the first to back off, saying, "Let's get you naked and to bed, I'll be in after I clean up and we'll be all set for morning sex if you'd like… I just really want you to get some good sleep. You been burning the candle at both ends and it's starting to show, lover."

I couldn't disagree, even though I wanted to, so I didn't. I just let him take care of me, slipping me out of my clothes until I was as naked as the day I was born, tucking me between the cool, crisp sheets of his wonderful bed which quickly warmed with my body's own heat. Of course, I think that was partially thanks to how hot and bothered he made me. From his touches to his glances to the way he kissed me, I almost wondered how I would ever fall asleep, now.

"Get some rest, I'll be back in a flash," he murmured and gave me one last lingering kiss. I settled in and closed my eyes and I guess I needn't have worried. I was out cold in the span of two seconds.

WHEN I STIRRED the next morning I was lying on my stomach. I turned my head on the pillow and blinked at the perfect curve of his toned hip and ass, the blankets pulled into his lap as he sat up against the head-board, glasses perched midway on his nose, a book resting in his big hands as his true blue eyes skimmed the words on the page.

Oh my God, it was sexy. Incredibly sexy and totally irresistible. I wanted to wake up like this every morning.

"What is it this time?" I asked quietly and he chuckled.

"Peter Pan."

I hummed my appreciation and asked, "Read it out loud?"

He did, and I closed my eyes, listening to the timbre of his deep voice, and it was the best way to wake up. His voice caressed over my nude back like rich fur as I stretched luxuriously and soaked in every word.

He left off at the end of the chapter and closed the hard, leather-bound copy with a soft thump. I opened my eyes as he set first the book and then his glasses on top of it on the side table by his side of the bed before he scooched down to put a warm hand against my skin, smoothing it down over my back from my shoulder to my behind, cupping my ass in his hand and giving it a squeeze.

My hips bucked involuntarily off the bed, pressing that handful of my ass into the palm of his hand even as my pussy gave a pleasure filled throb of desire.

"C'mere," he ordered softly and I turned on my side, sliding closer to him, pressing my chest to his and hooking one leg high on his hip, his erection pressing against my stomach as he urged me closer with his hand on my ass.

"I want to cut your hours some at the *10-13*, babe," he murmured, and I froze.

"What? Why?"

"So I can take you out more, live this life of ours," he growled, nipping the front of my shoulder. I groaned and let him slide me under him. I lay flat on my back as he engulfed me with his larger, much warmer, frame and relished the heat of his body against mine.

"I like the sound of that, actually," I murmured.

"You do, huh?"

"I do," I whispered against his mouth and then we were kissing and there wasn't much more talk as he slipped his thick cock inside me, pushing into me slowly, letting my body adjust to the sudden shock of his girth.

I wound my legs around his hips and pulled him closer with them, a hand on his ass; the other arm across his back. He was so much in control, so careful and exacting, so much more natural and at ease with me. His acceptance of us made an 'us' so complete that it felt like I'd found the other part of my soul.

We made love quickly and he fixed me breakfast while I was in the shower. I didn't have nearly as much time as I wanted; it was a performance night, so there was no practice, but I had all my other errands to run, laundry to do, and everything else that had been neglected during the week with my grueling dance and waitressing schedules.

It felt a little like I was giving up or failing reducing my hours at the restaurant but I had to admit defeat just a little. It was too much, and Skids was right, the increase in salary with the dance company meant I could conceivably quit working at the *10-13* altogether. I didn't want to. I liked working there, so cutting back on my hours to just two days a week it was. I would have Sundays and Mondays off with Skids, work Tuesday and Wednesday with him, take Thursday to do my errands and I was already off Friday and Saturday nights in order to dance.

When I went into the kitchen and dining area of Skid's apartment, he was plating up some eggs, scrambled with cheese, just like I liked them.

"Sit," he urged and I took a place at his small table. He set the plate down in front of me and said after a gusty sigh, "We should talk about last night."

"I know. I'm sorry I interrupted your –"

"It's not that at all, babe." He shook his head and sat across from me with his own plate. "I wouldn't have had it any other way, you being here with me. I just don't want there to be a next time. Want me to go with you to get a restraining order?"

I thought about it. "My roommates said he was going on about apologizing and he didn't want to leave."

"They call the police?"

"No, I don't think so."

Skids grunted and finished chewing his bite of toast, "They should have. Next time –"

"I hope there won't be a next time," I said.

"Be that as it may, better to be prepared. I'll call Yale and see what you need to do. Pick up the paperwork myself."

"A piece of paper won't stop him from coming near me," I said gently.

"No, but it'll make it a hell of a lot easier to prosecute his ass when he does."

I couldn't argue that point, and I was pretty sure it went without saying when guys went all whacked-out and started up with the stalker-ish behavior, the law wasn't exactly on a lady's side when it came to stopping them. Still, I would be a good girl and do what I was supposed to.

I sighed and Skids reached out and grazed my cheek with his thumb.

"It'll be all good," he said.

"I know, just always thought my first weirdo would be a deranged fan-type, not a fellow dancer."

"That's a fair point," he said.

"So, when you going to take me on our first real date?" I asked slyly, more in a bid to change the subject than anything.

"Gotta think of something we'll both like, first."

"Mm, okay," I said, swallowing my mouthful of the orange juice he'd poured for me.

"You gotta run?" he asked.

"I do," I said, pouting.

"Okay, be careful for me. Supposed to get freezing rain today."

"This winter is turning miserable," I said.

"That it is."

"Call me later?" I asked.

"You know I will," he said, and smiled at me in a way that warmed his eyes to bright summer skies.

"Miss you already," I breathed.

He smiled a bit wider and said, "Miss you already."

Aww, I think we found our first 'thing' as a couple. I loved that.

16

S kids…

I lifted the Styrofoam clamshells stacked and secured in their takeout bag and turned back to the bar, holding them out for Angel as he reached it.

"Thanks, man."

"Busy night out there, huh?"

"You know it. Oh, hey, these are for you and Reflash. Tickets to Claire's thing on Thursday."

"Oh, thanks!" I opened the envelope out of habit and said, "There's three tickets here."

"Duh!" he called, walking backwards. "Coco?"

My face split into a genuine grin and I called out, "Thank you, brother!"

"You bet, Chief!" He shot a half-assed salute just as he pushed back into the door and rolled along the glass out onto the sidewalk. He dashed through the sleet, into the passenger side of his rig and slammed the door. His partner gave him a fist bump and reached across him to wave out the passenger window and they lurched into motion, likely to find a parking lot somewhere they could hoover their dinner between calls.

I picked up the receiver on the bar phone and dialed Coco's number by heart. She answered on the fourth ring and said, "Hello?"

"Hey, beautiful."

"Oh, hey! What's going on with you?"

"Nothing much. Say, what have you got going on next Thursday night?"

"Just laundry and chores, why?"

"Think you can get them done earlier in the week?"

"Yeah, why?" I loved how her voice took on a shade of barely-suppressed excitement.

"Well, I was thinking about taking my lady on a date."

"I think that sounds awesome, what time should I be ready?"

"Talk about the particulars later? I'm working the bar and it's fairly busy. I just didn't wanna wait to put a bug in your ear about it."

"Sounds good, it's a date. I'll let you get back to it."

"Alright, babe. Love you."

"Love you, too."

"Ah huh, bye-bye now."

I hung up feeling pretty good about things and went in back to give Reflash the heads up.

"I dunno," he said loudly, and raised his voice even higher, "These mooks don't get their act together, I'm liable to think they'll burn the place down without me!"

I laughed and went back to my bar, calling back over my shoulder, "You're on your own for the most part – I'm making a date night of it with Coco."

"Good!" he shouted. "I was getting tired of being your hetero lifemate! Maybe I need to find a gal of my own!"

"You're married to your work, don't lie."

"You know that's right! Aw, come on! That's the third time this guy's sent his food back, what now!?" Reflash cried.

I went back out to the bar and couldn't stop grinning my fool head off, slinging drinks for the yuppie crowd right up until last call.

17

$\mathcal{C}$olette…

I ended the call and tossed the phone down on the bed, sticking my sucker back in my mouth and pulling my magazine back over in front of me.

"A real date, sounds nice," my mother mused aloud, and I rolled onto my back and hung, back arched, upside down off the end of her hotel room's bed.

"Ooo, I like that one," I said around my sucker, and she turned back to the full-length mirror and turned to the side, admiring the dress she'd tried on.

"Don't change the subject," she said. "Where are you going, what are you doing? You make it next to impossible to live vicariously through you, darling."

I rolled my eyes and she put her hands on her hips and arched a brow. My mother had never been fond of that habit and honestly, that's why I did it.

"I wish I had anything to tell you, but he didn't say. It was busy in the bar."

"Ah." She wiggled out of the dress and laid it on a much smaller pile of ones she was likely to keep, then sat down beside me.

We'd done a spa day on her dime and I was as polished and pampered as I could get from head to toe. A two-hour hot stone massage had left me relaxed and feeling lazy and we were just chilling out in her swanky hotel room relaxing before she had to go. She was leaving in the morning – had to get back to San Fran and her boyfriend for their Christmas, which was some kind of European vacation kicking off next week, even though the actual holiday itself was the week after next.

Jacque was alright, older than me but younger than mom, probably juuust in that territory of defining her as some sort of cougar. I think he was way more serious about her than she was about him, and it made me feel a little bad for him. We were just close enough in age it made family gatherings a little awkward and he wasn't always the most articulate – read 'not creepy.' Sometimes he would say shit and it would send my skin crawling, even though I knew he didn't mean it that way at all. Part of it was a language barrier, I think. He was very French to our American.

I'd tried to bring it up to my mom that he made me uncomfortable sometimes, but she'd always just kind of blown it off. It hurt our relationship a little, at least in my eyes, but she was pretty oblivious to it and I know it didn't do me any favor, keeping it quiet and not pressing it, but it was what it was, I guess. I didn't know if it made me more of an adult keeping it quiet to spare hurt feelings on her part, or less of one for ignoring my own. Maybe Skids would have some insight. It certainly fell under 'conversations to have with your nearest and dearest.' I made a mental note to talk to him about it and see what he said.

"Ah, new love," my mother said with a wistful sigh. "What I wouldn't give to be your age again and in it."

I laughed and said, "Trouble in paradise with Jacque?" I asked.

"Not at all," she said and mock-pouted. "Sometimes I find him entirely too agreeable."

"Good lord, Mom. You're honest-to-God the only woman I know who wants to fight with her boyfriend. I honestly don't understand it."

She smiled at me and wrinkled her nose. "I don't like to fight with my lovers, darling, but I do enjoy a spirited disagreement from time to time. Keeps the passion alive."

I fought not to roll my eyes.

"Isn't that the same thing?"

"I don't think so," she said.

I laughed and shook my head, biting into the soft, chewing gum center of my lollipop, the candy shell having thinned, giving a satisfying crackle between my teeth.

"What about your new beau?" she asked. "No disagreements?"

I shook my head, "Not yet, still like brand-spankin'-new. I hope we can disagree amicably and not fight or argue. I'll leave all that to you."

"You're just like my mother," she said and sulked slightly.

"Mellow?" I asked.

"Boring," she answered and I scoffed, pulling the pillow out from under my chest and swinging it at her. She broke into a peal of laughter and swatted me on the ass, getting back up to try another garment.

She was a born shopper, my mother. Another thing that hadn't really rubbed off on me. I mean, I enjoyed shopping but only with her. Any other time I just couldn't be bothered, really.

I was going to miss her, and both was and wasn't looking forward to her departure. My mother was like a sugar rush. She came around and everyone got all excited and hyper but eventually it petered out and the novelty wore off.

Oh, my God, that sounded awful, even in my own head. I loved my mom to death but sometimes I wished she would be more a mom and less my best friend.

It could get awkward sometimes.

Like with how much she'd flirted with Skids. My mother was a natural flirt. Didn't even realize she was doing it. Or, just about never realized she was doing it. We'd only had one spot of trouble with one of my boyfriends admitting he had a crush on her and believe me; that had ended that relationship. I guess I was a little worried that things were so new with Skids that if she stuck around he might take an interest in her over me on account of they were closer in age.

"Hey, Mom," I said, and she paused and arched an eyebrow in the mirror.

"What's wrong?" she asked at the expression on my face and I had to hand it to her. If ever there was a time I needed her to flip that switch between mom and best friend this was it and she did so with aplomb.

I sighed, hesitated for a minute, but I could never hold out with her for long. She waited me out and I spilled the beans about Skids, about my worry and how I felt just awful for even thinking it. She smiled at me and smoothed some of my hair back from my face.

"You are so grown up, Coco," she said with a sigh. "I think your new man knows that. I fully admit being a momma bear with ulterior motives the night I came for dinner at your new man's bar."

"Oh?"

"Mm, your momma laid it on thick, but he didn't budge, baby girl."

"You tested my boyfriend?" I squeaked.

"Of course, I did! I had to make sure, didn't I?"

"I don't know whether to be mad at you or –"

"Oh, you have every right to be mad at me. I would expect nothing less, but you know as well as I do, I love you, my heart… and I had to be sure."

"Ugh," I pressed fingertips into my eyes and rubbed. "That's so –"

"Dirty? Underhanded? Manipulative?"

"Yeah."

"You're my only child, and I admit, I don't know how you managed to turn out as well as you did with me as a mother," she said with a sigh.

"You're just sticking to what you know," I said unhappily. It was true. Dance world was ridiculously shady like that.

"It's true," she said, a bit ruefully.

"Okay, truce." I held up a pinky and she locked hers with mine. "No more 'tests' okay?"

"No need, he passed the one I was worried about the most."

"You know I'm going to tell him, right?"

Her mouth dropped open. "You better not!"

"Mom!"

"How did I raise you to be so honest? I thought I taught you better than that."

I laughed and said, "You did; consider it my major act of rebellion."

She sighed, "Well-behaved women –"

"Rarely make history," we finished together and fell to pieces, cracking up laughing.

"You always did march to the beat of your own drum," she declared.

"We put the 'fun' back in 'dysfunctional'," I agreed.

I smiled and she hugged me before flinging a cloud of chiffon in my face.

"We have to find you something to wear on this date."

Crap. My life-giver could and would use any excuse to shop.

"HEY YOU," he said, opening his door.

"Hi," I murmured, stepping over the threshold and into him. I raised my lips up in offering and he closed the gap, kissing me soundly as he swung the door shut behind me and twisted the deadbolt without looking.

He hummed in appreciation against my lips and broke the kiss saying, "Missed you."

"Missed you, too." I felt my voice deepen slightly, husky with desire. His kiss always managed to light me on fire.

"So, what brings you over?" he growled, voice just as laden with want.

"Honestly?"

"Always," he said without hesitation, despite the one-word question being rhetorical.

"My head's full, and I just wanted to cuddle up and use you as a sounding board."

"This is going to sound real juvenile, but I'm hard as a rock, mind talking with me cuddled up inside you?"

I laughed and he gave another growl and came for me, lifting me, shrieking and laughing, carrying me right for the bedroom.

Oh. He was serious! Well, I could get on board with that. After all, I'd feel a lot less guilty about using him if he used me right back.

"Hmm." He set me on my feet and pressed his lips to the side of my neck, his whiskers tickling my skin and sending goosebumps marching down my arms.

I reached up, swaying on my feet, and put my arms around him as he slipped his hands under the hem of my sweater, putting them against my body, stroking sensually along my ribs, grazing his thumbs along the band of my bra as he flicked his tongue against my pulse point.

"Oh." I gave a throaty moan which just encouraged him, his arms slipping around my back, hands on my jeans-clad ass, pressing my body to his as he woke every one of my senses.

"God, you smell good," he rumbled against the side of my neck, sending pleasurable little shockwaves through me, echoing down from that erogenous point in the hollow of my neck, pinging off my clit and traveling through my figure.

I gasped, my fingers wandering to the hem of his shirt, walking it out of his waistband, suddenly desperate to have his warmth beneath them.

His arms went around me, his hands grabbing my ass, practically lifting me to my toes as he walked me back towards the bed. He shoved my jacket off my shoulders and off my arms; I lifted his tee over his head, taking the flannel he had on over it with it. He raised his arms, letting me take it and once his hands were free, they went to my back, working at the clasp on my bra as he crushed me to his chest.

We went tit-for-tat. He'd steal an article of clothing, and I would take one of his, until nothing lay between us but the slightly chilly air of his bedroom.

Not for long.

He pulled me against his body and we fed at one another's mouths, hungry, ravenous for each other's kiss, for as much physical contact as possible. My blood danced through my body, warm with his body's heat, my ardor pirouetting across the stage of my heart as he kissed across my jaw, against my throat, down the side of my neck, turning me to melted chocolate in his arms, rich and decadent as he worried that arousing spot on my neck that sent my pulse into hyper-drive.

His fingertips skimmed along my flesh, sending delightful trails of tingling heat sweeping down my body that settled into a throbbing aching need at the apex of my thighs.

"God, I can't get enough of you," he rumbled against my stomach as I buried my fingers in his silver hair and dragged his mouth to where I wanted it.

He darted his tongue against the folds of my pussy lips, hot, pink, wet I threw back my head and moaned. He chuckled darkly, the sound painting my walls slick with want as he planted a hand in the center of my chest between my breasts and shoved, sending me flying back onto the bed.

He wrapped his big arms around my thighs and dragged me bodily over the bed, my hair fanning out along the deep, forest-green velvet comforter. His mouth was hot and wet against my cunt as he teased at my lips, using his lips and tongue with practiced experience to bring me to the brink in a few lapping strokes.

"Oh, God!" I cried to the ceiling, my voice strained.

"Ain't no one here in this room but you and me, babe."

Holy shit, that was sexy as hell.

I didn't have time to dwell on it, though, because he was pushing his thick middle digit inside of me, stroking my walls slick with my passion for him, searching out the spot on the roof of my sex, that slightly-roughened patch right there…

"Oh, God, right there!" My voice came out high, strained, a whining plea and he didn't disappoint, latching his mouth onto my clit, stroking his finger over the inside of me as I gripped it tight and tighter, the ecstasy climbing to an unearthly height.

"That's it, lover. Come for me," he ordered gently, and though it was gentle, it brooked no argument.

That was fine. He would get none from me.

I felt my back bow, my pelvis lift as his lips around my clit teased it just so with the tip of his tongue, and I died and went to heaven.

I vaguely remember crying out, my body crashing to the surface of his cloud-like bed as pleasure surged through me like electricity, like heat lightning through the clouds. It was barely contained by my edges, crashing into my skin from the inside, redoubling in intensity before arcing back into my core.

I vaguely remember squirming under his hold, barely remember reaching for him through my haze of euphoria, but I wasn't done. I was close, so very close, and I needed him inside of me.

18

*S*kids…

I was hard to the point that a deep ache was starting to settle into my balls and I couldn't hold off anymore. I had to be inside her, needed to feel her hot, silky walls, slick with her orgasm, envelope my cock, her body tensing, fisting it gently and drawing me in. God, every time I slid into her it felt just like coming home.

I lay over the top of her, smoothing her hair out of her face tenderly, rolling my hips slowly as she twined her legs around my waist. Her breath trembled as it passed between her sensual lips and her blue eyes slipped shut as if she listened to music only she could hear. She was so beautiful I didn't think there was a sonnet, a poem, a classic writ lovely enough to capture it, to do her justice. Trust me, I'd read them all to know.

Her pussy was sleek and tender how it gripped me and all manner of wild and magic sensation took root in the base of my cock, growing and filling me out from my center, euphoria and a subtle grace I'd never known spreading through my limbs as I slowly and almost lazily made love to her.

The moment was lovely, a touch dark, and oh, so deep. I couldn't and wouldn't ruin it with talking.

She held herself to me, her arms around me, and I just couldn't get deep enough. She let me go, let me kneel in worship and press her battered feet to my chest, and the expression on her face as I thrust that much harder, that much further into her body, was of such sweet surrender my heart ached supremely.

That was it for me. That was the moment I tumbled so deeply into love with her, I didn't think I would ever see the light of day again. All it took was that one, sweet, innocent look of sheer surrender – I would do anything for her.

Her body arched, her pussy tightening, and I bit my bottom lip savagely trying desperately to hang on, to not go off half-cocked, so to speak. I needed her to finish, wanted so badly to feel the ripple and pull of her body around mine, to die the little death by her side, in unison, two souls traveling as one to the gates of heaven.

I got my wish. She drew tauter than a bowstring, frayed so beautifully and fell back to the bed her body unwinding like satin ribbon from a spool, pooling on the coverlet in a languid radiance. A smile played on her lips even as she pressed her hands to her mouth to suppress a joyous giggle.

I pulled them away, her blue eyes flying wide, startled, and I wanted to feed whatever son of a bitch had told her or made fun of her laugh after sex his teeth. I knew someone must have done it. She wouldn't try to hide it otherwise.

I kissed each one of her palms in turn and whispered, "Don't you ever hide that laugh, that light, from me."

Her face became stone, a surprised look etched deep for several seconds before her fine features softened and she reached for me. I obliged, lowering myself over her, her legs slipping off to either side of my hips and parting just a little bit more, my over-sensitive cock shifting inside her causing me to grunt in sweet agony. She cupped my bearded cheeks between her hands and rose up as best she could to meet me halfway. The kiss she bestowed upon me held the copper taste of heart's blood from my savaged bottom lip and it held such a power, such a finality to it. She may have been young in body, but her spirit, the soul contained in it, was older than time and probably far older than my own.

She gave a satisfied sigh and a decadent little moan and hugged me to her, her lips playing along my shoulder and the side of my neck in light little nips and kisses.

By God, it stirred a fire in me, enough of a fire that this old man was ready for a round two.

"WHAT ARE YOU READING NOW?" she murmured sleepily from beside my hip. I lowered the book to my sheet-covered lap and freed the hand closer to her from beneath it so I could run it down her back, beneath the sheet and claim a handful of her ass.

"Poetry."

"Mm, who?" She stretched, long on her stomach, and it reminded me of a cat, lazing in the sun, though it was the middle of the night. No sun to be had, the cloud cover out there so thick that the usual white-blue hue of moonlight through the window was stifled. The eerie blue light of the electrics reflected off the fresh snow and ice, casting deep shadows in corners and fanning across my ceiling, the warmth of the yellow light from my bedside lamp barely beating it back.

"Frost, ironically," I responded.

"I like him," she purred.

"Yeah?"

"Mm-hmm, found him through English class when we covered "The Outsiders"."

"Ah, yeah. "Nothing Gold Can Stay. "" I flipped through the book and found the poem and read:

"Nature's first green is gold,
Her hardest hue to hold.
Her early leaf's a flower;
But only so an hour.
Then leaf subsides to leaf.
So Eden sank to grief,
So dawn goes down to day.
Nothing gold can stay."

I GLANCED AT HER, her cheek pressed to the pillow, eyes shut; a serene little smile painting her lips as she soaked in the words, basked in my voice, and that sensation was back. The one where it felt like my heart was crushed by my ribs as it grew two sizes too big to be contained by my chest.

I would carve it out and lay it at her feet if she asked me. These intimate moments meant that much to me.

I'd never shared my love of literature with my ex-wife. She had been interested in a lot of the same things I had been, just not the written word. Not the classics.

"Read me another?"

Coco's tremulous voice banished all thoughts of my ex, the timid fragility of her tone making me smile.

"You like that I read to you, huh?"

"I love that you read to me."

"One more," I said, "but then we talk about you."

"Me?"

"You said you wanted to use me as a sounding board."

"Oh, right! That. You're very distracting, you know."

I chuckled.

"I'll own it. I derailed that particular train of thought. What's up?"

She pushed herself up into a sitting position and fluffed the pillow to put at her back. I lost my easy smile at how so very serious she'd turned all of a sudden and started to worry about what could be wrong.

Coco hugged my arm with both of hers and leaned her head onto my shoulder, prompting me to softly close my book and give her my undivided attention. I stared off into space, listening to her as she spilled about her mixed feelings when it came to her mom and the exchange we'd had at the bar.

I chuckled and said, "So I passed her little test, did I?"

She lifted her head from my shoulder and looked up at me, her mouth a little 'o' of surprise.

"You knew?" she asked.

I laughed. I hadn't at the time, really, but hindsight being 20/20 and all…

"Not when she was there. Your mom is slicker 'n owl shit, I'll give her that, but looking back, I had to guess."

"So you're not mad?" she asked.

"At you? Never. At her? Nah," I shook my head. "You're her only kid, right? Kind of comes with the territory."

"Seriously? Just like that? No drama?"

I laughed and shook my head. "No drama required, beautiful. I am, and always will be, a cop at heart. We're used to people lying to us, the cause good, bad, or indifferent."

"That almost breaks my heart a little," she confessed.

"Don't let it, it was the job. Look on the bright side: as a bartender, I'm getting all the truth I can handle and then some."

She laughed and cuddled closer, laying her head back down on my shoulder. I joined in, I couldn't help it; her laughter was infectious.

"She has her own boyfriend, although I think she's less serious about him than he is her," she said, and something about the way she said it pinged my radar.

"Oh yeah?" I asked casually, opening the door for her to elaborate. She didn't hesitate, and I could tell she'd had this sitting on her chest for a while.

I listened, and immediately didn't like her mom's boyfriend, but I believed her when she said the schmuck was likely oblivious to it. I turned my head and kissed the top of hers.

"Solution to that one is easy enough," I said to her. "I just go with you whenever he's gonna be around."

"Seriously?" she asked.

"What kind of a crap boyfriend would I be otherwise?" I asked.

Some of the tension leaked out of her and she smiled at me. "I don't think you could be a crap boyfriend even if you tried," she said and her voice had dropped, kissed by that sultry little tone that drove me wild.

"Gonna have to agree to disagree with you there," I said, and set my poetry aside, reaching for her. She giggled as I attacked the side of her neck with kisses, her gasp turning into a moan as I really started to work at turning her on.

19

Colette…

I gave a little shimmy and tugged down, just above the hem of my off-the-shoulder grey cable-knit sweater dress and sighed. I turned this way and that, butterflies taking off in my stomach as I wondered if the ensemble was somehow inappropriate. Skids had said to dress for a date, not too chic, but nice. I'd chosen the simple sweater dress with its long sleeves for warmth. The off-the-shoulder look would be fine outdoors with the addition of my classic pea coat.

The dress fell just above mid-thigh; a short two-inch expanse of thigh covered by black pantyhose gave way to thigh-high black suede boots that hugged my slim legs. I loved them because they were flats, and super warm and comfortable.

I was nervous, but I knew I looked great, my hair done in soft beachy curls, makeup understated, lips coated in a nude gloss. I wore a simple white-gold necklace, a thin chain with a circle at the end, white diamonds taking up a third of the rim, a smaller, rose gold circle in the open center of the larger circle. Matching earrings hung from each lobe, a circle hanging from a length of thin chain with a single diamond set in the edge of each circle. The set had been an early Christmas gift from my mother, just before she'd left, a reminder that no matter where she was, no matter where I was in the world, she held me in her heart.

I missed her with a sudden pang that quickly faded when I heard one of my roommates answer the apartment's front door. I froze and listened and smiled when I heard Skids' voice, answer their greeting. A knock fell on my bedroom door, which the mirror was affixed to.

"Coco," Bridgette called.

"Yeah!" I called back.

"Your date's here."

I don't know why I just didn't open the door. I mean, I wasn't even sure why I was so nervous! The man had seen me naked countless times by now, had been inside me, and here I was worried about how he would think of me dressed?

I smiled at myself wryly and opened the door. Bridgette smiled and bit her bottom lip, excited. She bounced her eyebrows at me in approval and stepped aside so I could see Skids and Skids could see me.

He took my breath away.

Standing there in the doorway so proud and so tall, the suit he wore stylish and fitted, a deep midnight blue and of a fabric so fine, it held almost highlights or a faint sheen to it. The shirt beneath it was open at the collar and a deep black. His eyes practically glowed from the color pairings, his beard was perfectly edged and trimmed, his hair freshly cut.

He looked distinguished, handsome… foxy.

Oh, my God. I realized. *I was totally going out with the epitome of a silver fox. Yay, me!*

His eyes roved over me just as mine roved over him, and his smile was to die for. I felt a special thrill that he liked what he saw, and was so enamored with his sparkling blue eyes and the love and light in them, I completely missed the red and white roses he held in his hand, the stems stripped of their thorns and tied with a beautiful white satin ribbon.

We met halfway and he pressed the fragrant blooms into my hand and murmured, "These are for you. My God, you look lovely."

"Thank you," I said, my voice low, the heat of a blush coating my cheeks as I realized my roommates were all standing around the living room and kitchen staring at us.

"You guys are too cute," Genevieve said.

A little semi-hysterical bubble of laughter rose to the top of my voice box. I mean, how embarrassing. Skids walks through the door and it's like my brain decides to go out to lunch without me and leaves my ovaries in charge. Too bad, really, considering they explode anytime he's around me.

"I'll put those in some water for you," Bridgette said helpfully, taking the roses, and then added, "You kids have fun, now. We won't wait up."

I rolled my eyes at her and took the hand Skids held out. He checked his expensive-looking silver watch and said, "The car's waiting downstairs, we should get a move on."

Jess handed him my coat from the back of the couch. Skids gave him a nod and held it open for me and I slipped it on. Before I could say anything, Genevieve put my clutch into my hands.

"Thanks," I said.

"Don't expect she's comin' home tonight," Skids said and there was laughter.

"Night you guys!" I called over my shoulder and they all called back their good nights. Then it was just me and Skids striding down the hall to the stairs.

"I mean it," he said, opening the car door for me downstairs. I paused and he looked me in the eyes and said, "You're beautiful."

I smiled and got into the waiting warmth of the black town car and slid all the way across the leather seat. He got in beside me and told the driver, "Thanks for waiting."

"Where are we going, exactly?" I asked, curiosity eating at me. I twined my fingers through his.

He held my hand, raising the back of it to his lips.

He kissed it and said, "I told you, it's a surprise."

I gave him tight lips and he laughed at me.

"You're no help at all," I declared.

He grinned seductively and said, "I'll make it up to you. Promise."

All I knew was the plan was dinner and a show of some kind. Not a movie, but a show. I couldn't get anything more out of him no matter how much I picked, pestered, or begged.

The car took us through Old Town to the heart of downtown, and out the other side. It was an old industrial district that was flipping slowly but surely into more of an arts and entertainment sector. These warehouses were old, as in old wooden clapboard and brick structures circa the late 1800s, maybe early 1900s. They were places that weren't on the historic registry but had been kept up enough so as not to be completely falling down. Likely, no one had attempted to demolish them because there would be an outcry and they would then be put on some registry somewhere – who knew. I digress.

We pulled up in front of the doors of the middle warehouse in a row of three, the buildings much longer than they were wide. The entryways of them were greatly modified with glass doors and windows and small but opulent-looking lobbies. It was an enchanting mashup of old and new and I admit I was so captivated by it, I didn't immediately realize it was Reflash who opened the car door for me in order that I may step out.

"Hey, y' made it!" he cried holding open his arms for a quick hug.

I smiled genuinely and said, "Hey you!" before giving him a tight hug.

"They letting people inside yet?" Skids asked, eyeing the line.

"Yeah, yeah, come on. Guys are holding our place."

"Oh, shit," Skids said, and we hurried to our place in line.

"Coco, you know Youngblood and his woman, Chrissy. Yale and Aly, Golden and Lys."

"Yes, hello." I smiled and greeted them.

"Hi," Aly said and smiled really big. Everyone looked so dressed up and classy, a far cry from the casual attire or uniforms I usually saw them in at the *10-13*.

"Backdraft and Lil are already inside," Chrissy said. "They're saving our table."

"Oh, so it's literally dinner and a show, like at the same time?" I asked.

"Yeah, didn't Skids tell you?" Youngblood asked.

"Didn't tell her a goddamned thing, now shut up. It's supposed to be a surprise!"

We were hustled into the lobby off the sidewalk and I was grateful that it was warm inside. Skids took my coat and handed both it and his to the coat check lady, shoving the tickets she handed back into his pants pocket.

We were led into a vast, dark room, a single flame at the center of each round table illuminating it. We went to the table Backdraft was standing at, Lil, his slight, blonde, and sweet girlfriend sitting beside him. We took seats and I smiled and nodded back to everyone, greeting them in turn, more than a little nervous about making a good impression. I mean, I hadn't realized Skids was so ready to have me involved with his friends! It meant the world to me, but I was almost paralyzed with fear at just how much I wanted them to like and accept me. I didn't want to do anything that could be construed as wrong or insulting.

"You okay?" Skids asked, low in my ear. I smiled and nodded.

"Fine!" I said quickly. "Just want everyone to like me," I murmured in his ear.

He chuckled and kissed my temple.

"Everyone will love you just fine, just be yourself," he reassured me.

I nodded and looked around, listening vaguely to the chatter around the table, standing with everyone else when Narcos, Driller, and Everleigh arrived. They took the final three seats at the table just next to ours, where Reflash had sat, so they were just behind me and Skids.

There were fifteen of us, all attached to the club, and the tables only seated a dozen. There were some poor people already seated at this table of twelve with us who we didn't know, and they just sort of kept to themselves, turning in their seats to view the big round stage in the center of the room.

Waiters marched from the recesses around the big, open space and brought the first course to the tables. It was a fixed menu; I had no idea what I would be eating, but I didn't care. I was busy looking around the room, above the stage, to the second floor.

Ornately carved wooden railings ran around the open space, candlelight winking at regular intervals, shadowy people looking down from the tables seating two. It looked cozier up there, more intimate, but the view down here was better.

A salad was set before me and I murmured thanks to the waiter who'd brought it, startling slightly when he smiled from behind an ornate Venetian mask, black and gold, long-nosed, and almost operatic. He withdrew his white-gloved hand and bowed at the waist. His tux was all crisp white shirt, the jacket deepest black and high-waisted, with long tails at the back. He looked every bit the staunch and fancy servant from a bygone era and things seemed so very utterly posh as the waiters and waitresses, all in their identical serving outfits, melted back from the tables and disappeared through doorways and down hallways set in the walls between candled wall sconces, the white sticks a little too perfect, a little too uniform, electric flames dancing within flame-shaped bulbs at their tips.

Safer, but it ruined the ambiance just the slightest little bit.

"Good evening." A woman's voice came over the speakers and we all looked up to the stage. Where had she come from?

"Welcome to Tiatro del Notte. My name is Grace and I'll be your storyteller this evening."

She was beautiful, regal, standing on stage in knee-high riding boots, velvet fitted leggings, and a coat that was part coat, part dress, part corset. It hugged her trim waist, the skirt of it flaring at her hips and cut high in the front and long into tails in the back. Lace spilled from the fitted sleeves over her hands as she gesticulated gracefully, as her name implied. Her face was elegantly hidden by a black lace mask.

She strode in slow, even strides around the stage, striking in her white shirt beneath the black coat with its edging of silver rope-like embellishment and its shiny, elaborate silver buttons.

The blue-white light of spotlight came up to illuminate Grace as she spoke.

"Tonight, a tale of forbidden love, of loss, and a reminder that not every tale, fairy or otherwise, has a happy ending. Poignantly, we begin with a young couple, wild and free, and totally in love…"

She raised an arm in a flourish and the lights shining down on her at the edge of the stage went out as a spotlight at the center came up, presenting a couple, a girl in a white dress, a halter, clinging to her strong upper body, the skirt flowy and falling to just below her knees, reminiscent of the dress Marilyn Monroe wore, famously, above the subway grate.

The man was muscular and tall, holding up a great silver hoop between them, leaning forward as the music began, a haunting melody, hypnotizing notes. The couple stole a kiss and then he stepped into the hoop and they began such a dance between them, so full of skill, so full of heart, so filled with sensuality and beautiful erotic imagery, I maybe made it three bites into my salad before I was thoroughly captivated by what I was seeing.

Skids nudged my elbow lightly with his to remind me to eat and I jolted slightly, blushing faintly as I took another bite of my food. The salad was wonderful, mixed baby greens with a light vinaigrette that was definitely white, the flavor light and bursting with citrus and hints of pear and peppercorn over my tongue.

The rest of the evening was magic as performer after performer – dancers, acrobats, and more– played out the doomed love story on the stage. The tale was haunting. Idealistic young lovers, torn apart by circumstance and war. His return to find her changed; of course, he was changed, too – her spurning, and then the final act. Silks the color of fire swept down from the ceiling, Claire cradled in them, her costume fitted and black, as she represented the young woman coming into her own, a phoenix rising from the ashes, bursting forth through the flames of her trials and tribulations into a strong and independent creature that no man could capture or claim.

The whole series of performances was so beautiful, so poetic, and just so unbelievable and Claire's performance was the perfect finish. The food had been sumptuous. What they had here? It was perfect, pure, an incredible feast for the senses. I wanted to know if there was any way I could be a part of it at some point, because, *Wow*.

Everyone at the tables was on their feet, applauding, cheering, and whistling, loud in the dark. The performers all returned to the stage and the MC – excuse me, '*Storyteller*' – recited each of their names, and it was like rolling credits.

I was astonished, grateful, and almost moved to tears.

"How did I not know this existed?" I asked Skids, finally finding my voice from being so speechless.

"That's just it, babe. This was their soft opening. Their trial run."

"Well, they fuckin' nailed it," Reflash said from beside us and the lot of us just couldn't stop chattering about it as our plates were cleared and people began to move for the exits.

We waited in line at the coat check and when we reached the front of it, Skids dug the tickets out of his pocket and handed them to me. I handed them to the girl and she said the most embarrassing and awful thing.

"Aw, you brought your granddaughter! That's so sweet! Hang on, I'll be right back with these."

Skids and I exchanged a look, our eyes wide, and we couldn't help ourselves. We burst out laughing. I think we were honestly just grateful that none of the rest of his club, or as they referred to themselves, squad, was close enough behind us to hear what she'd said.

She returned with our coats and Skids held mine open for me. He stopped, paused, took a deep breath and said gently, "She's my girl-friend, not my granddaughter, and I know your heart was in the right place, but you really shouldn't make assumptions."

With that, he dropped a few dollars in the tip jar, took up his coat in one hand and my hand in his other and walked us out to the street.

Golden and Lys came out behind us, and so much for his squad not hearing. Golden was the one to say it.

"Think I'm gonna start callin' you Pappy from now on after that," he said with a wink to Skids.

"Fuck you, man," Skids said, shaking his head, laughing. All I could do was blush a scarlet to rival Claire's fiery silks.

"Please don't," I clipped out.

Lys burst out laughing and was all "Awww! Come here!" She hugged me and I hugged her back and tried valiantly not to let my eyes mist further with my humiliation.

Skids drew me away from Lys and hugged me tight to his chest. He looked me right in the eyes and said, "Don't. No one can make you feel inferior without your consent."

"Eleanor Roosevelt," I finished, attributing the well-known quote to the first lady who'd said it.

I sniffed and shoved the rising tide of embarrassment down.

He was right. She didn't know and she didn't matter. I didn't think I was going to be this sensitive about it, but then again, this was honestly the first time we'd faced such a thing.

I knew it wouldn't be the last, however, so I'd best toughen up now.

"Don't let it get to you," Youngblood said, cradling Chrissy close.

I smiled and nodded while Skids used an app to get us a car to take back to his place.

We all ended up at the *10-13* talking about the show and what we loved and the like, waiting for Angel and Claire to arrive. When they did, it was to another standing ovation and I found myself calculating what it would take for them to come see me at the ballet.

I would love to have them all, for as loving and supportive as they were of the performing arts. It touched me in ways I couldn't begin to describe.

There were drinks, a nightcap to a perfect evening, and then we retired upstairs to Skids' apartment.

I set my clutch on the entryway table and he took my coat from my shoulders, sliding it down my arms.

I sucked in a sharp breath as his lips brushed the skin between my shoulder and neck, his breath warm and scented with the strong coffee he'd drunk downstairs to top off his evening. I'd had a bit of whiskey in mine; the warmth was spreading through my body and relaxing muscles I hadn't realized I'd held tensed.

I cuddled back into my lover's chest and closed my eyes asking him softly, "Do you think they liked me?"

"Mm, you'd know it if they didn't. The boys, they ain't shy about making their opinions known. Give it a little more time, I think they'll love you like I do."

I turned in the circle of his arms and twined my arms around his neck, sighing contentedly at the intimacy of our contact. I said to him, "No one could ever love me like you do."

He grinned down at me and nodded slowly. "You're damn right about that."

I tipped my chin and raised my lips and he didn't hesitate to kiss me.

20

*S*kids…

Life was good. Better than good, in fact. Winter melted off into a beautiful spring and before the Indigo City Bay Ballet's run of The Nutcracker was through, Coco somehow managed to score the whole squad tickets to go see her.

She lied like the devil about it, too, saying she didn't spring for it out of pocket. Of course, if that was the case, she wouldn't have asked Reflash for the extra shifts. We knew better, my best friend and I, but decided not to call her on her bullshit. Just accepted the club-wide Christmas gift and went and saw her.

I loved watching her up there, dancing for us. She was beauty, she was grace, she was everything to me, and I took her home and ravaged her good for it.

I loved my girl so much. She wore her heart on her sleeve and was so bold and daring. We'd run into some flak about our age difference but come the second round, she had her fists up. She was kind, but she didn't hesitate to break it off in the guy's ass. The girl had some Irish diplomacy. She told that dude to go to Hell in such a way he went off packing, looking forward to the trip.

I was proud of her. Prouder still that when the weather turned decent she was the one to ask about when we were going riding. We went out once a week together. It wasn't about the destination; it never was, just more about the trip. She never once complained about Reflash coming with us, and they got along like two peas in a pod. It did my heart good that my woman and my best friend got along so well.

She was spending more than half her time here at my place with me, anymore. Her things were finding their way into the corners of my drawers and the edges of my closet. I liked it, it felt good, things naturally progressing like they were.

She was back in practice for the next production, a run of *Sleeping Beauty*. She and her Madame had put their heads together on how to spice up some of the choreography and had worked it out to add some aerial to the production. While they couldn't get Claire to hire on with them herself, they had hired one of Claire's male students, a kid who was almost as adept as she was at the silks by then, to play the dragon that the evil queen sent out in opposition to the prince.

I was so impressed with her, and felt luckier with every passing day. We didn't argue; we never fought, though we did disagree from time to time. I realized it was everything a relationship could and should be and I was grateful that I was getting to experience it at all, though I found it so damn late in life.

"What you thinking about?" Reflash asked, wiping his hands on the kitchen towel over his shoulder.

"Just feelin' good and feelin' fine, man."

"Coco," he said flatly, but he was grinning.

I smiled back and laughed.

"That obvious, huh?"

"Yeah, and it looks good on you, brother. I'm glad as hell to see you happy again."

"Feels good," I said. "I'm glad it didn't come down to an ass-whoopin'."

Reflash laughed, "Me, too. Pretty sure I would have gotten my ass kicked."

"Yeah, but you would have done it anyway."

"Damn right, I would. You were bein' a damn fool."

"Yeah, well, that was then and this is now," I said, straight up.

"You got that right!" he called out, turning to walk back into his kitchen. We were opening up for the lunch crowd. We'd cut out breakfast, except for our brunch on Sunday mornings, which was Reflash's specialty.

Business was as strong as ever, we had just decided to cut back a bit to live life a little more. We were finally at the stage with our place that we could do that, and we'd worked hard to be there.

For the first time in my life, it was like everything was falling into place and everything was as it should be. I felt like I could finally coast.

The bell above the door chimed and I looked up from my last-minute bar prep as Coco shut it behind her. She turned, and positively glowed when she saw me, and I felt my own heart swell a few sizes at the sight of her. She immediately came over and put her hands on the bar hoisting herself up and leaning forward on them to peck me on the lips.

"Hey, beautiful. What's going on?"

"Nada," she said in response and lowered herself back to the floor. "Practice was great, but just the same ol' same ol' other than that. What's going on with you?"

"Not a whole lot. You get whatever that thing was figured out yet?"

"Yep! Orion figured out how we could do it and the Madame seems happy with it so we're going to run through it a few times and see if it'll stick."

"Awesome, need to run upstairs?"

"Yeah, I'll be right back down."

"No problem, got your keys?"

"Of course I do!" She blew another kiss at me and went back out to go upstairs, shower, and change for her shift.

"You're one lucky son of a bitch, you know that?" Reflash yelled from the kitchen.

I grinned to myself and tossed the cuts of lime I'd been working on into their little bin.

Hell, yeah, I did.

A FEW HOURS LATER, the bar was hoppin', and I was sweatin'.

I would swear, I felt like I was comin' down with something all of a sudden, which was weird. I'd felt fine all day.

I turned, and it was getting a little hard to breathe all of a sudden. I paused at the register and put a hand to my chest. Swear to Christ, I'd never had a cold or whatever come on so fast, but it felt like an elephant was sitting on my fuckin' chest.

"Skids, what's wrong?" Coco asked from across the bar and I turned my head to tell her nothin', that I was gonna be fine, just must have been something I ate, you know? Not to worry her or anything.

But the words never made it out of my mouth. This crushing pain went through me and lanced down my arm, and I staggered.

"Skids!" Coco cried, but I was already losing focus, the rubber anti-fatigue mat rushing up to meet me.

I don't remember shit after that.

21

*C*olette…

"Skids!" I screamed out and I didn't care about anything else. I put a foot on the bar stool and climbed onto the bar. I jumped down into the well beside him and tried to help him sit up, screaming "Angel! Somebody call an ambulance!"

Our barback reached for the phone, and I got Skids half into my lap.

"Skids, babe, baby, talk to me." I slapped at his cheek lightly and he opened his eyes and let out this helpless little groan that left me distraught.

I don't know what made me think it, but 'heart attack' crawled across my brain like red lights crawling across a reader board, and I reached into the cubby by the register for the bottle of aspirin we kept there. Aspirin; he needed to chew it, I remembered. We'd all sat around talking about it one night, Angel quizzing me on first aid, and I remembered if someone was having a heart attack, you made them chew aspirin. I shook a few tablets into his mouth and covered it with my hand so he couldn't spit them out.

"Chew, baby, come on, chew!" I screamed at him frantically and his jaw began to work even as he made the worst face imaginable, though from the pain or the flavor I couldn't tell you.

Suddenly Angel was there, leaning over us.

"Good work, Coco Puff. Skids, man, look at me," Angel called. "You gotta stay awake man, you gotta stay with me."

He took Skids' pulse and tried to get his breathing to slow. I sniffed, grimacing, tears sliding out of my eyes, crowded, too many people in the narrow space.

"Get him up, come on, we gotta get him up!"

The confusion was real. Cody, the barback working tonight was babbling into the phone; I was trying to help Skids up; Angel and Reflash were on either side and in front of him, hoisting him up to get him out from behind the bar. Spilled alcohol soaked into my work slacks, pungent and awful and I didn't care. I helped where I could and didn't know whether to go to him or stay back.

"Coco!" Skids called and I went, staying at his side, staying out of the way. He looked up through heavy lids, his skin ashen and his lips almost blue and said, "I love you. I love yah, babe. It's gonna be okay."

"Of course it's going to be okay," I said through fresh tears. "We're all here, we've all got you."

God, what a nightmare. His eyes slipped shut and Angel, his fingertips pressed to the side of his neck, cursed and ripped open his shirt. He leaned over him and I was dragged back by Golden as Angel started working furiously, pumping on Skid's chest, the most awful crackling sounds emanating from him as he worked.

I cried out, anguished, and was passed off to Claire and Lys, Chrissy joining us, the three women holding onto me, and I very nearly collapsed myself.

"Come on, Skids! Don't do this to me, come on! Don't do this to me, man," Angel chanted and I was firmly in the clutches of the coldest, the iciest, fear I'd ever felt in my life.

❧

I DREW A BREATH.

> *"I looked and saw a sea*
> *roofed over with rainbows,*
> *In the midst of each –"*

I paused as Reflash slipped into the room and he waved at me to go on, and so I did.

> *"two lovers met and departed;*
> *Then the sky was full of faces*
> *with gold glories behind them."*

My face flamed; I wasn't used to anyone else listening. It was supposed to be just for me and Skids, our poems and classic writing, but things were different now.

He was asleep, well, comatose. They'd put him in a medically-induced coma to get his heart rhythm under control or something. Every time they talked about it, it would all just blur together in a jumble of medical jargon that made no sense to me. All I knew was that he was asleep, and that I wanted him to wake up – but we had to wait. We had to wait and hope and pray – and I was getting to the end of my rope.

"That was nice," Reflash said, encouragingly and I gave him a strained smile and nodded. I was trying not to weep again. I was so scared.

"What was it?" he asked after the silence went on too long.

"Ezra Pound's "The Sea of Glass"," I answered.

"Got any others?"

I nodded and pressed my lips together, stroking my thumb in little circles against the back of Skid's hand, careful of the IV tubing taped to it, nearby.

"You guys read to each other a lot, then?" he ventured and I knew he was just making small talk, or trying, but I didn't trust my voice not to betray me. I was so thin, so brittle, I was afraid if I spoke my voice would crack and I would crumble right behind it.

"Look, Coco, you gotta eat something. Go back to Skids' place and get a shower, maybe get some sleep. He wouldn't wanna see you this way, babe. Trust me on that."

"I'm not leaving him," I declared, and sniffed, hot tears trailing down my cheeks.

It was the third day and they had already started weaning him off the drugs keeping him unconscious, it just took time…

"At least come with me to the cafeteria," Reflash pleaded.

I shook my head, but I wouldn't look at him. I stared intently at my lover instead, willing his fluttering lashes to open for him to fix those bright blue eyes on me and to smile. *I would give anything for you to wake up right now. To wake up and to be okay…*

Reflash sighed, and it was a tired, gusty thing, full of irritation and defeat.

"So nothing yet, huh?" he asked, dropping onto the edge of the hospital bed, by his best friend's hip.

"Not yet," I whispered, my voice strained, more tears ghosting down my cheeks. I closed my eyes and more slipped free, my nose hot and stuffed, the skin of my cheeks heated and tight with the slick salty wetness.

"Hey, no, don't do that, huh?" Reflash shook a handkerchief out of his jacket pocket and handed it over.

I blew my nose and held the soft material wadded in my free hand, resting the back of it against the pages of the book of poetry open in my lap.

"I'm so scared," I confessed, and there it went, my voice cracking and the tears got through, pouring hot and fresh as I broke down into fresh sobs.

Reflash hugged me and put his hand on my back, rubbing useless circles as he said; "Don't be. He's a cop, they're all a bunch of tough bastards. Tougher than a lot of us, including us fire guys. Don't tell him I said that. He'd never let me live it down." He forced a little laugh and I could hear the strain in his voice; he was just as scared as me.

SOMETHING STARTLED ME AWAKE, but no one was in here. Usually when I woke up it was because a nurse had come in to check his vitals or to administer a nightly dose of whatever they were giving him, but not this time. This time it was silence. Just the whirring and occasional click of his IV machine pushing medicine and fluids.

I slowly lowered my feet to the floor from where I'd been curled in the chair and listened.

"Coco, that you?"

"Skids? Oh, my God! Are you awake?"

I picked up his hand quickly between mine and he winced, swallowing hard and asked, "Y'okay, baby?"

I bit my lips together, fresh tears, this time of joy, welling and spilling. I didn't even care he'd called me 'baby' instead of 'babe'.

"Of course I'm okay, are –you– okay?"

"Thirsty," he rasped.

"Hold on, let me call your nurse," I said and he twitched, his hand tightening around mine.

"No, don't go anywhere, not yet."

"I won't, I'm not," I promised and pressed the call button on the inside of his bed rail.

The speaker clicked on a moment later and a nurse's voice came through, tinny and overly loud. "Yes, can I help you?"

"Um, yeah, he's awake. He's thirsty, can I give him water?"

A pause and then, "I'll be right with you."

Skids jerked and turned his head, grimacing and reaching up to put a hand to his chest I stopped him before he could touch himself.

"Whoa, hey, don't do that," I warned. "Not yet. There's still staples."

"Staples?" he asked. "What the fuck they do to me?"

"They uh, they had to crack your chest open," I said and sniffed. "They had to massage your h-h-heart. They lost you three times," I knew my voice cracked and warbled with my tears but I didn't care. He was alive. He was here, his eyes open, his thoughts working, his voice soft in my ear once again, his hand warm, and solid in mine.

"Heart give out or something?"

"Yeah. Yeah, you had a heart attack. Your heart went into some kind of arrhythmia. It was bad, babe. Real bad." I sniffed. "I almost lost you."

He grimaced and the curtain was whisked back, the sound of it traveling along its rail super loud in the quiet hush of the night-time hospital ward.

"I'll need you to step out, miss."

"What? No!" I cried, and wanted to put up an argument but Skids winced and tried to sit up.

He said, "Go on, Coco. Just for a couple of minutes, I swear."

I stood from my place in my chair and said, "I'll just call Reflash, then, the um, the rest of the guys. Let them know you're awake."

"Thank you," he said and the nurse worked with him, tried to help him.

I went out into the hallway and pulled my phone from the pocket of Skid's over-sized house sweater I'd bought him for Christmas.

I called Reflash and when he picked up, he sounded groggy and I almost instantly felt bad for waking him up, but… but, Skids.

"Coco, what's wrong?"

"The opposite, actually. He's awake."

"He's awake?"

"Yeah, um, the nurse is in with him now."

"I'll be right there." He hung up and I lowered the phone and leaned against the wall heavily, breathing in and out slowly, the antiseptic hospital smell a constant assault on my nose.

It seemed like it took forever for the nurse to do whatever she needed to do for Skids and for her to come back out and let me in. I went to his side immediately and he looked at me, his expression so serious, calculating, the wheels clearly turning. He finally closed his eyes and bowed his head, shaking it slightly, overcome with an emotion I couldn't readily identify. I needed him to speak. I needed him to say something, but it wasn't about me – it was about him. I sank into the seat by his bedside and reached my hand through the bed rail. He grasped it immediately, threading his fingers between mine and giving it a firm squeeze and I felt some tension ease out of me.

"How long have I been out?" he asked.

"Almost four days," I answered him honestly.

"Shit," he said softly and I let him think, let him try to wrap his mind around it.

"You been here the whole time, haven't you?" he asked.

"Close. I did go to practice, but I've been doing shit. As soon as it's been over, I've been right back here."

"Babe…" His voice filled with something akin to disapproval and I hated to hear it.

"Shut it," I said. "I wouldn't be anywhere else."

"Where'd you sleep?" he asked.

"Right here; it sort of folds out," I said, patting the arm of the chair by his bed.

"I'm gonna kill Reflash," he muttered.

"He's on his way, and good luck with that. You need to rest," I murmured. "I'm here. I'm right here."

He reached over with his free hand and touched my face and I closed my eyes and felt the stricture of fear ease around my heart.

He was here. He was with me. He had lived.

We were going to be okay.

22

*S*kids…

She was hopelessly devoted to me. She was there at the hospital every day for the week more I was in it. My heart rhythm was being a bitch, they were trying to get the medications right, and I just wanted to fucking go home.

Through it all, Coco was a champ. She was also a pain in my ass. Wouldn't listen to me. Wouldn't fucking go home for any length of time and I practically had to yell at her before she went home for the night and slept in her own bed. She deserved way better than sleeping in a chair at an old man's bedside.

I struggled internally, now more than ever, with doing this to her; condemning her to a life with me and my failing body during what was supposed to be the best years of hers. It wasn't right.

I loved her for it, I loved her deeply, and it was because I loved her I came to the soul-crushing decision that this couldn't go on.

I couldn't have her taking care of me. It wasn't right.

Still, despite my decision, there never seemed to be a good time to say it. That, or maybe it was more a matter of I lacked courage in my convictions.

She doted on me. It tore out a piece of my soul every time I looked at her and thought about life without her – but I couldn't do it to her. I knew what was right and what wasn't and I just couldn't do it to her.

She unlocked the door to my place with her set of keys and I tried like hell not to imagine the look on her face when I asked for them back.

I knew how much it would hurt her, but I also knew how much pain I would be saving her in the long run.

God, I had let myself believe – I had let this go on for far too long.

You always were a selfish bastard. The voice in my head held the echoes of my ex-wife's voice and it made me angry. I hated myself, loathed myself so incredibly deeply over what I did to us. I wasn't about to make the same mistake twice. I wanted Coco with everything that I was, which told me that it was precisely the time to let her go.

"Bed or chair?" she asked softly, once we were just inside the door.

"Chair," I grunted and she gave a nod and spotted me over to it. It was annoying. My chest hurt from having it cracked like an egg, and being bedridden for almost two weeks sucked now that I was moving, because man, I had muscles that wanted none of it. It'd taken it out of me just coming up the stairs and I couldn't wait to get cleared to go back to the gym, to come back from some of this.

"What can I get you?" she asked softly, and I sighed out and put the footrest up on my recliner, wincing as things pulled in my chest when I worked the lever at the side of the leather seat.

"A glass of water, maybe?"

"Coming right up," she murmured and kissed me, a quick press of lips to my own. I closed my eyes and savored the sensation of her lips against mine, knowing it would likely be the last time…

"Yo, man, how you doing?" Reflash called, coming through the front door we'd left standing open, waiting for him.

"Good, I'm good," I said and he marched over and pulled the ottoman over from in front of my other chair and sat down on it so he could face me. Coco came in with a glass of water and handed it to me. I drank greedily and set it, more than two-thirds empty, on the stone coaster at my elbow, on the little table between the two chairs.

"You want your glasses?" she asked, and I nodded.

"Best bring 'em over here, so I got 'em handy," I said and my best friend was searching my face.

He saw it. I knew he did, because his expression grew stormy, his usual put-out with me. I waved him down and he scowled even harder.

"Don't you even think about it," he muttered.

I scowled back.

"Think about what?" I demanded. "You all of a sudden psychic now or some shit?"

"Don't need to be to know that look."

"Later," I declared.

Coco stopped cold by my chair and slowly handed my glasses case down to me. She studied us both and asked, "Did I miss something here?"

"He's gonna be a dumbass," Reflash declared.

"I am not."

"Are too," he shot back.

"What's he trying to do?" she asked, but her gaze was fixed on me.

"Nothing," I lied, and Reflash crossed his arms over his chest and raised his eyebrows.

"Skids?" Coco asked, and her voice was very soft, already holding an edge of sadness.

She knew. She already knew.

"I'm just thinkin'…" I cleared my throat of the knot that was suddenly in it. "I'm just rethinkin' us," I said, and tried hard to keep a lid on the sudden ugly burst of emotion in the center of my chest. The feeling was so profound, such a physical one, I put a hand to it – over my fresh pink scar running down the center of it between my pecs. A physical reminder of just what a fuck-up I'd been on just about every level. My past, back to haunt me.

"Well, you can just 'rethink' your ass back to center," she said.

I blinked and looked up at her sharply, but not before I caught Reflash grinning out of the corner of my eye.

Shit. Neither one of them were going to make this easy. That put some steel into my backbone.

I sighed and let my eyes close, not wanting to see her face when I broke her heart.

23

*C*olette…

I thundered down the stairs, tears painting my face in makeup and ruin.

"Coco!" I didn't turn, but slammed out onto the sidewalk into the late spring sunshine, my chest heaving. I put my hands on my knees and tried to catch my breath as Reflash's footsteps hurried down the carpeted steps behind me, the glass door framed in ancient, thick, hunter-green painted wood swinging shut just before he reached it.

He cursed and pushed it open, and I looked up at him with my shattered heart making a mosaic of pain behind my eyes.

"Ahhh, fuck." He put his hands on his hips and hung his head. "Stubborn son of a bitch," he grumbled.

"I can't even," I said. "He really means to do this to us?"

"He's a hard-headed idiot. Give him some time, he'll come around."

I shook my head, hurting so badly I just wanted him to hurt, too, and so I lashed out at the wrong person.

"Don't bother making excuses for him. He wants to be that way, fine! I'm done!" I snapped. I started walking away.

"Coco!" he called at my back. "Come on, don't be that way! You know how he is!"

I raised a middle finger over my shoulder and didn't look back, but before I turned the corner to dash across the street, I already felt bad. Reflash was stuck in the middle, had always been in my corner, and still was – he didn't deserve that but by the time I glanced back down the street, the door to the stairs leading up to Skid's apartment was already swinging shut. I walked a few blocks in the direction of the apartment I shared with my friends and pulled out my phone.

My mother answered on the first ring.

"Darling! So glad you called, how is your man? Home from the hospital, I take it?"

"Mom…" My mournful tone trailed off into broken sobbing as I leaned heavily against the brick of the building behind me.

I WAS HOPING he would call me, but nothing came through. I was miserable. The first day, I thought was the worst. The second day proved to be even more awful; by the third day I had given up hope, but my mom had blown into town and that had somehow made things better.

There were few things in life that couldn't be fixed, at least temporarily, by your mom, best friends, an endless stream of romance movies, and ice cream on the couch. Unfortunately for me, by the time we reached that phase of the break-up, there was a knock on the door that made things infinitely worse.

"I've got it," Bridgette declared and went to get the door.

All of us had our heads turned in that direction, and my heart plummeted when I realized it was Reflash, not Skids, in the doorway. His expression was so sympathetic that tears pricked the backs of my eyes almost immediately and my mother gave my hand a tight squeeze before letting it go.

I got up slowly and Bridgette drifted into the kitchen when I approached the door. Reflash had a couple of gym bags, one in each hand, and my shoulders dropped.

"Hey, yeah, not my first choice, either, kiddo."

"So why are you here?" I asked, taking first one, then the other, and dropping them just inside and to the side of the door.

"My idiot best friend talked me into it. Figured it'd hurt worse if you saw him standing here."

"How is he?" I asked softly, swallowing hard around the lump in my throat.

"An asshole," he said with a snort and I gave him a look like *Tell me something I don't already know.*

"He's doing better, ah, they got his ticker workin' with meds, but he's probably going to have to get a pacemaker or some shit. Won't be back to work right away, if you wanna maybe help me out for a couple more weeks?" He winced and I could tell it cost him to even ask.

I nodded, "I can do that, but you know why I have to quit."

"I know, and I'm really sorry. I've known Skids a lot of years – a lot – and I gotta tell yah, he's the absolute king of keepin' himself miserable."

I bit my lips together and didn't say anything, and Reflash nodded.

"Anyhow, I'll let y'all get back to what you were doin'. If he missed anything that you want back, just let me know."

I started to cry, I couldn't help it, and so I simply nodded, not trusting my voice.

"Really wish you wouldn't give up, too," he said softly and I sniffed.

"I haven't," I said and rubbed the tip of my nose with the back of my hand. "I just have enough self-respect to know that if someone doesn't want me, it's not worth trying to make them."

He sighed and stuffed his hands deep into his pants pockets, hanging his head.

"He does, more 'n anything, I promise you that. He's just got some issues and a hero complex bigger 'n I've ever seen. He really thinks he's doing the right thing by you, and good luck convincing his dumb ass otherwise."

I stared at the gym bags on my entry's floor and said, "He sure has a funny way of showing it," even though it wasn't fair. Reflash had already said he'd been talked into it; that it was supposed to somehow spare me some more pain.

"Yeah, well, I'll see you around, kid. I gotta get going."

I nodded. "Thanks for bringing these by, I guess."

"Sure, no problem. You try to have a better night."

Not bloody likely.

"Thanks, you too."

I shut the door and paused for a moment before turning around. Bridgette stood in the kitchen, my mother and Genevieve stared from the living room and all of them had such sympathetic looks on their faces that it really drove it home that this was it. He was gone. No matter how much my heart savagely rebelled against the notion.

God, how I wanted to listen to it, but right now that just seemed… I don't know. Foolish? Immature? Out of touch? Take your pick.

"Hey, how are you doing?"

Claire.

I stopped and turned at the corner of the bar, my heart giving a fractured ache anytime I needed to go to it for something and Skids wasn't standing behind it. I sighed and turned to her, and I didn't even bother to hide the deep, aching, tired hurt of missing him.

Her face fell into lines of concern and deep empathy and she said, "Reflash said you quit?"

I nodded. "I've already over-stayed my two weeks' notice to help him out, but the minute Skids is supposed to be back, I'm out of here. I don't think I can do it."

"I don't blame you," she said, hugging my arm awkwardly in solidarity. "All of us are really upset," she said and I nodded. She rolled her eyes slightly and said, "No, really. We think he's being super stupid and we're all hoping he'll change his mind and you two will find a way out of this."

I shook my head, "Even if we could, do you think I could trust him not to pull this shit on me every time things got even remotely hard?"

"Oh, trust me, I feel you on that one," Lys said, sidling up. "You tell her yet?"

"Tell me what?"

"Look, the dinner theater you saw me perform at a while back?"

"Yeah?"

"Wildly popular and looking to expand into the rest of the week, they're looking for a ballet dancer for Monday, Tuesday, and Wednesday nights. I figured with your performance schedule at ICBB, it might work for you, so I, maybe, threw your name into the hat?"

I blinked. "You gave them my info?"

"Yeah, please don't be mad I did it without asking. It just came up and I thought of you and I thought it might be a great fit and –"

"I'm not mad!" I cried, and gave her shoulder a squeeze. "I love that you thought of me, thanks. It might just be the thing."

"Of course," she said.

"I'll have to check with the company and my contract, there may be a non-compete clause or something in the way, but I'll check with the Madame and what-have-you, and hopefully I'll be prepared before they even call."

"That'd be great. They really are a great troupe of performers. I wish I could actually perform there more, but my classes have taken off at the Thin Blue Line and so I've been sending my more-advanced students."

"Hey, that's great about your business, though!"

"Yeah, thanks. So you'll think about it?"

"Oh, definitely," I told her as Brandon loaded my tray with drinks.

"Excellent!" Lys declared with a smile. "Come hang with us if you get off your shift before we leave."

"For real?" I asked.

"You're our friend, too," Claire declared with a frown.

"Okay… thanks. I will."

I got back to work before my tables could revolt and thought the whole time about the exchange.

I was going to take up Claire and Lys on their offer when I got off work in the next hour but when I turned away from my final table, turning it over to Kristy to finish up, Skids was there, standing near the bar, just off to the side, waiting for me.

"What do you want?" I asked when he followed me back to the office, silently.

"Needed to see you."

"About what?"

I expected him to say to get the keys to his place back, but I'd handed them to Reflash at the start of my shift. I didn't honestly know why I'd hung onto them the last couple of weeks.

"See if you're okay," he said softly.

"Nope. Far from it. Not that you need to worry about it, tonight's my last night working here and you can have your space back free and clear."

"Coco–" He grabbed my hand and I twisted it gently free of his grasp. Hurt flickered across his face, but he should have thought of that before.

"Don't, you're getting exactly what you asked for, or do you regret that decision?"

"I don't regret it," he lied and I could see it in his eyes. He missed me as much as I missed him and I wanted so badly to ask him, *then why?* But I already knew the answer. His macho fucking toxic masculinity bullshit.

I stood to my full height and stalked up to him. He looked down at me, puzzled and I captured his face between my hands and stood on tiptoe, plastering my mouth over his. He caved immediately, lips parting, tongue caressing mine and I let the kiss go to a fever pitch because *God I missed him so much,* before I tore my mouth from his, both of us breathing hard, both of us panting as we stared each other down.

"What the fuck'd you do that for?" he asked, shocked.

"Because I love you," I said, and making up my mind to follow my heart, added, "and you may be willing to give up on us just like that," I snapped my fingers and he jumped slightly at the sharp sound. "But I'm not." I jabbed him in the lapel of his motorcycle club vest and as a coup de grace told him, "So, get your fucking shit together and come find me."

"Colette?" he asked, confused, as I reached the office door with my purse and light jacket.

"It's 'Babe' to you."

And I walked out.

Ball was in his court.

24

*S*kids...

I sat at the bar in our silent, closed restaurant and waited for my best friend to get his ass out of his kitchen. While I waited, I twisted a rocks glass around on the bar top. It had two fingers of my old favorite whiskey in it and I watched the light bounce around the amber liquid and facets cut in the glass. I was tempted like no other time to drown the pain in her eyes in this old comfort of mine that'd damn near taken my life.

The doctors had whole-heartedly, no pun intended, attributed my heart attack to my past of heavy drinking. Some shit about the way the fats reacted in my body with all the alcohol running through my system. The science was legit, and I was damn lucky to be alive, and yet here I was, in some ways, wishing I wasn't.

"Ho, whoa, because that's a good idea." Reflash walked the length of the bar and plucked the glass out of my hand, knocking back its contents.

I raised an eyebrow and he asked, "What number was that?"

197

"One. Saved my ass again."

"All the times since you got sober that you were tempted, I've never seen you that close to falling off the wagon. Talk to me, man. I don't like this side of you."

He put the glass in the sink and the bottle back on the top shelf and sighed, coming back down off the small stepstool I kept back there for the shorter employees.

He leaned heavily on the bar and waited me out. I sighed.

"She's only twenty-two, partner. She has her whole fuckin' life ahead of her and me? I only got a handful of good years left."

"What? Shut the fuck up, you jackass. We're gettin' old. We ain't old yet. You sittin' there actin' like you're seventy-four is just Goddamn ridiculous." He shook his head.

"Truth is," he said and he stopped. I frowned and he looked me right in the eyes and said, "The truth is, I'd kill to have half of what you got."

I frowned and demanded, "What the fuck you talking about?"

"That girl loves you. Fiercely. It's one of the most beautiful and hardcore things I've ever seen, and you're sittin' there acting like she's Donna."

I scowled and he glared right back.

"She's not," he continued. "And while I know you weren't no bowl of roses when things came to an end with your wife, there was shit she was doin' to you, expecting outta you, that was way out in left field. I don't think it was so much the job to drive you to drink as it was her lack of supporting you when you needed it the most, man."

I stared at him in disbelief. I never knew he thought that way. About Donna, about any of it. You would think out of all these years, both before and after I got sober, it would have come up – but it didn't.

"Point I'm trying to make is, Coco is everything and then some that Donna's not and wasn't. You love the same things, she wants to be there for you. I mean, did you know, it took us two days just to get her to leave your side long enough to get a shower? She sat there by your side in her work uniform reeking of bad alcohol for two fucking days. It took a team effort, a bunch of us from the club sitting with you and Youngblood and Chrissy, and the rest of the girls to practically carry her off to get herself cleaned up. In the end, she still didn't leave the hospital. Pasquale and some other nurse Youngblood has an in with hooked her up at one of the empty room's showers."

I sat back in my seat and put my hands flat on the bar to keep myself from reeling.

"Only way I even got her to go to her ballet practice was to guilt the fuck outta her. Declare you would be disappointed if she didn't go. Her friends still had to bring her clean clothes. She'd go right from the hall to there and back again and wouldn't budge unless one of us was there by the phone to let her know if you woke up. I ain't seen nothin' like it."

"You're right, I didn't know," I said.

"That's because you had to go off all half-cocked. You didn't even think for a second about what she wanted or what she was feeling, and man," he shook his head, "that was some bullshit."

"I didn't want to be cruel –"

"Yeah, well, you were. I can count on one hand and have fingers left over the number of times I've been truly disappointed in you, man." He shook his head and said. "That one, took the top spot. You're number one," he declared and held up his middle finger.

I laughed, I couldn't help it, and Reflash smiled and put his hands back down on the bar.

"You wanna get outta here?" he asked. "Go for a night ride?"

"Shit, yeah. How long has it been since we done that shit?"

"A minute," he agreed, "but I think both of us could use a dose of wind therapy, so let's get our knees in the breeze already."

I nodded and got up and he shrugged into his jacket and cut as he came around the bar.

"She kissed me, y'know, when she left here."

"Yeah?"

"Back in the office."

"And?"

"And I miss her. More than the job, more than drink, more than I've missed riding, more than anything. I miss her."

"So what're you going to do about it?" he demanded.

"I don't know yet. You wanna grab a shower and a change of clothes upstairs?"

"Fuck, yes, I smell like myself and my kitchen."

I nodded and we went out and around to the street-level door.

"She gave me these at the start of her shift," he said and held out a ring with two keys on it. I took them and bounced them in my palm, sighing. I used the one to key us in down here before we both trooped up the stairs. I was winded at the top. I'd been cleared to go back to some moderate exercise, but damned if my ticker didn't like to complain.

A pacemaker was definitely in my future, probably a lot sooner than I liked. My heart just didn't want to maintain its normal rhythm after the heart attack. It'd stopped on me enough times and long enough that they'd cracked open my chest and had to pump it for me manually while they cleared the blockages in two of my arteries. It'd been a hot mess, and I was damn sure grateful to still be here.

Reflash took a quick shower and threw on some spare clothes he kept in the dresser in my spare room. He came back out running a towel over his hair and asked, "You ready to go?"

"Yeah, man. Waitin' on you."

"Well, wait no more."

We went down to the alley and the bikes, locking up behind us. I had to frown; there was an envelope taped to my speedometer, plain, white, and business-sized. I tucked it into the inside of my jacket and threw a leg over my bike.

I had a feeling I knew who it was from, and I just wasn't terribly ready for anything else right now. I wanted to ride. To feel the wind in my face and the pavement rush beneath my feet.

We started up our machines and I set a course. Reflash didn't say a word. Just rode with me, taking my cues as I took us back across the bay bridge and down the highway toward Baltimore.

I didn't want to take us too far. Didn't want to keep my pal out too late, either. He'd worked his ass off in the kitchen, and me? Well, I may not have done shit, but I still tired out quick.

I took us to Westminster Presbyterian and the burial place of Baltimore's literary great. I was thinking a lot about poetry lately. Well, that wasn't exactly true. I couldn't stop thinking about Coco, who was pure poetry, and the love we both shared for the classics. I backed the bike against the curb and Reflash followed suit.

"What the fuck are we doing at a cemetery?" he demanded. "You ain't got some wishful thinking going on or some shit, do you?"

I laughed, "Nah, man. Not at all. You know who's buried here?"

"No."

"The man himself, Edgar Allen Poe."

"Shit, really?" He peered around us at the neighborhood and said, "Don't look like much and the gates are closed. Why you bring us here?"

"Dunno, it's never really about the destination –"

"It's all about the ride," he finished with me and I nodded, taking off my helmet and running a hand back through my hair.

"Thinkin' about death and mortality?" he asked after a while.

"Some, mostly right after I woke up, but now it was mostly thinking about the literature."

"Yeah?"

I drew breath and recited something for him.

> *"And this maiden she lived with no other thought*
> *Than to love and be loved by me.*
> *She was a child and I was a child,*
> *In this kingdom by the sea,*
> *But we loved with a love that was more than love--*
> *I and my Annabel Lee--*
> *With a love that the winged seraphs of heaven*
> *Coveted her and me."*

His mouth drew down at the corners and his eyebrows went up.

"That's Poe?"

I nodded.

"No shit?" he looked impressed, then gave a nod and said, "Sounds about like you and Coco."

"Yeah, I was just thinking that."

We were silent for a moment until he shifted on his seat and pulled out a couple of cigars from the inside pocket of his jacket. He held one out to me, and even knowing I probably shouldn't, I took one. It'd been a minute since I'd indulged.

We did the usual ritual involved with a good cigar and lit up, leaning back and staring at the sky, picking out stars that made it through the light pollution, talking about love, the club, and my thoughts on stepping down as chief.

"You know they'll never go for it. It's not like you're dying, you're just a little crazy 's all."

"Crazy?" I asked and mused to myself about it, and finally had to nod. "Datin' a woman thirty-two years my junior, yeah."

Reflash snorted and said, "That's probably the most normal thing any of us have seen you do, yah chucklehead."

"How's that?"

"You think it's normal for a guy to be livin' as puritanical as you've been the last few years? You're not at work, you lock yourself up in your tower with all them dusty books."

"Hey, they aren't dusty. I dust."

"Exactly my point, man. Who dusts?"

I laughed a little and shook my head.

"I get out, go to the gym, and on rides," I protested.

"Yeah, but you ain't had a zest for life like you have the last few months, man. She's been a shot in the arm for yah."

He was right, I couldn't exactly deny it. My time with Coco had breathed new life into, well, my life.

I reached into my shirt pocket and pulled out my glasses, sliding them onto my face. Reflash looked over as I extracted the envelope out of my coat and slid a finger under the flap, tearing it open.

"What's that?"

"Dunno, it was taped to my bike when we came out."

I unfolded the single sheet of paper inside and raised my eyebrows.

"It's a poem."

"Coco?"

"Looks like it."

"What's it say?"

I read it out loud.

"To think that my eyes once could draw your eyes down for a moment,
From their lifting and straining up toward the opulent heights—
To think that my face was the face you liked best once to look on,
When fairer ones softened to pleading 'neath shimmering lights!

Regret you? Not I! I am glad that your proud heart disowned me,
The while it was lying so sullenly under my feet;
Since Love was to you but a snare and a pain, and you knew not
Its height and its depth, all unsounded, and soundless, and sweet.

Too dark was the shadow that fell from your face bending over me—
Too hot was the pant of your breath on the spring of my cheek!
I but dimly divined, yet I shrank from the warring of passions
So strong that they circled and shook me while leaving you weak.

Acknowledge! You knew not aright if you loved me or hated;
But you pushed me aside, since I hindered you're seeing the heights.
They were but the cold, barren peaks up which selfish soul'd clamber,
And for which they surrender the gardens of scented delights.

From where I am sitting I watch your lone steps going upward,
And to-night I am back in those nights that we knew at the start.
I think of your eyes dark with pain, full of thwarted caressings,
And suddenly, after these years, from my hold slips my heart!

But no matter! There's too much between us—we cannot go back now
I'm glad of it!—yes, I will say it right on to the end!—
I'm glad that my once sore-reluctant, tempestuous lover
Hasn't leisure nor heart now to be my most leisurely friend!

My lover! Why how you would fling me the word back in fury!
Remembering you loved me at arms' length, in spite of denial;
That the protests were double: each went from the struggle
unconquered:
The hour of soft, silken compliance was not on our dial.

You were angry for loving me, all in despite of your reasoning—
I was angry because you were able to hold your love down;
And jealous—because in the scales of your logic you weighed me,
And slighted me for the dry bread of a sordid renown.

So I laughed at your loving—I laughed in the teeth of your passion;
And I made myself fair, but to stand in you light from sheer malice;
Delighting to hold up the brim to the lips that were thirsting,
While I scorned to let fall on their dryness one drop from the chalice!

Alas, for the lips that are strange to the sweetness of kisses—
The kisses we dream of, and cry for, and think on in dying!
Alas, for unspoken endearments that stifle the breathing;
Since such in the depths of two hearts, never wedded, are lying!

You say, "It is best!" but I know that you catch your breath fiercely.
I say, "It is best!" but a sob struggles up from my bosom;
For out of a million of flowers that our fingers are free of,
The one that we care for the most is the never-plucked blossom.

Yet, O, my Unbroken, my strong one—too strong for my breaking!—
I am glad of the hours when we warred with each other and Love:
Though you never drew nearer than once when your hair swept my
fingers

And their touch flushed your cheek as you bent at my side for my glove.

Never mind! I felt kisses that broke through the bitterest sayings.
Never mind! since caresses were hid under looks that were proud.
Shall we say there's no moon when she leaves her dear earth in the
shadow
And hides all her light in the breast of some opportune cloud?

Yet this germ of a love—could it ever have bourgeoned to fullness?—
For us could there ever have been a sereneness of bliss,
With the thorns overtopping our flowers, turning fondness to soreness?
Ah, no! 'twas a thousand times better it ended like this!

And yet, if I went to you now in the stress of your toiling—
If we stood but one moment alone while I looked in your eyes—
What a melting of ice there would be! What a quickening of currents!
What thrills of despairing delight betwixt claspings and cries!"

It was by Laura Redden Searing, another Maryland poet. I'd read her before but I don't think I'd ever encountered one of her poems that moved me like this one just had. Hell, then again, nothing I'd read by her had the circumstance at hand to move me. I was moved, alright, though. As the kids Coco's age would say, I was shook.

"Wow," Reflash said, breaking me out of my reverie. "That was hot."

I snorted and laughed and he cried out, "What? I was serious!"

"Alright, alright," I said and we both had a bit of a laugh.

I sighed finally and said, "Hey, 'Flash."

"Hey, yeah, what?"

"Thanks for never giving up on me, man."

He huffed a bit of a laugh and said, "You ain't never given up on me either."

"Never will, my man. I never will."

25

*C*olette…

"Colette, these came for you." I looked up and turned, holding out my hands for the dozen roses.

"Thank you, Madeline. I appreciate it," I said kindly, and the female valet smiled at me before backing out of the dressing room.

I set the heavy leaded crystal vase on the dressing table and admired the white blooms edged in crimson, the tight buds fragrant, and so beautifully unique I sat for several moments admiring them. Finally, I plucked the white envelope from the plastic trident tucked in among the blooms.

I opened it and withdrew – not a card, but a carefully tri-folded piece of what appeared to be a heavy parchment. Written on it was a poem, and I immediately knew who it was from. Only Skids would know the first poem we'd ever discussed, months ago.

> *Nature's first green is gold,*
> *Her hardest hue to hold.*
> *Her early leaf's a flower;*

But only so an hour.
Then leaf subsides to leaf.
So Eden sank to grief,
So dawn goes down to day.
Nothing gold can stay.

Ugh. Didn't he think I knew that? Of course nothing gold could stay, nothing good in life was indefinite. I sighed and threw down the paper, putting my face into my hands, pressing my fingertips into my eyes. I knew he was older, I knew he was going to grow older and pass while I had so much more life left in me. Why couldn't he get it through his thick fucking skull that I didn't care? I wanted what time was given to us to be with him.

I loved him. I loved how he smiled, how he looked at me and I felt like I was the only woman in the world. How when he kissed me, the stars fell from the sky and I felt like I would never be cold again. How he read to me, and how any time I asked he wouldn't stop – even though I knew he sometimes grew tired of it.

I lived for the timbre of his voice in the close dark of night, reciting poetry in my ear as his hands slid over my body, filling me with such a grandeur and warmth.

I missed his hard body against mine. I missed breathing him in. I missed how I felt nothing could touch me or harm me when he held me. I missed learning new things just about every time we talked about anything. How he didn't laugh when I didn't know something, but rather how he taught me.

I missed sharing my day with him, I missed sharing my life with him, and I wished his stubborn ass would realize that he missed me, too!

I'd felt it in our last kiss. The longing and the yearning. The way he'd cupped my cheek, caressed it with his thumb unwittingly as his tongue tangled with mine and he fed from my mouth as if it were the fountain of youth.

God, why did he have to be this way? Wrapping himself in misery, shrouding himself in it like it was some kind of old familiar cloak?

Why is he so afraid to be happy? I wondered.

I picked up my phone and dialed the *10-13*. Brandon picked up.

"Cormorant Bar & Grill, this is Brandon. How can I help you?"

"Yeah, Brandon, hi… is Skids there?"

"No, ma'am. Can I get Reflash for you?"

"Yeah, put him on."

I waited and a few seconds later Reflash picked up in the kitchen.

"Yeah, what's up?"

I frowned.

"How did you know it was me?"

"I didn't. What's up, Coco?"

"I just got a dozen roses from Skids."

Silence on the other end of the line for several heartbeats.

"And you called me?"

"No, I was calling him, but he's not there."

"Well, duh, sweetheart. He had tickets to the ballet tonight. Might wanna get out there, he should be out front if he hasn't lost his nerve."

I frowned harder and thought *Yeah right*, but what I said was, "But the poem he sent was "Nothing Gold Can Stay"."

"I ain't into all that – hey! I told you not to do it that way! C'mon man! Coco, I need you to get to the point, these mooks are killin' me up in here tonight. It's like I got a bunch a damned barely-trained monkeys runnin' my kitchen."

I cringed slightly and said, "I just wanted to ask why he was so damned attached to his misery." It was like she was a better lover than me or something, the bitch.

"Your guess is as good as mine, sweetheart. Talk soon, I gotta go." He hollered something unintelligible to someone and the phone clattered onto its receiver and went dead in my ear.

I let out an explosive breath I hadn't realized I'd been holding and ended the call on my end before staring at myself in the mirror, makeup half-off, rhinestones still glued to my skin in places, glittering in the net around my hair.

I made a face. It was supposed to make me look magical and ethereal. Instead, I felt like an overzealous drag queen had gotten to me with a be-dazzler. Lord knows, Pasquale loved his rhinestones. Skids had taken me to one of his drag shows a few weeks before his heart attack. I'd loved it. Hadn't laughed so hard in a while. Neither had Skids.

God, I missed seeing him happy. I missed being happy, myself.

"Shit or get off the pot, Coco. Either win him back or flush him," I murmured at my shattered, makeup-streaked reflection. I was tired. I danced almost all of my emotion out on stage and wore myself out every night I could, mostly so I would be too tired to think about how much it ached having him ripped from my life.

His parting words still burned like acid thrown across my consciousness…

"You're just a kid, you don't know what you want."

I closed my eyes and sighed.

Problem was, I did. I knew exactly what I wanted. *…and you always want what you can't have.*

I finished attacking my face with makeup cleansing cloths until it was as scrubbed free as I could get it without a shower, bordering on raw in some places.

Swiftly changing into my street clothes, I just wanted to go home. I hesitated and couldn't bear to leave them, so I swept the card and poem into my hands and tucked the scrap of paper inside the envelope, tucking it back between the tines of the little plastic holder-fork before I hefted the heavy crystal vase and hugged it to me, walking to the exit.

You can only imagine my surprise when I stepped around the edge of the building from the performer's entrance to see Skids. He was parked under a street lamp at the curb, the light gleaming softly along the chrome curves of his motorcycle, his hair slightly mussed, and his shoulders hunched as he stared at his hands pressed to his gas tank.

I stood frozen, staring at him and how heartbreakingly handsome he was to me under the sweeping light from the old-fashioned street lamps, when he turned his head and caught sight of me. He straightened, his shoulders easing down and the look on his face was almost of exquisite agony.

But it didn't have to be that way.

I took a faltering step in his direction, but the fear of yet more rejection stayed me. The performer's entrance crashed open behind me, peals of laughter from the other dancers leaving for the night, my roommates among them, startling me.

I jumped again at the loud crackle and roar of Skid's bike firing up. I turned back to look and watched as the club logo on his back faded into the dark as he rode away from me.

I swallowed hard and felt my eyes mist and wondered, not for the first time, who the real adult of this so-called relationship was and realized, if I were being honest, it was neither one of us.

"Hey, Coco, you okay?" Orion called and I nodded.

"Yeah, I think so," I answered and walked in the direction my friends were headed, a quiet stone among their incessant joyous babbling, as we flowed along the sidewalk towards home.

~

"I really don't like that man anymore," my mother said to me, voice crackling over the line.

"I don't know that that's entirely fair," I said with a sigh.

"Oh? Like he's being fair to you?"

"I'm not exactly being fair, either," I confessed miserably.

"Coco Colette," she said with disapproval. "What did you do?"

"Nothing! I just keep pushing things, you know? The idea of 'us' and that this could, should be fixed."

"You're not giving up."

"Nope."

She sighed and sounded genuinely worried.

"Baby, you've always taken on every challenge that's been presented to you head-on, but this might be one challenge that isn't a challenge at all. If he doesn't want a relationship, you have to let it go."

I gave an exasperated sigh, "If he doesn't want a relationship how come he keeps coming to see me dance? He's been on the ticket roster three times since we broke up, and why the roses? Why would he wait to see me like that? I think he misses me. I think he honestly can't, or won't, make up his mind –"

"I think he needs to shit or get off the pot. This isn't fair to you or him, and like any man he's acting like a giant man-baby and he needs to get over himself."

I laughed and said dryly, "Tell me how you really feel?"

She sighed and said, "I really feel he ought to leave you alone. He made his bed and he should lie in it. I also feel that it doesn't matter what I say, you're going to do what you're going to do anyway, and I honestly wouldn't have you any other way. My darling girl, I raised you to be whatever you wanted to be. To be with whoever you wanted to be with. Nothing about that has changed. I may worry, and I may fret, but I have never, not once, ever been disappointed in any decision you've ever made – well, except for that one time you allowed yourself to be photographed in that awful bubblegum-pink monstrosity of a dress."

I laughed and immediately knew what she was talking about; it'd been an absolute horror of a design and I hadn't known what I'd been thinking, in retrospect. Then again, I'd been seventeen, and… "Be grateful that's the only teenage rebellion you got out of me."

"Oh, I am, trust me. You give me a heart attack with some of the decisions you make, like your insistence on staying with this man when he is so obviously beneath you at this point –"

"Mom!" I cried interrupting her. "Too soon."

"Oh, for Pete's sake!"

"Who's Pete?"

"You're insufferable, girl."

"But you love me."

"More than life itself, my darling." She sighed, and it was a heavy thing, before she said, "You only have one heart, Coco. You must protect it."

"I am," I whispered softly. "I'm fighting for it as we speak," I said, turning the page in the poetry book I had open in front of me on the bed.

"I love you."

"I love you, too."

26

S **kids…**

I opened the door, frowning when it revealed Coco on my doorstep. She stood with a book in her hands, but I couldn't tell if it was one of mine or not. I stuck my head out into the hall and looked down the stairs and asked, "How did you get in here?"

"Reflash keyed me in," she answered. "Now move, we need to have a chat."

I raised an eyebrow and against my better judgment – which I'd been going against a lot lately – I stepped aside.

"What's with the book?" I asked.

"It's poetry," she answered, and looking around seemed satisfied that at least some things hadn't changed around here.

"Here." She thrust it against my chest and I winced, putting up my hands to catch it. "Take your pick. I figured if all else failed today, I could use the book itself to beat some sense into that thick skull of yours."

I blinked and laughed slightly at her audacity, but also partially at the fact that her proclamation was funny as shit. She wasn't having any of it and I realized it was as if I'd crossed some imaginary line she'd drawn in the sand and this was a genuine, come-to-Jesus type of meeting about to go down.

"Sit down," she said, and pulled out a chair for me at my own table. I lowered the book to the table beside the chair as I sank into it. She eyed me from where she stood looking sharp and sexy cool in a light wool skirt, spring sweater, and long raincoat despite the fact it was dry out there. She shrugged out of the coat and hung it on the back of a nearby chair, revealing the sweater to be sleeveless.

Her hands on her slim hips, she demanded, "Why won't you just talk to me?"

I sighed and turned my head, and again, she was having none of it, grabbing my chin roughly and bringing my face 'round to look at her. I blinked and suddenly couldn't focus on anything but her glossed, slightly-parted lips.

"Seriously," she said. "What are you really so afraid of?"

I snapped my eyes to hers and struggled with the question, but finally exhaled sharply and said, "Everything."

She let my chin go, and stepped forward in her heeled knee-high boots, sinking down into my lap, straddling the tops of my thighs, her arms going around me and her eyes fixing mine, her gaze both calm and barely-contained, the rest of her expression unreadable as she asked softly, "There, now. Was that really so hard?"

I nodded. Yes. Yes, it was.

"Just talk to me," she whispered. "Barring that, just fuck me until whatever this shit is, it's out of your system."

"Pretty sure it doesn't work that way," I said, but my hands had already traveled from her hips up under the hem of her sweater, caressing the sweet skin of her torso, like softest satin under my hands, warm and alive.

God, I missed her. Fuck, I was a damn fool in not being able to stay away.

"It works whatever way we say it does," she said. "But it'll only work if we're in it together, because let's face it, we suck at being apart."

She was right. We really did. Seemed like no matter how hard we tried, we were two magnets pulling each other back together.

"I fuck everything up that I touch, babe," I murmured and her eyes slipped shut.

"Seems like the only time you fuck everything up is when you're not touching me," she responded.

"I can't do this," I said, anguished, and she opened her eyes and fixed me with her gaze.

"Stop overthinking everything," she said, her voice filled with exasperation, and it was impossible to retort because her mouth was suddenly on mine and I was a drowning man.

Her hands swept from my shoulders to the sides of my face and she held me to her without really doing it. I could have pushed her off. Could have put a stop to it at any second but I couldn't. I wanted her just too damn bad – I just didn't want to leave her, didn't want to die on her, didn't want to destroy her completely.

The emotions were strong and fierce and I was caught in the maelstrom of them. I tore my mouth from hers and panted, pressing my forehead to the center of her chest.

She put her arms around me and held me lightly and murmured once more, "Just talk to me. I'm right here. Just tell me what's going on in that head of yours."

"I don't want to be the end all of be all's for you. I don't want to get you wrapped up with a broken fuck like me, then shuffle off and die and leave you holding this awful mixed bag. I love you too much to do that to you."

"And I love you too much to not make the most out of whatever time we have, so for the love of God, will you please meet me halfway and respect that I may be young, but that I know what I want?"

Fuck me, she had a point, but also, fuck me I didn't know if I could cede control like that. It already did things to me, not all of them unpleasant, when she took control like she was doing right now. It both excited me and it scared me some. I couldn't remember a time I could count on a woman with my heart without disaster ensuing and it hit me like a bolt from the blue – that wasn't Coco's fault. That wasn't her problem, and judging her by the actions of others from my past wasn't doing anything for our future. It was just fucking everything up and I had to admit it to myself.

I'd been miserable so long, was I afraid to be happy?

Yes.

Did I want that?

No.

I wanted her. I wanted that smile, those sparkling blue eyes. I wanted inside her, to listen to her moan, I wanted to watch her give herself over to me, and I wanted to watch all the jealousy show up in other motherfucker's eyes when they looked at her while she was with me.

I wanted her. I wanted this. No matter how much I didn't think I deserved it, my actions spoke louder than my words and I just couldn't stay away.

And bless her fuckin' heart, her keen mind, and her empathetic ways for knowing the difference and for not giving up on me. I'd fucked up twice now, and I was a law-man. A firm believer in the 'three strikes and you're out' laws. They certainly applied to more than just felonies.

"I'm so sorry, babe," I whispered, and turned my face up to hers for a kiss.

Our shit just proved, just went to show, age didn't mean shit when it came to anything. Especially matters of the heart.

"Just stop giving up so easily," she murmured, and molded her lithe body to the front of mine.

"Deal," I whispered and she sealed it with a kiss that raced fire along every nerve and through my blood, my heart skipping a beat and seizing up in my chest, sending a flash of panic through me – because wouldn't that be my dumb luck? Reconciling with my woman just in time to pitch my dumb ass into another heart attack.

I didn't let the fear ride me, but rather rode it, putting my arms around her, dragging her up my thighs to put her sex above mine, glad as hell my dick was cooperating and rising to the occasion. The doctors had warned me that some of the medication I was on could inhibit getting and maintaining a proper erection and told me to let them know if it was a problem. It'd been yet another crushing blow to my damn ego, and yet another reason I'd pushed her away.

"God, I need inside of you," I breathed against her chest, pushing the soft, angora sweater out of the way. She lifted her arms and I swept it over her head and let it fall to the floor. She looked striking in it, but I still preferred her in nothing but one of my shirts – if she had to have anything on at all.

I kissed between her small breasts, and felt the throb and flutter of her own heart beneath my lips, through the delicate cage of her ribs. The sensuality in her touch as she buried her fingers in my hair, the way her nails scratched lightly against my scalp, the shivers that sent down my spine, were unparalleled.

I trailed my fingertips up her back in a targeted strike, finding the clasp to her nearly-pointless bra, just another scrap of material in my way. I unclasped it and did away with it. She let it fall to the floor, her hands immediately returning to the back of my head as she clutched my mouth to her breast and I worked the nipple between my lips, grasping it lightly with my teeth to play my tongue over it.

She arched her back, thrusting her breast into my mouth and it was the hottest thing.

Hotter still when I smoothed my hands over her thighs and under her skirt to feel around only to discover that, no, she wasn't wearing a thong, she was wearing nothing at all beneath the skirt.

My blood heated so quick, I swear that it evaporated. To know there was nothing between our bodies except my own clothes nearly gave me a fucking stroke, forget another heart attack. I pulled her down against me and moved her back and forth by her hips and she groaned against my mouth.

I couldn't stand it, scrabbling at my belt, working the worn leather through the metal buckle, as she scooted back and tried to give me the room I needed to get my cock out. It was a frenzied few minutes as I worked the front of my pants open and she stood just long enough for me to shove them down to my knees before she lowered herself back over me to sit atop my thighs.

I kneaded the tops of her thighs with deft fingers, squeezing the taut muscles, working my hands up and down her legs, shoving her skirt up and back against her stomach so that I could feast my eyes on my body disappearing into hers as she lowered herself over me, her pussy hot and wet, gripping me with surety as I slipped inside her.

She was like silk against my raging hard-on and when she settled back into my lap, looking down at me with heavy lidded eyes, we just stopped for a moment. Either that, or time did, I couldn't really be sure. I looked up at her as she looked down at me and she bit her bottom lip, uncertainty chased through her eyes by her vulnerability, and I hated it. Hated that look on her face, directed at me, the fear that I would somehow hurt her – again.

It killed a part of me, but not my boner. For some reason, that grew even harder inside her.

"Rock for me, babe. Fuck me like you want to, like you came over here to do," I growled and she did, her body writhing over mine perfectly. She moved, sinuous and graceful, muscles rippling alluringly under her skin, that ripple echoed around my cock as she worked me damn-near into a frenzy, both of us panting, our skins quickly becoming dewed with sweat, sex perfuming the air, my kitchen suddenly sultry and warm.

She came into my place and I swear, just her presence here, she turned it into a home and I suddenly felt like I needed her here, with me, all the time, to keep me straight, to keep me from being such a dumbass – but of course that hadn't stopped me before.

I was such a fucked-up mess of a human being – still – and I needed to fix my shit because it wasn't just hurting me. These insecurities, these notions of mine, I had to deal, I had to communicate, or I was going to lose this right here and I couldn't fathom letting her go again. I'd tried twice, I'd failed; and I never failed at anything I put my mind to, so this meant something.

"Oh, God," she said, her voice low and breathy, her body tight and welcoming, her eyes closed, her hands buried in my hair as she rode me.

I pressed my lips to her skin just over her heart again. I let myself go, burying my face against her chest, kissing and licking as I felt that fine trembling in her that heralded her first orgasm. It was just a first blush of motion, scarcely there, but it built swiftly until she shivered uncontrollably in my lap. The sensation of her, on and around me, drowning in her ecstasy, was a hard act not to follow, and my control wasn't infinite.

"That's it, beautiful, come for me, you've got it," I growled and she threw her head back and cried out, her hands dropping from my head, her nails biting through my tee shirt, the pain sweet and adding that edge that sent me over into madness. I stood up with her wrapped around me, my hands beneath her thighs, and laid her down on my table, driving into her with no mercy.

She bit her bottom lip and gazed up at me from beneath her lashes, her legs falling open, encouraging me to ride her, the sounds of our feral panting echoing back from the ceiling, the sharp report of our bodies connecting, flesh slapping, pinging back from the walls.

"Harder!" she cried, and I gave her what she wanted.

It was the kind of dirty, cathartic sex that cleansed the soul and we both needed it, gave ourselves over to it, and let ourselves be consumed by our passion for one another.

I was good. I could die a happy man, right here, right now, with this angel stretched out beneath me to take me home.

<h1 style="text-align:center">27</h1>

Colette…

We ended up naked and in his bed, and there was no place I'd rather be. We lay half-dazed in each other's arms, my cheek pressed against his pec, the raised line of pink scar tissue from his emergency open-heart surgery right in front of my nose. I traced patterns on his skin, through the smattering of silver and white hair on his chest, and trailed the tip of my middle finger lightly down the seam of his scar, the skin shiny and pink, soft and raised. He shuddered beneath me and grabbed my hand with his free one, the other splaying flat against my lower back.

"That feels weird," he said, and I frowned slightly and pushed up just a bit so I could look down at him.

"What does it feel like?" I asked.

"Like little electric shocks," he said. "Like there's something in the scar and you're running over it with your fingertip and when you do, sparks leap but not like in a good way. More like a 'shuffle your feet across the carpet then you touch me' kind of a way."

I wrinkled my nose. "That's weird!" I declared.

"Mm-hm," he sighed, and it didn't sound happy.

I pushed up further into a sitting position and gripped my shin with both my hands, like holding onto a railing. I stretched my hips slightly, out of habit, while I asked him,

"What's wrong now?"

"I got lucky, I guess, and I don't know how to talk about the fact that," he swallowed hard and reached up, teasing some of my hair back behind my ear. "That it might not always be like this. That I might not always be able to –"

"Stop, just stop," I said, and sighed harshly. "That you might not always be able to get it up?" I asked.

"Yeah."

"You know you don't need an erection to orgasm," I informed him.

He laughed and shook his head, and said, "How would you even know that?" he asked.

"I had several late nights with nothing but my phone and Google MD to keep me company."

"Oh, yeah?"

"You were sleeping," I said, and reached up to trail my fingertips against his cheek. I was keeping my distance otherwise, expecting he was going to change his mind yet again, that at any moment, this was going to turn into another mistake and he'd ask –or tell– me to go.

"What's wrong?" he asked.

I knew I couldn't keep my sad expression off my face or out of my eyes.

"Scared that you're going to say this was a last hurrah. Expecting you to kick my ass out the door – again."

"I am such an asshole," he muttered, and sighed deeply.

"I can't argue there," I said and shifted, hugging my knees.

He reached up and put a hand atop one and gave it a squeeze.

"So what do you want to do?" he asked me.

I could tell he meant it, that he really wanted to know what I was thinking.

"Depends, are you going to listen to me?" I asked. "Because if you're just going to blow me off, what's the point?"

He bit his lips together and tried to keep from smiling, but I caught it. Rolling my eyes, I let out an exasperated sigh and went to get up.

He caught my wrist and said, "It's not that, I swear."

"Then what?" I demanded.

"I'm just proud of you, is all."

I sat back on my haunches, confused, and raised an eyebrow.

He laughed slightly and said, "You're giving me hell. I admit, I deserve it, but I'm proud of you that you're doing it and yet you still aren't giving up. I don't want to give up – I thought it was what was best." He looked away from me, staring into a faraway distance that wasn't there. "For you…" he shook his head and sighed turning back to me. "But you're not a child, and you're not some little woman in need of the big bad man to protect your feelings, and I've been an asshole, and I can see that."

I pressed my lips together and nodded.

"We have to do better," I murmured. "Both of us. At communicating."

He nodded and reached out for my hand. I gave it to him and he laced his fingers between mine, shaking it loosely back and forth.

"I can get on board with that," he said and his eyes were locked with mine, the sincerity and determination in them causing the stricture of caution around my heart to ease.

"Yeah?" I asked, and hated how my voice trembled slightly with emotion.

"Yeah. Now come here."

I went to him and straddled his hips like he indicated, looking down at him, my fingertips playing along the seam of scar on his chest, unbidden. He caught my hand and shifted slightly beneath me. I could feel him growing hard beneath the sheet against my sex, and a throbbing ache of desire pulsed faintly from my core.

"I said get down here," he said playfully, a smile on his lips and I leaned forward and put my mouth against his as his hands began to roam warmly over my skin.

"LET'S GO FOR A RIDE. Just you and me," he murmured, velvet-soft into the dark sometime later. I felt like Jell-O with how many orgasms he'd given me and barely had the energy to cuddle closer to his side beneath the warm nest of blankets.

"Tomorrow morning?" I asked with a yawn.

"No," he answered, a hint of a smile in his voice. "Now."

"As in right now?" I asked, laughing. "Aren't you tired?"

"No, strangely enough. I'm feeling pretty good, wide awake."

"I am going to be so sore in the morning, but against my better judgment – sure, okay, where are we going to go?"

"Destination doesn't matter," he murmured. "Just the ride."

"I don't know," I said lightly, stretching like a cat. I smiled and finished with, "The destination for this ride was pretty important."

He laughed and laughed, and I figured we were both a little sex-drunk for it to be that funny, but still…

"I don't have any clothes here suitable for being on the back of your bike," I said, pouting.

"Well, that is a problem, now, isn't it?" he asked, reaching up and caressing my cheek.

I nuzzled my face into his hand and said, "I could take a car home and be back in nothing flat."

"Nah, I don't want to let you out of my sight." He was quiet for a time and said, "Tomorrow morning, we'll get you home and changed, and I'll take you out to this breakfast spot that's a decent ride away."

"Okay," I agreed softly.

We did just that.

The next morning, we showered together and got dressed. I took a car home and he followed, pulling up behind it at the curb and dismounting as I got out of the back seat, thanking the driver. He made a shooing motion with his hands and I bit my lip in an effort to stifle my grin at the light of excitement in his eyes.

We'd only ever really gone for a ride with the rest of the club in a big group once spring had fully taken hold. It'd still been cold, but had been nice. Now that the weeks had gone by and the sun was out, things had grown significantly warmer and I was really looking forward to it.

I keyed my way into my apartment's front door and slipped inside. My roommates were gathered around the breakfast table and all stopped and stared in my direction.

"Walk of shame?" Jesse asked with a crooked grin.

"Nothing to be ashamed about," I said, and made my way toward my bedroom.

"Not unless you were with that geezer," Genevieve commented, sticking a spoonful of oatmeal in her mouth.

I stopped.

"One, he's not a geezer, and two, you guys can stop hating him now. We're working things out. In fact, he's waiting for me downstairs. We're going for a ride."

They all exchanged looks and I frowned.

"What?" I demanded, cutting through the thick silence.

"Just –" Bridgette couldn't seem to find the words, so Genevieve spoke for her.

"Just, are you serious?" she demanded. "Coco, the man has broken your heart twice now."

"I know that," I said softly.

"So we wouldn't be very good friends if we didn't have some misgivings," Orion said plaintively.

"That's fair," I said cautiously.

"Orion's right," Jess said. "I don't get it either. I mean, if dude was our age and had put you through the mixed signals and ghosting on you like that, you'd have kicked his ass to the curb."

"So?" I said defensively.

"So why does this guy get so many chances?" Genevieve asked, her expression turning a bit stormy.

I sighed and felt my shoulders drop.

"I don't know," I said simply. "I can honestly tell you that this is it. This is his last chance, but as for why? I can't explain it in any way that would probably satisfy anyone here. It's just a feeling… a knowing I have."

They all looked at me with the same worried expression and I felt just awful. They'd been there to pick up the pieces both times Skids had let me down, but I didn't know how I could explain that we were talking, really communicating now, and that this time would be different. I just knew it, could feel it deep in my soul, wanted to go with it and follow this through – but I didn't know how to do it without my friends, and I could see plainly they meant to give Skids no quarter.

It was a predicament. How to tell them that I knew this time would be different without betraying some of Skids' more deeply-kept secret hurts and anxieties. The ones he had confessed to me and had entrusted me to keep secret.

"I want to be able to tell you how I know," I said when the silence had dragged on for too long. "But to tell you would mean betraying a trust that's been placed in me, and I'm not comfortable doing that."

They exchanged looks, their worry softening to uncertainty, and I sighed and palmed my face.

"Augh! I know you guys don't have any reason to trust me where Skids and his track record are concerned, but I feel like this is something I need to follow through on. I don't like the idea of giving up on a relationship so easily – that's not me, and it's not the very grown-up thing to do, now is it?"

"I think this goes way beyond grown-up versus childish, honey," Bridgette said with sympathy.

"Seems to me, dude didn't think much of giving up on you guys when the going got tough."

"Both times I think it was fear," I said and even though I knew it was, I didn't want to speak much further out of turn.

"What's a badass like that have to be afraid of?" Jess asked, leaning back in his chair.

I shook my head, "I've already said too much, and he's waiting for me downstairs."

"Seriously?" Genevieve asked, nonplussed.

"Seriously," I said and I went into my room, shutting the door behind me so I could change.

I was stuck between a rock and a hard place, between my friends and the man I loved, and I had to admit, to myself at least, I was almost afraid of coming clean to Skids about it. Afraid he would try to set me back on my shelf and that he wouldn't want to play with me anymore, like I was some sort of wind-up doll.

It was an unfair thought, but I had it, none-the-less. With a big sigh, I took stock of myself in the mirror and deemed myself suitable for an extended ride. Perhaps it would help us both think, and by extension, sort some of our weird shit out.

When I went back out, everyone looked, but no one spoke. It was uncomfortable, like none of us really knew what to say to each other anymore. I sincerely hoped it was just a slightly rough patch and that everyone would get past it and work through it and we would all end up being okay in the end.

Skids looked up from his phone and his face fell when he saw me. I guess I hadn't schooled my expression enough, but then again, I wasn't exactly trying to hide my emotions or anything. I think both of us were far too guilty of hiding far too much from each other. We needed to be more open, more honest, not less.

"What's wrong?" he demanded, and turned in his seat on the front of his bike.

"My friends are a little less than thrilled about me trying to patch things up with you," I said honestly, and his expression dropped again as my words sank in.

"Ah, shit. babe," he reached out and gripped my arm lightly, a reassuring touch above my elbow. "I'm sorry."

"As long as you don't try to drop me for my own good again, I'm sure it'll be fine. You do, after I spoke up for you in there, I may damage my friendships irreparably with them. I mean, they have a right to be annoyed with us at this point. They have been the ones to pick up the pieces, after all."

A muscle in his jaw ticked and he nodded, he got up off his bike and faced me squarely and pulled me into his arms, holding onto me tight.

"I didn't think about the fallout," he said. "Jesus Christ, I fuck up everything that I touch."

"Hey!" I argued, leaning back and looking him in the eyes. "You do not."

"I've made you so unhappy," he tried to argue back, caressing the side of my face.

"By your absence," I said. "Never by your presence."

"You sure? I mean really sure?"

I smiled and said, "I'm more, I'm really really sure."

He smiled and laughed and stroked his thumb along my cheek one more time before reaching for the helmet on the seat.

We rode all day, first to a brunch spot that made French toast out of banana bread drizzled in caramel sauce and a smattering of fresh banana slices. It was decadent and to die for, and Skids was good, sticking to eating healthy with a spinach and egg white omelet, only stealing one bite from my plate for 'dessert.'

We took a ride from the brunch place out to the historic London town and Gardens, walking hand in hand through the ornamental plants and pathways, speaking quietly, opening up about things like we never had before. It was beautiful, and put both our hearts and minds at peace for a time – which was worth its weight in gold, to be honest.

"You think we're going to be okay?" I asked with an apprehensive sigh as we headed back for his bike.

"I think we're going to be more than okay, babe." He brought the back of my hand to his mouth and placed a kiss there, pulling me into his side and wrapping an arm around my shoulders.

I sighed and leaned my head against him, wanting to believe him more than anything.

28

———————

*S*kids…

"Walk me up?" she murmured, breathless against my lips. I pressed mine to hers just one more time – or what I meant to be just one more time, but I could never leave it at just one taste of her. We kissed, making out at the curb like a couple of teens, and finally broke apart again, laughing softly at our infatuation.

"Yeah," I murmured and checked to make sure I was parked outside the load-and-unload zone, where the bike could sit without being ticketed. Parking was a premium in Old Town Indigo City, and the city was almost always hard up for cash.

I walked with her, hand in hand under a sky turned ominous, and no sooner did we step inside her lobby's glass door, than the sky opened up, just pouring.

"You're my good luck charm," I told her and she bit her bottom lip, suppressing the smile the slight compliment had given her. It'd like to break my heart that she did that, that somehow, some way, she'd got it into her head that I didn't want to see her happy, that I didn't want us to be happy, and I couldn't say I blamed her much for that.

I'd screwed things up six ways to Sunday. I knew that. I was still trying to figure out the why of it, and I had to come to the conclusion that I just wasn't done punishing myself for the past, which was damn foolish. Just because I felt like I deserved to be unhappy didn't mean I needed to make Coco miserable.

It was just me, allowing history to repeat itself, and I had to do better.

She wasn't my ex-wife. Far from it, in fact. She wasn't my job, either... she was my heart, she was my happiness, and I had to admit to myself that enough was enough and that I deserved that happiness.

We'd talked about a lot of things today, and I felt good about life. She was right, God love her, today was the first day of the rest of our lives and it would be the same tomorrow, and the day after that. Each day would only be what we made of it, and not all of 'em were bound to be good. We just needed to get to where more of the days were good. Even if, for a while, they just were better than the day before.

"Come in and stay a little while?" she asked, shoving her key into the lock.

"Aw, babe, I don't know... your friends..."

"Will need to get used to it," she murmured, and shoved open the door. She took my hand and drew me inside, but it looked like nobody was home. I relaxed some and let her lead me in. She took my coat and cut, and I let her, watching as she hung it from a set of hooks on the back of her bedroom door. She did the same with her jacket and pushed the sleeves of her blouse up to her elbows.

I found myself unconsciously mirroring her with my gray Henley, rucking the sleeves back over the swell of my forearms.

"Um, tea?" she asked.

I nodded.

"Yeah, that would be nice," I said. "Got any of that red, orange-flavored stuff?"

She laughed lightly and said, "Took a liking to my ruby-orange-ginger herbal huh?"

"Better than a lot of them," I agreed.

I stood in the entry to her little kitchen and talked with her, bantering about the tea while she loaded a teapot with the blend she liked, pressing down on the tab of her electric kettle to get the tea water going.

I watched her move through the small space, light on her feet, graceful in the heavy boots we'd gone out and bought together some weeks, hell, probably a couple of months, back. The leather pants we'd bought on the same trip fit her like a second skin. She was so incredibly sexy without even trying and already I was hard, my cock restricted by my jeans, my boxers not doing much to curb the growing discomfort of my dick's prison.

"Why are you looking at me like that?" she asked with a knowing smile.

"You know why," I said softly and it took everything in me to stay rooted to the spot. To not go to her, to not peel her out of every strip of leather, every scrap of lace I knew she wore underneath.

"Maybe I like to hear it," she murmured, and for long seconds, the only sound between us was the water heating.

"You're probably one of the most beautiful creatures I've ever laid eyes on," I told her. "I still can't understand what you could ever want with a son of a bitch like me. I won't ever understand."

Her face went from smiling to an expression that said she ached for me, crumbling into lines of confusion and pain.

It was likely a thing we would have to agree to disagree on until the end of time, but when she stepped in my direction, her lithe body shimmering across the space between us, hips swinging provocatively, I knew I couldn't ever push her away again. I would never get used to her loving me, wanting me, but that I never wanted to get used to such a miracle, either.

She wound her arms around my neck and I palmed her slim figure, running my hands down her hourglass shape from her breasts to the erotic flare of her hips, her lines subtle and sleek as compared to a more curvaceous woman, but there was no comparing Coco to anyone. She was so beautifully, selflessly, uniquely, and kindly herself.

Her lips were sweet, her kiss like honey against my tongue, her taste exotic and feminine, a balm to my battered and weary soul more than alcohol ever was or could be again. The way she molded her body to the front of mine was pure bliss. The way she let her fingers do the walking, caressing the hot, hard length of me through my jeans drove me fucking wild.

"Bedroom," she said against my mouth, and all I could do was grunt an assent and let her lead me there.

I had to laugh when I remembered her bed was a single, and she grinned and spun in a delicate pirouette to face me saying, "Whether you're on top or I am, there's plenty of room."

"Babe, I'd fuck you standing up if that's all I had to work with." I kicked the door shut behind us and watched her as she took a step back from me, doing an erotic little strip-tease for me, the devil in her eyes.

God, she was perfect. A princess in the streets and a harlot between the sheets, and I said, "How fucking lucky am I?" unable to keep the awe out of my voice.

She came back to me, nude and perfect, dropping to her knees in front of me, her fingers pulling my boxers and jeans down. Looking down at her ready to take my jutting cock into her mouth sent an electric thrill down my spine, when she put some food for thought into my brain.

"Ever think that might be some good karma, finally coming back your way?"

No.

No, I had not – and I didn't think I would ever really think again when her satin lips wrapped around the head of my dick and her velvet tongue took its time exploring the head.

"Oh, fuck, yes, angel. Just like that," I said and tipped my head back, letting myself go.

Jesus, the way she fucked me with her hot little mouth was enough to send me straight to heaven before my thoughts and rough hand sent me right back down to hell.

"Fuck," I groaned. "Like that, yes, right there, just like that." I couldn't keep my mouth shut, just kept telling her how fucking good she was while I tried like mad to hold myself still, to let her do her thing, to not twine my fingers through her flaxen hair and thrust my cock over that hot wet little tongue of hers into the back of her throat.

It was hard to do, keep still, especially when she reached up with her hand and fondled my balls just the way I liked.

"Fuck, you're gonna make my ass cum," I warned her, and she knew by the strain in my voice how very close I was. She knew right when to stop. To stand up, put her hands on the wall over her bed, leaning over, thrusting her pink pussy at me in offering.

Shit, it was hot, the level of dirty this girl got with me, how she let me fuck her hard, how she begged for more, how she clenched around me, and as I pounded into her, the wild and feral cries that spilled from her throat.

God, it was lovely; she got so down-and-dirty she made me feel clean, and I hadn't felt that way in so long.

"Harder," she cried, her voice cracking, and I obliged her, but it wasn't enough, it almost could never be enough.

I gripped her upper arms, pulling her back onto me as I thrust forward and I knew it was intense. I felt myself go deeper than I'd ever gone, bottoming out against her cervix. She shot up, back arching, crying out with this beautiful animalistic sound and her sweet pussy gushed with her orgasm, her muscles contracting wildly around my shaft, drawing me in tight, her pussy fisting my cock and wringing it dry of every last drop of my own orgasm. She collapsed to her lavender bedspread with me on top of her, still inside her, our knees digging into the carpet at her bedside, my chest pressed to her heaving back.

I was worried I'd maybe hurt her, until the giggling started, bubbling out of her between heaving breaths.

"You okay?" I asked.

She laughed, less hysterical and more centered and huffed out, "Yeah. Oh, my God, yeah!"

I chuckled then swallowed hard as my heart tried to skip a beat as it raced in my chest, tripping over itself in glee.

"Mm," she hummed in pleasure as I ran my hands over her back and body, her skin slightly and unnervingly cool to the touch.

"You sure you're alright, babe?"

"Mm, hmmm…" she huffed a few more breaths, and I realized she was drunk on our love. "Never better."

I backed off her and pulled from her body carefully, shuddering at the over-stimulation, soaked where my body had made contact with hers. A special kind of messy fuck, but then again, messy was the best kind of sex there was. Messy meant you were doin' it right.

"Ever try anal?" she asked suddenly, and I choked and coughed, sputtering.

She looked at me over her shoulder, a mischievous sparkle in her eyes, and I had to laugh.

"Another time, babe. You'd like to give me another heart attack at this rate."

We don't want that," she said, arching provocatively, offering her lips up to mine. I kissed her back and smiled against her lips.

To die in her arms would be the sweetest death I could imagine at this point, but she was right. I'd already visited death's door once and I only had a finite time left with her.

I wanted to use it for all it was worth first.

COCO WAS LAYING on the couch, her head in my lap as I absentmindedly stroked her long hair and read to her from a Dickens' classic. She may not have been curled in my lap like a kitten, but the effect was much the same. Her eyes were closed, her breathing deep and even, her face relaxed in slumber.

That was how her roommates found us when they came in through the front door, their somewhat boisterous conversation dying at the sight of me on their couch. I held the book in my hand, three fingers and my thumb gripping it closed, index pressed to my lips to beg silence for the woman still so soundly asleep in my lap, the warm silk of her long hair trapping the fingers of my other hand.

"Someone mind turning down her bed?" I asked softly.

"Uh, yeah, sure…" her girlfriend, Bridgette, broke off from her boyfriend and went for Coco's room.

I set the book aside on the wide arm of the couch I was fetched against and carefully I eased her into my lap further. Lifting her slight frame from a sitting position was a challenge, but I managed, and I took her in to lay her down and tuck her in.

Her friends kind of watched from the living room, through the open doorway as I pulled blankets over her and kissed her goodnight.

Her friends, Bridgette, Orion, and Jess all looked apprehensive. Genevieve looked like she wanted to serve my balls up on a plate. I couldn't blame any of them. The best I could do was remain polite and weather what storms would come, to earn back their trust through action and time.

I shut the door to her room softly after retrieving my boots and carefully lifting down my jacket and cut from the back of her door and went back out to put my boots on. I laid my jacket and cut over the arm of the couch, over the book I'd been reading and sat down.

Everyone kind of just stared at me awkwardly, mute.

Genevieve was the first to break, asking me pointedly, "What are you even doing here?"

"Genevieve!" Bridgette hissed quietly in that motherly tone of voice that meant none other than *Oh, my God! Don't be rude!*

Respect was given where respect was earned, and looking back, I certainly hadn't done much to earn it. Hell, the first time I was ever here I yelled at these kids in their own home; any subsequent time, I'd never strayed in past the front door or past a polite nod or hello as I picked Coco up for something or other. Granted, these other kids were her age, and not her parents, but that didn't mean they didn't deserve half a pour of respect more than I'd given 'em.

"It's okay," I said. "I was here at my lady's invite. I'd expected to be cleared out before y'all came home, but had a hard time leavin'."

A blush overtook Bridgette's face while the color drained from Genevieve's. The boys even colored a fair bit at the implication. I pulled on my last boot and stood up.

"I'll be getting out of your way, then," I said picking up my coat. The book slipped to the floor and I bent and picked it up, setting it aside on the coffee table.

"That Coco's?" Orion asked and I nodded.

"Indeed it is, will it be alright there?"

"Yeah."

"Good deal." I shrugged into my coat and fixed the collar. "Y'all have a good night, now," I said and kept my back straight as I went out, all of their eyes burning a hole in my back.

"Wish I could wish you the same," Genevieve said, dour, and again Bridgette tried to admonish her.

I looked back and said,

"It's alright, now. I deserve it." I shut the door on their startled looks.

It'd stopped raining outside and I was glad there were only like eight or so blocks for me to go to get back home. I did my best to wipe off the seat with a hand towel I kept in one of my saddle bags, but it wasn't a very good effort and my ass got wet anyhow.

I got waylaid by a bunch of the guys waving at me through the windows of the *10-13,* and so I took a detour inside.

"Skids! Where you been all day, man?" Oz asked from one of the tall tables by the dart boards. Blaze lined up his next throw behind him as I slid onto a stool opposite Backdraft.

"Took my lady for a ride, wound up back at her place as it started rainin'. Waited out the showers there. Why, you jealous?"

"Depends. Where'd you ride through?" Oz asked with a crooked grin, and of course, he couldn't help himself. He asked, "And how old is she this time?"

"Still twenty-two, still blonde, petite, a ballerina and –"

"More pussy than you're hittin'," Blaze said from behind him.

The rest of the guys laughed at Oz's expense and I had to nod to myself. That was a good one, I had to admit, even if I didn't like anybody dimming down Coco to just her lady bits. She was far more to me than just a good lay.

"While I can appreciate some good old-fashioned horsing around, if y'all wouldn't mind treating my girl with a lot more respect than that, I would highly appreciate it," I said, tipping a nod to my bartender, who set about pouring me my usual coffee.

"Hey, no offense meant, Skids. We like her and we're glad you're working things out. Right, boys?" Backdraft asked, pointedly, raising his eyebrow to look back over his shoulder at Blaze.

"Sorry, Skids. Didn't mean anything by it," Blaze muttered.

"You'll get it someday," I said with a wink, and he winced and put his hands over his gut like I'd delivered him a low blow, which I had. Blaze had been out fishing off the dating pier but kept coming up short, something he'd lamented about more than a few times at the old barstool confessional.

I stuck around for a while, letting my ass dry out from the ride, drinking my coffee, which I should have made a decaf, and playing a round of darts with my boys. In the end, it'd been a real long fuckin' day and I was dog-tired and ready for bed. Thank God I'd already done the whole shower thing over at Coco's. We'd been a fair bit of a beautiful mess after that hardcore fuck session.

I went to bed alone and found I couldn't readily fall asleep.

I missed having her there in my arms just a bit too much.

29

*C*olette...

"For what it's worth, I don't think he's going to dick you over again."

I looked up sharply from my breakfast plate at Orion while Jess gave me an apologetic little shrug and got up to follow Genevieve into their room where she'd disappeared after slamming the door.

"I don't think he will, either," Bridgette said.

"You guys, I feel really bad. I never meant to make any of you feel uncomfortable in your own home," I said, and shifted in my seat uncomfortably.

"She had no right to say that," Bridgette said, making a face.

"It's your home, too," Orion reminded me gently.

It'd been a tense breakfast, and that was the understatement of the year. Genevieve was pissed at me. I don't think I had ever seen her so heated over anything else in my life.

I didn't even know what Skids had done or said. I'd been dead asleep when they'd come home and I'd slept hard, deep and dreamless the whole night through. Exhausted, not just from the ride and great sex, but from all the mental and emotional gymnastics of the day before. Relationships were work and anyone who told you otherwise was likely not very good at them.

I'd woken up on cloud nine that morning, feeling more optimistic about life than I had for weeks. That was, until I'd stepped out of my room to the tense roommate situation.

We'd been sitting in silence around the table, eating our meal, no one really looking at me or talking to me, until Genevieve had exploded. She had yelled at me about having Skids in the apartment after they'd made it known they didn't like him, screamed across the table at me about what a selfish asshole I was being, before storming off to her and Jess's room and slamming the door.

I had sat quietly for several moments, hot tears collecting on my bottom lashes, simply staring at my breakfast plate until Orion had said what he had.

I suddenly wasn't very hungry anymore, and I didn't know what else to say, so I got up and cleared my plate and went quietly into my room to get dressed.

Orion and Bridgette were in the kitchen when I emerged, clearing the rest of the dishes, and the apartment was deathly quiet. They both cast sympathetic looks in my direction as I slipped out into the hall, just wanting to be away from all of them and generally feeling like a horrible person.

I called my mom. I knew it was super-early on the west coast but I needed her opinion on the drama. She picked up, sounding groggy on the other end, and asking immediately, "What's wrong?"

I dissolved into tears, unable to hold them in any longer and told her everything as I walked, about trying to patch things up with Skids, about the household melting down over it. She listened quietly through it all, which was unlike my mother. Usually, she had a lot to say.

I waited, the silence stretching out for long moments, to the point I had to check the screen on my phone to make sure the call was still connected.

"Mom?" I asked.

"Yeah, baby. I'm still here." She sucked in a deep breath and let it out on an explosive sigh, and finally said, "I'm proud of you. Sometimes I have a hard time believing you're my child. You have such a poise and grace, such a forgiving heart and a willingness to see things through and try, even after you've been hurt. None of those are qualities I have ever been accused of possessing."

I snorted and said, "Of course you have them. You raised me, right?"

"Sometimes I think the opposite is true," she said with a slight laugh. "Now, all of that being said, I can see both sides of this particular issue with your roommates."

I listened, hearing her out before I let myself get upset.

"Okay," I said, an indication she should go on.

"On the one hand, this man has broken your heart not once, but twice. Your friends have been there each time to pick you up, and I am sure they are frustrated with him and by extension, with you for trying to work things out. That being said, they, like you, are young and they haven't figured out that when you have found that person worth fighting for, that's what you do. You figure things out, you pick your-self up and you work things out."

"That's exactly how I feel!" I cried.

"As for the things Genevieve said to you? The last time I heard you were current on all of your rent and bills, and from what you described, Skid's presence was fairly unobtrusive."

"I mean, none of them were even home when he was there! And it's not like he's a kleptomaniac or anything. He's a retired cop, for Christ's sake."

"Precisely. I think this may or may not have more to do with Genevieve and something from her life or her past than it actually has to do with you or Skids. Have you tried talking to her?"

"No, not yet. This literally just went down, like five minutes before I called you."

"Okay, and where are you now?"

I let out a breath and said, "Honestly? Walking."

I could hear the sly smile in her voice when she asked, "Walking where?"

"Well, I honestly think I need a hug, and you're not here, so…"

She sighed and it sounded sort of miserable. She asked me, "So, has the man gotten his head out of his ass?"

"Mom!"

"Don't 'Mom' me, answer the question!"

"I believe so, for real this time, yes. But I do have to admit, he's fooled me at least once before."

"I don't honestly think that's true," she said. "The first time he had a reason to be afraid, for you both. He isn't a stupid man, Coco. I've met plenty to know the difference."

"Mom!"

"Ah, ah, ah! I wasn't done."

"Okay."

"The second time…" She sighed. "After a major life-altering event such as a heart attack on the scale that he suffered… I can understand his reluctance to continue any sort of relationship. I can also appreciate that even though he broke your heart, he did so from a place of love in his own. I can also imagine it wasn't easy for him being all alone in a vulnerable state like that."

"That was the same conclusion I came to," I said softly, knowing full well I was precisely my mother's daughter even though she hadn't given herself any credit in attributing her list of accomplishments towards me, to herself. I mean, I had to get it from somewhere, and I didn't exactly have a father to speak of and she did raise me on her own, so…

"I just want you to be happy, baby. I know that most of the time it isn't possible, but when you're with him and things are going well? You're the happiest I have ever seen you, and I want that for you."

"And what about you?" I asked, pausing at a corner to wait for a cross-walk signal.

"What about me?" she demanded.

"When are you going to find someone who makes you happy?" I asked, still detesting her boyfriend.

She laughed lightly and I could tell it was forced.

"Darling, I am perfectly fine with Jacque."

"Are you sure?" I asked.

"I'm sure," she said and then classic mother, deflected. "Besides, we're talking about you, not me. Now, where are you?" she asked.

"Almost there," I told her.

"Alright, then if you're safe and you don't feel like crying anymore, would you mind terribly if I went back to sleep?"

"Not at all, thanks for talking to me, Mom."

"Of course," she said. "Ta-ta for now."

I smirked and ended the call just as I drew up in front of the downstairs door to Skids' place. I pressed the buzzer for his unit, which was only one of two – the other was vacant and used for storage. His voice came, gruff, over the intercom, telling me that I'd woken him.

"Who's there?"

"It's Coco," I called out clearly, and the door buzzed for me. I opened it up and by the time I reached the top of the stairs he was at his front door in nothing but his boxers and a white tee shirt, looking warm, rumpled, and delicious.

I practically threw myself into his arms, and he folded me against his chest and stepped back into the sanctuary of his place, swinging the door closed behind us and shutting out the outside world.

"What's the matter?" he demanded and didn't let me go. If anything he held me tighter and I closed my eyes and breathed him in.

"Coco, what's wrong?" he asked, his voice a bit strained as his worry climbed.

I wanted to lie to him and say 'Nothing.' I wanted to say to him that I just missed him was all and have a pleasant do-over on breakfast with him, but we'd both agreed we needed to start playing for the same team and that meant being honest. Even when it was painful.

"My roommate and I sort of had a blow-up over you, and my feelings are really hurt," I said and he smoothed a hand over my hair.

"What happened?" he asked.

"Might help me if you told me exactly what happened when you left last night," I said. "I'm still kind of unclear as to why she's so upset. I mean, I know you, and I know you wouldn't have been rude or anything – so what happened?"

"You're right, I wasn't. At least, I didn't think I was. What did she say?"

"Nothing, really…" I told him about coming out for breakfast, about how everyone was really tense and quiet, how no one would really speak to me, and then how Genevieve blew up at me.

"Okay, was anything said before that?" he asked.

"I mean, they weren't happy with me giving you another chance," I said. "They said as much before I left yesterday, but I didn't think it was as bad as all of that."

He leaned back and sighed some and said, "You finish your breakfast?"

"No."

"Alright, then. Let's make some and unpack some of this."

"I only have an hour or so, I have practice today."

"No problem, babe. I'll get you there on time."

We cooked together, talking things over. I could tell that he was bothered by the way I was being treated, and I was honest when I said I wasn't looking forward to practice.

"Think maybe you're too close, you know, between work and home?"

"Maybe," I conceded. "I just don't understand what's going on with Genevieve all of a sudden, though. I've never seen her so angry, and I don't know why she's so angry with me."

"You ever stop to think it may not even be about you?" he asked.

I nodded, and confessed, "I feel like a horrible friend that I don't know. I've been so self-absorbed and I've missed so much… I mean, I should know, shouldn't I?"

"You ain't a mind-reader, babe. You can't know what she hasn't told you."

"Also true."

I sighed and he reached across the table and covered my hand with his.

"You guys have been friends for a long time, just give it some time. It'll either work out or it won't. Doesn't mean any of you are bad people, it's just a part of growing. You never stop. Even at my age."

He smiled at me then and I smiled in return.

"Well, maybe you can teach this new dog some of your tricks," I said and he laughed.

"This old one is open to learning some new ones," he said with a salacious wink, and I bit my bottom lip, my smile growing impossibly big. He chuckled and told me, "Come by the *10-13* for dinner tonight. Decide if you want to crash at your place or with me here." I looked at him and he held up his hands, "No pressure! I'd just like to be with you is all."

I nodded and said, "I'll think about it."

PRACTICE WAS, as I predicted, stiff and a little ugly. I did my best but even the Madame called me out on some simple mistakes – missed cues and missed marks. My roommates kept to themselves, talking quietly, casting looks over at me until I wanted to cry at the unfairness of it.

By the end I was exhausted, not so much from the physical activity as the mental and emotional gymnastics of trying not to let the cold shoulder bother me. I was surprised, when I stepped out of the locker room ahead of Bridgette and Genevieve, that Orion and Jess stopped me in the hall as I tried to pass by.

"Hey, Coco, hold up a second."

"You guys, honestly, I don't think I can take much more today. I'm just going to head to the *10-13* for some dinner and I'll probably stay with Skids tonight so you don't have to be uncomfortable around me."

Both of them blinked and exchanged a startled look.

"We were just going to say, it's not you," Orion said.

"Genevieve's pregnant," Jess declared.

I blinked in surprise myself.

"Pregnant?" I squeaked.

"Hormonal as all get-out already," Jess said, and looked a little haggard.

"Uhhh…" I dragged the word out, unable to tell if I was supposed to be excited for them or not. I mean, in the world of ballet, a pregnancy could be the end of your career and we were all in our prime.

I mean… pregnant? *Wow*.

"Um, I'm not sure what side of the fence I am supposed to be on," I said. "Are you guys happy? Excited? Give me something here."

"To be honest, I think we're mostly just scared. I mean, I'm really happy and excited, but she hasn't landed on a decision, so I don't want to get my hopes up too high. She'd probably kill us if she knew we told you, but you don't deserve to bear the brunt of things without knowing why. It's real unfair, and I know that." Jess looked genuinely distressed and I hugged him quickly.

"I don't know a thing," I said fast. "I'm going to the *10-13* and I'll stay at Skids'. Give you some space to deal and figure out what you want to do without the distraction. I love you guys, and I'd be lying if I told you this hasn't hurt, but we'll get through it, we always do," I told them optimistically.

"We'll deal with Genevieve," Orion promised.

"Don't be hard on her, guys. I can't imagine the stress and what she's going through." Except I could. My mother had done it. I couldn't imagine the hormonal nightmare, though. Thank God for my birth control and the fact that I didn't really have periods, thanks in part to it and in part to my body type.

"Thanks, Coco," Jess said, and I nodded and dashed down the hallway and around the corner feeling equal parts better and worse for the knowledge. I mean, I was literally the last to know; they'd all kept it from me.

Ouch.

I tried to sort through my mixed feelings all the way to the *10-13.* Skids had dropped me off that day for practice, and it was nice and still light out, though heading on toward evening when I left. I decided to walk, my bag slung across my chest, hands buried in my pockets as I walked down the cracked sidewalk at a brisk pace.

The walk was uneventful, though my heart thrummed like a humming-bird's at certain points along it, acutely aware I had none of my typical safety in numbers.

I was relieved when I spotted the old-fashioned hanging shingle above the bar's door and even more so when I glimpsed Skids behind the bar, back in action, smiling and moving along, pouring drinks and chatting up customers. The highlight of my day was standing outside in the gloaming, watching him finally notice me and the way the light in his eyes went supernova at the sight of me.

I felt such love from my head right down to my toes and I couldn't stop grinning like a fool.

I went in and went up to a vacant stool at the bar and clambered up onto it, putting my hands flat to the middle of the bar's polished wood surface and leaning in to greet my man with a quick kiss.

"How was it, babe?" he asked me, and moved away slightly to prep another drink.

"I have no idea what you're making, but I could use one of those," I said in reply.

"Eesh, that good, huh?"

"Oh, my God. I just could really use a drink!" I called after him.

"Coming right up," he declared and as soon as he sent the new waitress who replaced me packing with her tray of drinks back to her table, he set to work mixing me something.

"How's she working out?" I called, trying desperately to keep the subject off of me for the time being.

"Alright, I guess. You know, she's not you, but I think you're happier dancing, and where you're at is working out for you, so I'd like you to stay happy."

He laid down a bar napkin with an expert flourish and set me down a tempting-looking sweet drink. I took a sip and smiled in bliss.

"Okay, my night just got a whole lot better, thank you, lover."

"Anything for my girl," he said with a wink.

We talked where we could, mostly light banter or chatter between customers as the bar got busy. I kept my seat and Skids served me up something from the kitchen without me even having to ask or order. It wasn't on the menu but it was certainly delicious, and I made a quip about him spoiling me.

"That was all Reflash, honey," he said with his hands up, and I had to laugh.

None of the other guys came in that night, which I was grateful for. It meant that the minute things had calmed down enough that the bar could be manned by just Brandon, Skids felt like he could slip away – and he did, taking me by the hand and leading me out the front door and through the next leading to his apartment's stairs.

He couldn't wait. Just inside the old-fashioned wood door that was mostly glass, he pinned me against the stairwell wall, his hands on my hips as he bowed his head and captured my mouth with his, kissing me deeply as if I were an oasis in a desert and he were a man dying of thirst.

I hummed out in appreciation and he broke the kiss smiling, saying, "I need to give you these back," before pressing the set of keys that'd been mine back into the hip pocket of my jeans.

"You sure?" I asked quietly.

"I'm really really sure," he said with a wink, and I giggled and let him usher me up the stairs ahead of him.

Inside the apartment, he pulled me, with a squeal, into his arms, his mouth working mine expertly, stoking the fires of our passion for one another even as he divested us both of our wallets, keys, phones, bag, and jacket, all blindly making them go where they belonged, between the coat tree and the little entryway table by the door.

I giggled uncontrollably at his foolery which turned into a moan filled with warmth and surrender when he captured me around my body with his arms, pulling me close and safe in his embrace.

"I need a shower," I whispered as he kissed the side of my neck, wholly unenthusiastic at the thought of getting busy without one.

"I need one too; want to put it to the test?" he asked.

"Put what to the test?" I asked, with a sultry little laugh.

"Shower sex," he said simply.

"Oh, you're on," I declared.

We left our shoes by the door and he started the shower running. The steam billowed out into the hall as I opened up the doors to the laundry so we could throw our clothes straight in.

I joined him in the bathroom, kissing and stripping one another bare, fingertips gliding over, skin pebbling with gooseflesh in their wake. I sighed and let him grab me and haul me against his perfectly imperfect chest, the scar marring it a reminder to never, ever, take this life of ours for granted. He kissed and licked the side of my neck, setting his teeth gently into it, and I melted against him, so ready to be clean and to have him inside of me.

"Ladies first," he growled, whisking back the curtain and I marveled silently to myself at just how far we'd come since my first time here, huddled in the bottom of his bath, scared and incoherent with a drug-addled mind not of my own making.

He stepped in after me, pulling me immediately into his arms, his mouth melding to mine as he stepped forward, backing me into the punishing spray of his massaging showerhead.

I tried not to let our burgeoning sexual escapade waterboard me, laughing against his mouth as the hot water sluiced down our bodies.

"How in the hell does anybody fuck in a shower?" I asked, giggling, suddenly remembering why I'd never tried.

"Carefully, dirty, there sure isn't any real sensual love or finesse to it. Let me show you," he said, sweeping his hands down my arms, curving his fingers into the spaces between mine, his palms to the backs of my hands. He planted my palms against the cool tile of the wall in front of me.

He murmured in my ear, "Keep 'em right there," and then made a liar out of himself when it came to the lack of sensuality and finesse when it came to making love in a shower.

He swept his hands over my skin, grabbing the bottle of body wash and lathering me up, the sensation slick, warm, and causing my nipples to tighten, my clit to tingle with a first blush of arousal.

His mouth followed where the soap had been and was now rinsed away. Part of the cop he'd been peeked out when he gently kicked my feet apart as wide as they would go. He bent me further, pulling back on one hip while pressing a hand to my back.

"That's it," he said, pleased, his voice gentle and husky with desire.

He plunged a finger into my pussy and teased me, stroking in and out, causing me to whine and clench, desiring his cock to replace it to satisfy the craving that came roaring to the foreground of my body and soul. I thrust my hips back to meet the thrusting of his fingers and he chuckled darkly.

"You like that?" he asked, and slapped my ass causing me to jerk back into him more firmly.

"Yeah," I said, breathy.

"You want more?"

"Yeah."

He added another finger and I whined. That wasn't what I was talking about and he knew it!

He chuckled at me, the bastard, but just when I was about to protest he found my g-spot and stroked it just so and I let out a very different kind of yelp.

"There it is," he murmured to himself, and God he had me going, my clit erect and begging for attention there was no way to give it as he got me riled up, wound tight. Just when I thought I was maybe going to cry from the frustration, his fingers were gone and he started to shove his cock into me. I arched my hips, raising my ass in offering as he pene-trated me slowly, agonizingly slowly, inch by torturous inch.

"Ah, keep those hands where I can see 'em," he ordered when I attempted to bring them down off the wall. I replaced them, and as soon as I did, he thrust forward the last few centimeters, making me cry out.

God, I felt so full, so alive, so connected to him. The feeling was a glorious one, heavy with feelings of love intermingled with lust, shot through with desire and grace.

He started slow, the sensation of the hot water beating on my back, rivulets running over my flanks and down the front of my thighs a stark counterpoint to the heat starting in my core as he moved inside me, bringing me alive.

God, it felt so good, the subtle glow of orgasm growing brighter and brighter, maddeningly stalling out just before that glorious supernova that made me tremble and shake with joy. I moaned, I cried out, I shifted so frustrated trying to get exactly the right angle, the right spot, to no avail.

I closed my eyes and listened to him over the shower spray: the groans of satisfaction, the soft sigh of his breath as he let it out, and, occasionally, as he sucked it in when he found an especially potent sensation for himself. He played my body like a violin and held me on a high note, but not the highest it could be and I needed the crescendo so badly it almost hurt.

I whined and begged, told him I couldn't get there and his chuckle was almost cruel, but God, I loved and trusted him, and I needn't have worried. He reached up and took the showerhead down and pressed it to the front of me, between my legs, the shower spray tormenting my clit deliciously as he resumed his rhythm. I bit my bottom lip and groaned, a deep and guttural noise of devastation and desire as he built me up all over again, only this time, when I reached the summit of my climax, he shoved me over the edge right into that warm, beautiful bliss I so desperately craved.

30

S kids...

She was exhausted, as wrung out as any one person could be and sound asleep against my chest. I stared at the ceiling, my head stuffed with guilt to the point I was on the cusp of a splitting headache.

I was trying to rack my brain about how to fix things, and I could only come to one conclusion. I just didn't know if she would go for it, even though I felt it to the bottom of my soul that it was the right move to make.

I wasn't getting any younger and my nights to spend with her, like this, were limited. I wanted to spend every one of them that I could with her. I wanted to feel her beside me, the warm caress of her breath across my chest, the steady rise and fall of her back beneath my hand, the even cadence of her body's sleeping rhythm lulling me to a slumber of my own.

I'd died once before. I'd glimpsed heaven and I could tell you first-hand, it didn't even compare to this, right here.

It took me a long time to fall asleep, and when I woke, she was gone –

but not far. I could hear her singing to herself in the kitchen and something smelled damn delicious. I got up and pulled a pair of lounge pants on, shuffling my feet into my worn old sheepskin slippers. I made a quick pitstop in the bathroom on the way down the hall to drain the old lizard and smiled to myself at the clatter in the kitchen.

When I ducked around the corner I stopped at the edge of the hall and leaned a shoulder against the wall, my hands stuffed in my pockets, just so I could watch her.

She was wearing one of my shirts again. The sleeves were rolled to her elbow, the tail of it hitting her just above the knee. It wore like a damn dress on her and it was the hottest thing, watching her skip lightly between fridge and stove, adding veggies to whatever she had going on in the pan.

It was the height of domesticity and I had to admit just how much I missed that. Having a woman to wake up to. A woman cook me breakfast, because she wanted to, because she loved me.

"Move in with me," I blurted and she jumped, shrieking her startlement, one knee lifting to her chest, both hands going to her heart.

I had to laugh, pushing off the wall and going to her, arms open. She fell into them, panting, her arms going around me as she cuddled into my chest.

"What did you say?" she asked.

"I said, move in with me, babe. I want you here. Every night, in my bed, every morning, like this. It'll solve a bunch of problems with your roommates, with a lot of things. You'd be closer to Bayside Hall and —"

"You're serious," she said, all wide, surprised blue eyes, with her lush lips parted and inviting.

I resisted the temptation to claim them and simply nodded, my voice suddenly stolen by just how beautiful she was to me in that moment.

I swallowed past the lump it caused in my throat and said, "I feel guilty, about the situation with your roomies. I mean, if it wasn't for me –"

"Don't say that," she said, and looked distressed. I frowned. "Tell me you want me here because you love me, tell me anything but that you want me here because you feel guilty."

"Oh, shit." I hugged her to me, tightly. "Babe, no. That came out wrong. I want you here because I love you. Really, I'm not just saying that. I was awake for hours last night thinking about it. About how when I died, I swear I glimpsed heaven – saw the white light and everything – and how it didn't even compare to having you in my arms last night. I want that so bad, I wouldn't have it any other way, in fact."

She cuddled into me harder, her arms tightening around my waist, and I upped the ante, "Plus, with the guest room, your mom doesn't have to stay in a hotel she can –" I stopped cold at her little sniffle, realizing she was crying.

She looked up at me with tear-filled eyes and said, "Shut up and fucking kiss me, you jackass!"

I laughed and obliged her, lowering my mouth to hers the salt of her tears mingling with her fresh, sweet taste, echoes of the poem "Annabel Lee" stirring in the back of my mind.

> *It was many and many a year ago,*
> *In a kingdom by the sea,*
> *That a maiden there lived whom you may know*
> *By the name of Annabel Lee;*
> *And this maiden she lived with no other thought*
> *Than to love and be loved by me.*

Except it wasn't many a year ago; with any luck, it was many a year ahead…

I broke the kiss and reared up, putting my mouth out of reach of hers and asked, "Does that mean you're saying yes?"

She nodded, her blonde head bobbling rapidly on her shoulders, her hands going back to my bearded cheeks to drag my mouth down within reach of hers. I smiled on the inside, my lips otherwise occupied, and lifted her in my arms, spinning her with glee, a jubilant laugh spilling from her and eradicating any residual sorrow or gloom from the inside of my place.

I needed that. I needed her. Here, with me, every day to remind me what it really was to *live*.

EPILOGUE

olette…

"Wait, is that it?" Oz demanded. "Just that little bit of shit?"

I smiled and nodded. "That's it."

"Then what'd we bring the whole squad for? Jesus."

"Quit'cher bitchin'," Skids said. "Everybody knows you're just in it for the free beer."

"Yeah, but at least I showed up willing to work for it. God damn!"

Laughter ensued and I had to smile. There was just enough for one box to each man and a few hangers of clothes to each woman, and that was it. Bridgette and Orion seemed happy. Jess, too. He was just preoccupied with consoling Genevieve, who was beside herself, crying.

When I'd come home two weeks before and declared I would be moving in with Skids at the end of the month, they'd all sat in shocked silence. Genevieve had been mad at first, but then the other three had pretty much lit into her and I'd just gone into my room to let them all sort out their mess. I had packing to do.

They'd asked me over and over again if I was sure and I'd had to tell them yes. I didn't want them to be uncomfortable in their own home, but I wouldn't be made to feel uncomfortable, either. It'd taken some convincing that this was for the best, but in the end, it wasn't like they had much choice in the matter.

I was doing it anyway.

I'd even offered to keep helping if they needed it, at least for the next two months until the lease was in need of renewal and I could get myself off of it.

I'd started ferrying things to Skids' place a little at a time. Any clothing I took over stayed there, and I would bring a few books here and there, slipping them in among his on the shelves in his living room.

Eventually, things calmed down between me and my friends, and I'd told them it just made sense. The baby, which Genevieve had decided to keep, was going to need a room anyways. This would give them plenty of time to get it ready.

"You sure this is it?" Oz asked again, before heading out the door to join the rest of the caravan walking things the eight blocks to Skids' place.

"I'm sure," I declared. "And even if I did forget anything, it's not like I'm never going to be over here again," I said rolling my eyes.

"We have to have a pizza-and-ice-cream night at least once a month," Bridgette agreed.

"Solidarity in our women's issues," I agreed.

"Oh, fuck this shit, I'm out. I am not about to listen to this," Oz said, leaving out the front door past Backdraft, who laughed at him.

"Wow," Orion declared, while Jess struggled not to shake with laughter.

"Yep," I agreed. "He's pretty much always like that."

I made a sympathetic face and went to Genevieve and hugged her.

"I feel so bad!" she cried mournfully and I didn't know what to say to that. I mean, I understood why she'd had the attitude, being all hormonal, but in the end, it was a reason, not an excuse for her behavior. There was a difference.

"I know," I told her, holding firm to my personal boundary to not let her off the hook completely. I loved my friend dearly, but I wasn't willing to blow off her hurtful behavior and lie to her, telling her that everything was alright. She knew everything would be alright in the end, but she also knew that in order for me to believe that she was sorry for turning all *Mean Girls* on me, that the behavior needed to change – which it had so far, but it had been an ugly, ugly fight to get there.

I loved Genevieve like a sister, and family didn't give up on each other. I reminded her of that now.

"I'll be over later this week," I reminded her. "It'll be like I never left."

"I hate being all stupid emotional!" she cried.

I laughed some and said, "Me too! So stop crying, or you're going to make me start!"

"Okay, okay," she said, shoving me back, swiping under her eyes with her fingers.

I hugged everyone else and said my goodbyes and then left my old apartment with Backdraft at my side. We went down the hallway and he looked down at me from his lofty over-six-foot height.

"You alright?"

"Hm, me?" I asked, so preoccupied with my own thoughts I wasn't quite sure if he was asking about me or Genevieve.

He laughed and said, "Yeah, you."

I nodded and said, "I'll be okay. I'm just not used to her being like that, she's usually not so emotional. It's weird."

"Pregnancy hormones will fuck you up," he agreed.

I smiled and asked, "Something I need to know about Lil?"

He laughed pretty hard at that and shook his head.

"Not yet, but we've been talking about it."

"Oh?" I asked, intrigued, as we stepped out the lobby doors into the early summer sunshine.

"Forget I said anything for me, huh?"

I smiled and nodded. "You bet."

We chatted about other things on the walk to Skids' place, spotting Oz with his plastic tote of random things up ahead, the colors of the patch on his back catching the sunlight.

Skids was at home, keeping the apartment and street level doors propped, and sorting things as they came to the apartment. We'd spent the last couple of weeks discussing some changes to the place, namely a different paint color and some new carpeting – the 70's green had to go.

I spotted him at the street level, watching for me and Backdraft, who was my escort; he hated the thought of me walking the city streets by myself.

I smiled when I saw him, and Backdraft grinned and said, "You make the Chief happier than I've seen him in, well, I think, ever."

I felt my smile grow and my heart swell.

"The feeling is mutual," I told him, and then we were within earshot of Skids.

He called out to me, "Welcome home, babe," and then I was in his arms.

The apartments, his or the one I'd come from were just the places where I lived.

Home? Home was right here, in his arms, cuddled against his chest.

ALSO BY A.J. DOWNEY

The Sacred Hearts MC

1. Shattered & Scarred

2. Broken & Burned

3. Cracked & Crushed

3.5 Masked & Miserable (a novella)

4. Tattered & Torn

5. Fractured & Formidable

6. Damaged & Dangerous

The Virtues

1. Cutter's Hope

2. Marlin's Faith

3. Charity for Nothing

The Sacred Brotherhood

1. Brother to Brother

2. Her Brother's Keeper

3. Brother In Arms

4. Between Brothers

5. A Brother's Secret

6. A Brother At My Back

7. A Brother's Salvation

ABOUT THE AUTHOR

A.J. Downey is the internationally bestselling author of The Sacred Hearts Motorcycle Club romance series. She is a born and raised Seattle, WA Native. She finds inspiration from her surroundings, through the people she meets, and likely as a byproduct of way too much caffeine.

She has lived many places and done many things, though mostly through her own imagination…An avid reader all of her life, it's now her turn to try and give back a little, entertaining as she has been entertained.

Stalker Information:
www.ajdowney.com